# MENACE
## —UNDER—
# MARSWOOD

## Sterling E. Lanier

A Del Rey Book

BALLANTINE BOOKS • NEW YORK

Also by Sterling E. Lanier
*Published by Ballantine Books:*

HIERO'S JOURNEY

THE UNFORSAKEN HIERO

# A BEWITCHING INVITATION

"I have made the Tea of Dreaming." Danna Strom's amber cat-eyes stared into his from a foot away. "Drink. It will not harm you. I swear—by my medal of office." She drew the leather thong from her collar. On the end hung a flat medallion.

One side, much worn by time and use, bore a face. The chin was very square, and the large oval eyes wrapped around the round head to well on the sides. The ears, if that is what they were, were cones set high on the skull so that they were almost stubby horns. The forehead bulged.

There was only one response to such a gesture of trust—Slater tilted his cup and drank. As the hot liquid raced down his throat, its effect was instantaneous. Despite himself, he clawed for his holstered gun even as he slid sideways...

For Katherine Williams and Berwick Bruce,
alias Kate and Bear,
who are my future

# Contents

# CHAPTER 1

# The Fort
# in the Forest

SLATER AWOKE QUICKLY AND SAW THE MONSTER. IT WAS crawling slowly and inexorably onward, straight toward his head, the two terrible claws on the armored limbs waving gently in front of the pointed head, as four stumpy legs urged it on. From somewhere inside the dome-shaped, warty body came a clicking hum, too faint to be heard except in the silence of the small sleeping cubicle. The one great compound eye, centered in a forward turret and colored the dull red of a Martian desert, stared fixedly into the two brown ones of the young officer. Now it was very close indeed. Slater raised himself on his elbows, the sheet spilling down farther, and glared at the creature.

"How in the name of God you ever get a woman to sleep with you, knowing that horror is wandering around here, beats me," came a voice from the doorway. Fully dressed in battle gear, Lieutenant Helge Nakamura lounged against the lintel, staring with unconcealed dislike at the form on his friend's chest. The giant Norse-Japanese had no use for that particular pet of Slater's.

Slater extended a lean hand and plucked the two-inch snapper off his bare chest. Its legs waved feebly in the air, the two claws clicked audibly, and its inner noises grew more audible.

"Grabbit's all right," Slater said equably. "He never hurts anyone I like—do you, boy? He's hungry just now, so he came to Daddy. Must have cleaned out all the roaches and junk in the room. Much better than a cat, you know."

Holding the snapper by its midsection, he rose, walked naked across the room, and took a strip of tough meat from a tiny wall refrigerator. The snapper, freed on the plasteel of a tabletop, smoothly shredded the meat in its razor-sharp chelae and clicked the bits into the four-cornered mouth under the pointed front of its carapace until the last bit was gone. The two men watched in silence until the six limbs retracted into the body and a shutter fell over the great eye. Asleep Grabbit took on the appearance of a lumpy chestnut burr or an odd-looking brownish rock. Slater placed the tiny creature in a small flat box of impervium. Pressing the lid shut, he laid it on the table and began to dress, talking as he did so. It was time to report for the morning watch, and Nakamura had come to wake him.

"I know he's dangerous. Damned if I don't think those claws could cut the impervium if he tried. They certainly cut everything else. But he came to me out in the Ruck, and he never tries to leave. Never bothers anything but bugs and mice in the fort either. Perhaps I'm a bit nutty, but I can *feel* he likes me. Sometimes I even get the feeling he can talk, peculiar as it sounds."

"You've been in the Ruck too long, Slater. The base psych people will have a field day when you get debriefed. By then you'll probably be talking falsetto as well, if dear old Grabbit feels like a snack and your gonads are handy. He gives me the creeps. You know what happened to the first settlers before the domes were built."

"Yeah, but most of those snappers were full grown—the size of house cats." Slater buckled on his sidearm, picked up his helmet, and followed Nakamura out of the room. Ten minutes later they were manning the command post on Fort Agnew's wall, just over the main gate.

"Stinking Teef! Dirty Ruck!" Nakamura spat neatly over a corner of the parapet before continuing. "Why don't they throw the whole bastardly planet away and let the Ruckers have it for themselves?" It was not exactly a new idea but it cropped up frequently. The Ruck depressed some people.

Despite his last name, Nakamura was a dark-eyed blond, and over six feet two inches tall. Broad nostrils and very full lips were the legacy of his Herero great-grandfather. The Norwegian and Japanese ancestry, indicated by his names, were more recent. He scowled at his friend and slapped angrily at a cloud of stinging gnats that hovered in front of his face.

It was very quiet under the sun of the Martian summer. A few noisy insects piped and trilled in the haze of the near distance and some larger beast, probably a ferkat, screamed once at the edge of hearing. Fresh scents of growing things, of expanding, burgeoning life, drifted on the air from the surrounding forest. The temperature was a pleasant but moist 20°C. At night, however, it would drop to −20°C.

Senior Lieutenant Mohammed Slater smiled lazily back at his classmate. "Old buddy, you never stopped screaming for action at the Academy. Where else you going to get it, unless you meant a Girly Camp?"

Slater's jet eyes turned restlessly back to a sweep of the dark wood's edge. He was nervous for a reason he could not analyze but had learned to trust. An almost full-blooded Gilzai Pathan from the West Himalaya Republik, he had one recent English ancestor, the British grandfather whose name he bore. He pulled the green fibersteel helmet lower over his aquiline nose and wondered how many eyes watched from the Ruck. He saw nothing but knew that meant exactly as much. The UN Service Academy could only teach Mohammed Akbar Slater, six times great-grandnephew of the Faquir of Ipi, weapons technology and grand strategy. Tactics, especially those of frontier survival, had come to him with his mother's milk.

Fort Agnew was a thirty-foot-high, four-sided, open stone box with walkways and parapets running around all four sides. A small, crenellated tower rose at each corner, and a tall square keep with a platform for copters on top rose in the center of the two-acre area enclosed by the walls. The blue flag of the United Nations drooped from a flagstaff on the keep. Rumor had it that the fort's engineers had copied a plan of King Arthur's castle out of sheer laziness. But the fort simply reflected age-old answers to equally old problems. Beau Geste would have felt at home there.

The fort sat on an artificial mound. For two hundred yards around the walls, nothing grew but mutated grass and reindeer moss clipped to a height of six inches. Nothing could approach unseen because day and night the walls were patrolled by sentries using every sensing device the UN labs could turn out. For this was Marswood, also called the Teef—for Terraform—or more commonly still, the Ruck, from the Hindi for "Forest." It was commonly—and accurately—called the most dangerous duty in the Solar System, not from the impersonal forces of space and cosmos but due to human endeavor.

The first effort to Terraform Earth's almost airless, meteor-pocked neighbor had begun with a joint American-Russian enterprise in the late twentieth century. It had commenced with sending specially bred, iron-consuming bacteria to Mars in a large number of robot probes. These had thrived far beyond expectation, and their waste products were the oxygen and nitrogen compounds they released from the iron-rich, Limonite surface of the planet. In only ten years, a hazy, cloud-speckled atmosphere was visible in lunar telescopes. Then cargoes of mutated fungus spores and the gametophytes of hardy mosses were sent, and when those had taken hold, the seeds of arctic grasses and alpine shrubs followed. They too survived. The scientists responsible were deservedly proud. A new Earth was being given to the universe. The great distance from the Sun and attendant cold seemed to have been canceled out by two other factors, one being the incredibly rich virgin "soil," the other the benefits of really intense UV light due to the absence of a stratosphere.

But the third superpower had not been consulted. Communist China had been ignored by her Caucasian rivals. The successors of Chairman Mao, who held his beliefs largely undiluted, were faced with the prospect of seeing their more technologically advanced rivals, the capitalist Americans and the neorevisionist Russians, divide a second planet.

China soon launched its own cargo-carrying rockets.

All that was over two hundred Earth years in the past, but the results were before their eyes now. The two young officers, one with fascination, the other with dislike, watched the incredible, seething barrier of swarming plant life that surrounded them.

Kudzu vines, pale-green leaves ten feet across and stems a yard thick, grew almost as one watched, their tendrils battling with those of poison ivy of equal bulk. Mongolian thorn bush bearing bronze daggers a foot long struggled with twisted manchineel trees and giant saw grass that grew far over a man's head. Twenty-foot, poisonous hogweed, its touch an irritant, sprouted everywhere. Olive mounds of mutated prickly pear and the jade drums of giant barrel cactus elbowed towering euphorbias, whose scarlet blooms hid their spiky branches. Huge Martian thistles, their flowers turned an inexplicable orange, reared over a thousand Earth weeds, most of them now the product of random mutation, all adapted to subarctic cold and all thriving beyond belief. Only lasers or edged steel could penetrate the solid mass of the Ruck. Only the trained, the truly Marsworthy, could survive in the tangled immensity that was Marswood.

For the Chinese contribution to Martian life did not end with the plant kingdom. Shipments of animal life came too. Flies, fleas, lice, wasps, mosquitoes, poisonous beetles, spiders, centipedes, scorpions and mites; every unpleasant arthropod available was sent, not once but repeatedly. Most succeeded in establishing themselves. Many grew to large size with appetites to match.

So too did the brown and black rats, the Eurasian rabbit and the house mouse, as well as the Indian mynah bird and the European starling and, eventually, the dwarf goat. They were no longer dwarfs and were doing splendidly. Even certain aquatic imports had made it. When all these creatures were added to the inevitable dogs and cats from the first settlements, it was clear that planned Terraforming was as dead as Kelsey's nuts. The offended Chinese had exacted a mighty revenge from the nations they thought had tried to keep them Earthbound. The smooth colonization of Mars had become an empty dream.

Slater put down the monocular with which he had been examining the edge of the Ruck and continued the conversation. "We can't give it to anyone, stupid! We need it too badly! And you know it." He liked Nakamura but sometimes grew very tired of his griping. He hoped the big lieutenant would adapt. Still, it was a fact that some never did.

"Look, Helge. There are almost a million legitimate settlers on Mars now. They have a right to stay. Minerals like the cryolite we're guarding here are desperately needed back on Earth, where they're mostly exhausted. You know all that crap." He raised his monocular again and focused on a distant splash of color. A giant, chocolate-colored diurnal moth, triple the bulk of any on Earth, no doubt due to the low gravity, soared above the distant trees. As he watched, a dark bird the size of an eagle zipped up out of the growth, seized the huge insect, and dropped back again.

"Those starlings can be a bloody nuisance," Nakamura said. "Ever been near one of those ball-nest things they call a rookery? They go for your eyes."

Slater continued to peer through his glass, nagged by an increasing sense of unease. The fort was always under observation, but today it seemed more oppressive somehow, almost a physical weight.

"I could stand the damn birds, the bugs, the mother-stinging plants, and the cold, but people who live here and *like* it . . ." Slater ignored Nakamura's teasing. One reason that he never got very annoyed at Nakamura's grumbling was that the big blond was a good officer. His muttering never interfered with his watchfulness. Even as he spoke, he was scanning the forest. The two of them commanded the fort's western face for this watch, with Slater as the senior.

They were not watching for animals, save by strict biological definition. There were people out in the incredible fog-shrouded jungle, men and women. It was for, or rather *against*, them that Fort Agnew and fifty more like it, large and small, girdled the planet. For they were so savage and inimical that an army in permanent garrison barely sufficed to keep them within bounds.

The Ruckers, or Teefies, as the men of Earth called them, or the "pseudoindigenous and hostile clans" as one government handbook put it, were the newest subspecies of humanity. They were also a constant threat to the orderly colonization of Mars. In less than two hundred years, a complex barbarian culture of unparalleled ferocity had developed out in the wild, chill lands that still made up five-sixths of the Martian globe. In the beginning compounded of runaway South American miners, Nigerian farmers, and Russian and American military deserters, the Ruckers attracted the worst members of every culture to touch down on the new world. The fit had survived, the unfit had not.

There the restless misfits of an increasingly planned Terran economy had established a society of their own, one based on a virulent hatred of the off-planet civilization that had given them birth. Brown-skinned, leather-clad, and apparently totally irreconcilable, the Ruckers warred without letup on the people of Earth, their possessions, and their habitations. The Ruckers were as cunning and adept at survival as, for example, the ancient Apaches of the mother planet. More, for they utilized science when it suited them, preserved the arts of reading and writing, and were quite capable of copying advanced weapons or using those captured. Like my own Pathan ancestors north of the Khyber, Slater thought, not for the first time.

With so much of Mars covered by dense "undergrowth," the Rucker clans were usually invisible until they struck. No one had any real idea of how many there were. They made the forts and their garrisons an absolute necessity if the Martian surface was to be even partially utilized by Earth. So far, the battle was a draw.

We imported everything, Slater mused, even a vampire culture we spawned. We must need enemies since we breed our own.

The distant hoot of a bullhorn broke the dreaming hush of noon and caused the two officers to scan the perimeter of the fort with fresh interest. Below them, a crew manhandled two fieldpieces, air pom-poms, into position behind the sliding gate in the center of the wall. Other crews manned lighter compressed-air weapons, one in each of the two end towers and one in the middle of the parapet near where the two lieutenants stood. Nakamura bounced over to take personal command there. Slater adjusted his throat mike and laid his carbine within easy reach on the parapet.

The horn sounded again. One of the two daily convoys of refined ore was returning from the nearby cryolite mine.

"Check all weapons; convoy approaching!" Slater's voice boomed from a loudspeaker over the parade ground. Two squads under arms deployed in the square below and behind him, the standing reserve. On the battlements, all the men not attached to gun crews crouched with their air rifles ready. All weapons pointed at the one break in the greenery opposite the gate, the trail to the mines. Hacked clear during the previous watch, already twisting suckers and green fronds of vegetation had half concealed it again.

The hooter sounded again, this time close. The blunt brown nose of a light tank poked from the opening and the tank scuttled into the open, its twin-gun turret swiveling to cover a sector of forest wall as it did. It halted halfway between the Ruck and the fort and took station to cover the rest of the convoy. Two more followed and took up other positions. With their tracks completely concealed by plates of armor, they looked like great beetles. Sensors of different kinds turned restlessly on the turret domes.

Now the first big ore carrier, really a giant cargo-carrying tank itself, emerged into the clearing. It had a small turret of its own, but its bulk and armor were its main defenses. It headed straight for the fort at a slow pace. Another and another of the clumsy things rolled into the open. Then came a tank, the middle guard. The first ore carrier was now almost at the gate and a fourth was emerging from the green tangle when the attack began. The timing was lovely. Everyone had started, though ever so slightly since they *were* veterans, to relax.

Without warning, six rockets flew from stubby handmade bazookas and burst against the sides of the tanks. At the same time, clouds of smoke expanded like dirty balloons under the fort's walls. Through this murk bounded screaming fiends in camouflaged leather, each one with a specific job to do. More explosive charges struck the tanks and two of the towering ore carriers as well. But only two. Rucker techs tore their way into the other two with thermite and prybars, killing the crews in savage in-fighting. In hardly more than sixty seconds the battle was over. As the two captured ore buckets lumbered away, snipers hidden along the forest edge opened up on the wall defenses, which were already half immobilized by the acrid smoke. Nakamura fired his cannon alone, his crew dead or wounded, and caught one wave of the vanishing enemy in a shower of slugs. Slater and his six wall guards picked off a few more. The two tower cannons were rendered harmless by the dense smoke.

Trying not to overcompensate for the weak gravity, Slater clattered down the tower stairs and found the cannon crews at the gate choking and gagging from the greasy smoke, several bodies adding to the confusion. Curiously, Slater did not find the Rucker smoke too bad; something in it actually exhilarated him, something wild and pungent. Might be a hallucinogen, he thought, while he shouted for the reserves. He led the reserve squads into the clearing where shattered vehicles glowed dull red through the smoke, their crews mercifully incinerated. He turned at the curse and saw Nakamura behind him, one arm limp and bloodstained.

"The bastards killed Omatuk and Kusinen, my two best gunners!"

"Go look after your arm, you damn fool!" Slater looked back at the clearing, sick at heart. Four tanks and two ore carriers destroyed, two captured! *Captured!* Inside one of those reeking, burned-out tanks was a cinder called Lieutenant Wolf, the convoy officer, a good friend. How in the names of God had it happened? He knew only too well who would get the immediate blame. Major van Schouten, temporarily in command, was good at applying blame to others. Slater took a deep breath and coughed as a wave of smoke filled his lungs. Now the stench of cooked meat was uppermost. If only he had listened to his instincts earlier! He did not stop to query what he could have done. The Old Man had warned them never to be afraid of giving a false alarm or two, that in the field instincts were often the best guide.

The gate gunnery sergeant, Brown, his face now a normal color, came up and saluted again. "Sorry about the guns, sir. That smoke blotted everything out in split seconds and then they fired through it at close range." In grudging professional respect he added, "It was a nice bit of work for those wood rats." Slater wondered what had been in the smoke. The Ruckers were always finding new uses for the mutated plant life of their beloved jungle. Still odder was the fact that he seemed unaffected.

## CHAPTER 2

# Post Mortem
# and Mystery

A S HE HAD EXPECTED, THE AFTERMATH IN THE POST COM-
mandant's office was anything but pleasant. Two hours of
frenzied work by everyone on the post who could be spared
from the warning net or the guns had cleared up most of the
mess. The wounded were in the hospital and the dead were
laid away decently. A scorched pile of earth was all that marked
the place where the armor had been so cleverly ambushed. As
the officers, tired and stinking of smoke, sat in the commandant's office, they could hear the whine of distant jets looking
for the two ore carriers or anything else to bomb. No one
expected them to find anything. The operation had been too
well planned.

It was still very neat. Crawling under mats of grass which
had been woven into an aluminum mesh, a large party of
Rucker warmen had patiently wormed its way to the wall during
the previous night. Then they dug into the ground at the base
of the wall, somehow disarming the mines buried there. The

metal in their grass shields blocked the heat seekers on the walls. They were so close that it would have taken a genius to even think of looking for them there. They were in the one place no one *could* plant an ambush. Neat!

Major van Schouten, in command of Fort Agnew while Colonel Muller was away, was cordially detested by all of his juniors and knew it. A pink-faced, white-haired Hollander, he was fussy, excitable, and largely incompetent. He owed his rank to very strong political connections, but even they could take him no further in the service and he knew that also. Two review boards had recommended against his promotion. In three months a third would meet, and his compulsory retirement inevitably would follow. Enraged and frightened by the attack, van Schouten was still looking for a scapegoat.

"You're supposed to be a veteran, a trained man, Slater!" he yapped, his voice rising in shrillness as he sensed the unspoken disapproval of the others. "Taken in by a child's trick, by God, and causing the loss of seven vehicles! Can you think of any reason why I shouldn't have you brought before a court? You too, Nakamura? What in Hell were you doing to let all your men get shot down? Wait till the press hears about this, wait till—"

"Major, anyone could have been taken in by this one." The heavy voice of Captain George M'kembe cut in. M'kembe was justly famous for having killed three warmen in unarmed combat, an almost incredible feat and the reason for one of his promotions. A solid, silent, black giant, he usually kept quiet save for rhapsodizing to anyone who would listen about his family in Lesotho. Van Schouten hated his guts, since he was everything the major was not.

"All right, Captain M'kembe, we've heard your opinion. Which is not mine! What are we to do now, eh? Now that these idiots have lost an armored company for us? Tell me that, will you?" The pink face and the small pig eyes made the cropped white hair look false, as if they had been moved from another man, thought Slater.

A look almost of disbelief came over the unattractive face. It seemed finally to occur to van Schouten that no one could absolve *him*, the commanding officer, of the blame for the mishap. All of the officers present could see it happen. *He's just realized that a lifetime of excuses has come to an end. No hiding place up here. But he'll get me to slide down with him, or die trying.* Slater kept his face a rigid mask.

"The primary fault is those money-grubbing leeches over at Universal Mining." The acid tones of Captain Nasiban, the lean, balding adjutant, penetrated the room. "They have such lousy labor problems they won't let us garrison their cruddy mine. Afraid we'd see too much. Yet we have to take their mother ore *and* trek it through the Ruck *and* take full responsibility for it."

"That's enough!" The major's pudgy hand slammed down on the table, the gesture as ineffectual as his other mannerisms. "The government makes these decisions, I'll remind you. No criticism of higher authority under my command, please! And I'll also remind you that the big corporations pay a lot of taxes, including much of your pay. You all might show a little gratitude." He ran a finger around his sweating neck.

*We all might remember you have a cousin on the board of Universal.* Slater struggled to betray none of the contempt he felt. *What a ripe piece of flea dirt you are, Major dear.*

There was a pause, hesitantly broken by Ensign Rivera. He was the most junior present, a boy from the Altiplano of Peru, just out of the UN Academy.

"Why can't we, ah, attempt to trade some prisoners for the captured armor? We have four or five in the fort's cells."

It was typical that van Schouten was cheap enough to laugh at the boy, his usual sneering bark, reserved for those unable to answer back.

"Ruckers don't trade prisoners, son," M'kembe said gently. "They don't trade *anything*, except on Truce Days. If we didn't have those prisoners pretty well hog-tied, they'd commit suicide or kill some of us trying."

"You should have learned all that back at the Academy," the major added. "Well, let's have some real ideas! Can't any of you think of something that might delay the Committee of Inquiry?" Despite his attempt to be sarcastic, the despair in van Schouten's tone was mirrored in his face.

A sound from the waiting room behind Slater caught their

attention. The orderly sergeant's "glad to have you back, sir!" made all the heads turn to the door in welcome surprise.

It opened and two figures walked in, one behind the other. The first one brought every man to his feet at rigid attention. At sight of the second, hands clawed for the holstered sidearm worn with every uniform while on Mars duty.

"Easy! Stand at ease, I said!" Colonel Louis Muller, the commanding officer of Fort Agnew, whom all had thought to be on an Earthbound rocket a week earlier, walked around to where Major van Schouten stood spellbound. Amazed as they were to see the colonel, it was the other man who kept them all staring. Meeting glance for glance, arms folded across his barrel chest, rifle slung behind his olive-dyed leather tunic, fur hood thrown back, there stood before them a Rucker warman in full battle panoply. The pale-brown vees incised in his forehead proclaimed him a veteran warrior, while the short cloak of black feathers slung across one shoulder showed that he was also a konsel, an elected ruler. No such person had ever been inside the walls of an uncaptured Terran fort in the memory of anyone living. Indeed, it was rare enough to see a man of such rank even at the semi-annual Truce Fairs. The flicker of grim humor in the dark eyes told Slater that the irony of the situation was not lost on their strange visitor. Otherwise the Rucker stood quietly, his natural dignity a shield against the vengeful glances of his assembled enemies.

"I am reassuming command." Colonel Muller's quiet voice broke the silence. "This is Thau Lang, a chief and konsel of the Rat Clan of the True People. He understands Unit and is the official guest of the government, subject to certain limitations, which I will explain. He is to be treated with the respect due his rank. Is that clear?" Muller waved van Schouten out of his chair and seated himself at the head of the table while his officers stared at the Rucker.

Louis Muller was a squat little man with a pug nose and soft-brown eyes. His undress green uniform was usually wrinkled and he paid small attention to form, somehow always managing to escape parades, receptions, and official ceremonies. He looked rather dumpy and soft and his thinning brown hair, parted in the middle, lent him the look of a retired bookkeeper. He was fifty-five years old and had twice refused promotion to general. He never wore his decorations. He was the finest soldier on Mars, a man whom younger officers regarded as their ideal. His subtlety matched the Ruckers' at their best, and his bushcraft was their equal as well. He was about as soft physically as a ferkat and he could move so fast that he appeared to float away as one watched. Frequently he took his leaves in the Ruck, alone and without even a tent, as another might tour an Earthside forest reserve. To Slater, Muller's return meant the difference between night and day. Whatever happened now, all knew who commanded; the officers knew, too, that no one would be sacrificed as a burnt offering to those on high. Muller was merciless to laziness, stupidity, corruption, and anything that smacked of tale-bearing or political influence. But he was utterly fair. Now his quiet presence dominated the room as always, a thing that never ceased to amaze Slater since it was so effortless.

At Muller's command a chair was brought in by the sergeant and the Rucker chief was seated at the end of the table, next to Slater. Thau Lang's odor came to him sharply; it was not unpleasant, but pungent, a mixture of woodsmoke and herbs, leather and oil.

When the sergeant had closed the door behind him, Muller looked at his officers, his gaze slowly sweeping the table.

"All leave is canceled herewith, no exceptions whatsoever." Muller took out a pack of gum and selected a piece before continuing. Beside Slater, Thau Lang grunted once, as if clearing his throat. Muller quickly threw a piece of gum to him. The Rucker caught it with a flick of his wrist, opened it, and sat back chewing contentedly.

"There will be no inquiry into today's tragedy," he went on. "It is an incident, nothing more. No one is considered to be at fault. I have the plenary authority to dismiss the matter as a simple tribal action. Universal will make no complaint. Is this clear?"

"But the ambush—someone is to blame. Whose responsibility?..." The major's voice died away under the level gaze of his commander. *He*, van Schouten, had been in command during the attack; to any committee of inquiry he would be the chief culprit, and Muller's words had given the major an unexpected reprieve. He sat back in silence, his eyes glassy from the realization that he had a second chance.

"As of this exact moment, Fort Agnew is the headquarters for a new campaign," the colonel went on. "It is an enormous secret that a new campaign is even starting. Therefore, I impose the highest classification of military security. All mail will be censored from now on and letters will be completely rewritten if any hint of what we are doing appears." He paused, rose from his seat, and unrolled the big map of their operational hemisphere of the planet that hung on the wall behind him. All the forts were marked upon it, as well as the larger craters, now mostly lakes or marshes, the higher ranges of hills, the great gorges, the desert tundra areas, and the roads. There were few of the latter. Much of the map was utterly featureless, as unknown as it had been when the first scouts landed two centuries and more before.

"What concerns us is our own south half of the planet." The colonel's pointer flicked the map. "Here at the South Pole is Mainbase, Ares. The campaign will be coordinated from there, of course. The northern hemisphere will not be neglected. But all the signs seem to indicate that here we are of most importance. Look at our position. We are the center, or rather the south center of the ring of forts. The cryolite mines we guard are the farthest advanced of any concession granted in the unknown area.

"The first stage of the campaign will be an urgent search for information. We have far too little. Tragically little. We must seek new methods of getting it. And we have very little time." Muller's quiet voice was without emphasis, but a thrill ran down Slater's spine. No one had ever heard Louis Muller refer to anything as being urgent before. "We have half Earth's land surface in our charge," he added.

"Pardon, sir." It was Captain Nasiban. "What about this . . . uh, our guest here? I assume he plays a part in this."

"Correct. A major part. He is our ally, subject to certain limits that he and I have worked out and to which Supreme Command has agreed.

"Someone, some group perhaps, but someone or some persons inimical to us is known to be coordinating the tribes. They are being formed into an army for a concerted attack. The planetary defenses—and I repeat, this is Top Secret—are not geared to withstand such a thing. There is evidence, which I will discuss in due course, that the plans do not originate in the Ruck at all. However, the areas that seem to be the heartland of the coming attack are being sealed off. And not by us—by them, whoever 'they' are. Even low-flying aircraft are sometimes being downed in these areas. It took over a year for our base and Earth's computers to analyze a thousand apparently random incidents. What emerged was a pattern of great subtlety, but a pattern nonetheless—one of slowly and cautiously denying us access of any kind to large areas that seem to be strongpoints. The computers predict these areas can be nothing but centers for the development of massive arms buildups, arms and men too, of course.''

"What about our satellites? Do they report nothing, Colonel Muller?''

"Nothing, Ensign Rivera. But why would they if the enemy was careful? I must repeat, at the risk of overemphasis, that we have encountered nothing like this threat before. This is *clever*. You know the Rucker facility for digging. You know the subsoil of the planet is riddled with volcanic bores and other kinds of natural caverns. A chain of the latter connected by tunnels would render the satellites useless. Then there is the fog, the clouds, the rain, the snow. And the great canyons. For a better understanding, you should discuss the details with Captain Feng, the post intelligence officer.''

"What do you mean, sir, about plans not originating in the Ruck? Surely they could hardly originate off-planet? Who would gain?'' Van Schouten looked incredulous but he met the colonel's gaze without flinching.

"Well, Major, the United Nations *does* have a few dissidents, or so I have heard. There are lots of people back home who think that the World Government is not opening this place up to settlers fast enough. Plenty of worthless politicians get elected solely by promising a looser quota, by telling their voters that the Rucker problem is 'exaggerated.' Maybe some of them have a new source of muscle behind them, *neen*?'' A few Afrikaans words clung to Muller's tongue. Van Schouten had once implied that he and the colonel might have some common ancestors. Smiling politely, Muller had asked if he meant the Boers or the Hottentots. The subject was not raised again and the tale went all over the post in minutes.

"It is not our business to speculate about anything off-planet, particularly in the political area," Muller went on. "There are agencies that handle such things for the government. Our business is to find out who is arming the tribes *here* then squash the whole business. Now I will answer the next question before it is asked perhaps. What is a Rucker konsel doing in a UN fort, being given access to our innermost secrets? Is the government mad? Am I? I will let Thau Lang do the answering this time. I will say one thing before he starts. He is an old personal friend of mine." Muller sat back, his eyes twinkling.

They all turned to stare at the silent man in the oiled leather. The three vees cut neatly into his forehead below the black bangs told them all that he had killed many times. Though the clans warred among themselves often enough, it was a ritual warfare, using complex rules and conducted with as little loss of life as possible. Most warmen kills were of UN troops. The long, two-edged dagger he wore had probably been whetted in Terran blood. He met their glances with one as cold as any, his iron, clean-shaven face betraying nothing. Then he spoke.

"Let us make things plain, so that no one makes mistakes." His Unit was slow and rather harsh, but a child could have understood perfectly.

"I am here because my people are threatened. The True People, or as you say, the Ruckers, want no more offplanet settlers. This is *our* planet, and we have paid for it with our blood." His gaze seemed to grow remote, and they waited in silence for him to continue.

"But not all of us think like little children, and some of us have grown worried in the last few years. New weapons are appearing from the South, from down here. Chiefs who do not agree with the new thoughts are sometimes not heard of again. There is the continual talk of *uniting*, of becoming *one*, of thus gaining great strength and driving you Greenies out entirely.

"We became a people to *cease* being 'one'! All our laws

were framed to let us each be different. We have the personal records of the men and women who fled from the first settlements. They wanted freedom to be *themselves*, and they established the loosest set of rules by which people could still live together and yet be *alone*, in their own minds and spirits. If you do not understand me, I will go back to the beginning and say it again. Because you *must* understand, as Louis understands, or the whole planet will die. And my people will die first and most. They will all die."

The chief's voice had been rising in emphasis. No one else spoke. Even van Schouten realized that he was hearing something unique, a Rucker leader expounding their basic philosophy. Slater was awestruck but sufficiently self-possessed to realize the Rucker was an old man. Despite his sturdy form and deceptive movements, a fine mat of wrinkles appeared under the beige skin when Thau Lang spoke.

"I went to my friend Louis. He knows I speak for others as well as myself. The movement out of the southern area is bad. The True People are being *used*. The young men are being trained in ways which are against all that we have sought for ourselves. The Wise Women are being ignored. Two konsels have vanished in my clan area, which is far north of here, near your Fort Peron. They were of the group which thinks as I do. I have been threatened. Messages have threatened my life. Poison has been used in my food. I am a Taster and detected it. A man of the True People may use poison after he sends formal word of a feud. Or woman. They have their own rules, the women. But I am too old to have a woman try to poison me. And I have no feuds. So." He looked about, his face impassive.

"I am here to help. Whatever is behind this movement is no friend to the True People. The lessons come from elsewhere. Many of the weapons are new to us also, and I like what I hear of them as little as the lessons. Louis has lived in my clan-place. I have come to help him, and to give help. Of the two enemies, you Greenies are much the less, in my judgment. You want to pen us up and turn everyone into farmers of the dirt. What this new thing in the South wants, I have no idea, but something about it is foul. It is a concealed enemy that I think loves us no more than you, and has plans for us that are far worse. We will halt our warfare, those of us who feel this way, against you Greenies until we find and tear out the rot that has somehow sprouted down here. You will never find it without our help, that I can tell you. So you must forget that I have killed Greenies and you must let me forget that you have killed Ruckers. Once this is all over we can go back and kill one another properly." For the first time since they had seen him, he smiled. His teeth were fine but gray, not white, a Rucker characteristic, perhaps due to some mineral deficiency.

While they digested Thau Lang's remarks, Muller's voice broke in. "Show them the thing you brought, Thau Lang."

From a large, elaborately worked pouch slung over one shoulder, the old chief produced an object that he held out to Slater. It was a tapered metal tube about a foot long. One end was swollen into a ball. At the other, the smaller, was a fine hole. It looked like a distorted syringe of some sort save that the ball end was rigid metal. The metal felt odd. It was rather rough in texture and a bluish black in color.

"What is it?" Slater asked, handling the thing gingerly.

"A weapon. It is empty now. He who bore it was a young man, a warrior of the Ferkat Clan, which used these southern woods. That is, if his paint and harness were not a lie. He is dead and cannot tell us. If he were alive I could make him speak. The Wise Women of my clan could too. He tried to kill me with it, but he was noisy. The Ferkats should be ashamed of him, to miss an old man."

"It's an interesting weapon," Muller said. "Our techs are wild to disassemble it, but I need it too badly. It only had one load left, or maybe it's a single shot. It sprayed a cloud of tiny needles, apparently ice. If Thau had not had the reflexes of a youngster, one of them would have got him. Instead they hit a tree. Within each needle was some sort of corrosive muck. The tree was full of inch-wide holes in no time."

Feng, who now held the odd-looking thing, was obviously fascinated. "But if all of this conspiracy is so secret, sir, why did they try to kill the konsel with such a strange weapon? It would be bound to attract some attention."

"It was meant to, eh, Thau Lang? Lots of attention. Think for a minute, Captain, about what the konsel has just told us."

"My people were supposed to see me die in great pain from a weapon they knew nothing of," Thau Lang said. "But no one thought that the Greenies would ever hear of it. The lesson was for the True People only. A warning to obey the new commands from the South. Also it must have been thought that the weapon, whatever it is, would not be found, but only my body, full of large unpleasant holes." For the first time the chief looked sad. "My clan has some traitors. There is no other way this southern *stylyag* could have reached the hiding place near my cave. He had to have help from within my clan."

"Sir?"

"Speak up, Captain M'kembe," Muller replied.

"This weapon—ice gun or whatever. I am the arms officer and cleared for Top Secret. This is not a Terran weapon at all. I don't believe that we even have anything like it under development. It—it looks like some other, well, *alien* form of technology. It doesn't *feel* like a gun. It doesn't seem to fit the hand properly. How does it shoot?"

"I assume you mean where is the trigger, George. There is none. And you may take it from me that the Ares Base intelligence did everything *but* take it apart. We don't know *how* it fires. We don't know *how* it loads either. And, of course, we don't have the vaguest idea *what* it loads." He leaned forward and looked at the puzzled faces around the table before continuing.

"Surely some light is beginning to break through, gentlemen? Are you still not in the picture? Have the extraordinary precautions about this whole weird business not come home to you yet?" He smiled crookedly and then suddenly pointed at Slater. "Speak up, Senior Lieutenant! I can see that you, at least, have a thought."

Slater could only stammer, as the idea ricocheted around in his skull, becoming more improbable as each second passed. Finally the words got out. "The Old Martians!" There was a long silence. The colonel continued to smile dreamily, as if contemplating some lovely vision. His eyes refocused themselves on Slater finally and he spoke.

"That's right, my boy," he said jovially. "The Old Martians."

## Chapter 3

# *Danna Strom*

Colonel Muller smiled briefly then continued.
"I don't mean that I believe in Old Martians or, for that matter, Old Terrans either. Or ghosts, or the dust devil things my 'Tottie ancestors thought lived out in the Karoo desert. But Old Martians will do. Ares Base has a code name—*Project U*—for something labeled Unknown, Unpleasant, and Unwanted. Something that is apparently systematically killing Ruckers who disagree with it, *and* Terrans who are ignorant of it." Despite his casual air, the mild-looking little man was deadly serious. His officers had no doubt of that.

"We have to find it, you know," he went on quietly. "A concerted rising of even two-thirds of the wild tribes—*minus* any unknown technology, mind you—is utterly beyond the capability of the UN forces here to handle. Nor do we have the ships to evacuate civilians. We would have to use deterrents. *Ultima ratio regis*, gentlemen—the king's last argument. It used to mean artillery, back in the so-called civilized past. Now it means nukes, *and* bacteria *and* viruses. Since Thau Lang and a number of the other elders of the True People are not without a fair share of reasoning power, why, they

23

want this conspiracy stopped. Permanently." Once again the room was silent.

"This is all new to you. Regrettably, there is little time to digest it. Since I have some ideas and am also the commander of this post, I have been given a pretty free hand in this matter. Captain Feng, Lieutenants Slater and Nakamura remain. The rest of you are dismissed. I'll deal with each of you separately later. For the present, carry out your normal duties. Be alert. Those ore carts were not stolen for fun."

As the other officers filed out, the colonel remembered something. "Van Schouten, get busy on all those damned forms that came in since I've been gone. I don't want to see one by tomorrow except for my signature."

Thau Lang remained as well. Slater was surprised to find that the old konsel was studying him closely, making no effort to hide the fact. His iron visage was expressionless but his eyes were interested.

"Captain Feng." The colonel's voice brought their attention back to him at once. "What can you tell me of the five prisoners we now hold?"

Rucker prisoners, a rarity at any time, were cared for only by Intelligence guards and medics who had received special training for that duty. Rucker prisoners were homicidal, suicidal, and cunning beyond belief. The Rucker warmen did not surrender and their base camps, usually below the ground or in caverns, had only been found once or twice, by accident. Thus women and children hardly existed as a factor in discussing prisoners.

This was one reason that the two junior officers pricked up their ears. The last batch of prisoners had been brought in swaddled in cloaks, late at night and by helijet. Though no one could say who had started the rumor, every man in garrison was convinced that one of the captives was a woman. The fact that not a half-dozen women had been caught alive in the last fifty years made the story even more interesting.

"There are four men and one woman," Feng admitted. "All under restraint. They have been force-fed, but no interrogation has taken place." His black eyes met those of the colonel. "There is something odd about this gang, sir. They were caught in the open by a passing heli and knocked out by gas bombs. I'm more than a little suspicious of the whole thing. I sent a coded communication detailing my suspicions to Intelligence H.Q. in Ares but have had no answer yet, which also surprises me."

The colonel tapped his pocket. "I have your message and I'm your answer. I'm also your superior in your own branch for the duration of this emergency. You'll get a signal to that effect today from your people. From this minute, you report to me and to no one else. Understood?"

Feng appeared delighted. "That gives me great pleasure, Colonel. Just tell me what you want done. I'll do my best."

"Let's go see your prisoners for a start." Muller rose and the others followed him. "Thau Lang goes with us. He goes anywhere in this fort that he wants. I've cut orders to that effect. When he returns to his people, he will report nothing of what he has seen. On the word of a True Person." He strode out of the office, the others trailing in his wake, Slater and Nakamura staring at one another.

Prisoners were kept in the deepest section of the subbasements, directly under the central keep and its offices. Intelligence maintained a sealed section there, with its own special equipment. Of non-I-Corps personnel, only the post commander had the right of entry, and he seldom exercised it. The Intelligence branch functioned best when left to itself.

Feng identified himself through a pinhole and they went in, the guard inside coming to attention as the heavy steel door slid into its notch. Waiting for them at the entrance to the hospital section was the pet frustration of the unattached males on the post, Lieutenant (of Intelligence) Mohini Lal Dutt, all six feet of her gorgeous body in medical whites. She did not stand at attention, simply waved a pretty hand. The Benares Bomber favored each of them with a dazzling smile. Slater reflected that her I-Corps training showed in the fact that the smile sent to Thau Lang was no whit less gleaming and kind. As he trailed after the others into the security ward, Slater aimed a hand at the white-covered roundness nearest him, only to have it gently guided past. "No free feels, today, Dirty

Pathan pig," she breathed gently in his ear. He suppressed a grin and went on in. *One of these days, Mohini . . .*

The five beds were kept three feet from each other. The five occupants were conscious, but only their hands were free to move. Their bodies were wrapped in extended versions of the old straitjacket, each of which was secured to its bed in several places. The beds were clamped to the floor. An armed guard, carbine on hip, leaned against the wall at the entry end of the room. He paid no attention to the visitors and his eyes never left the prisoners. To a stranger, the precautions might have looked rather absurd. To a soldier familiar with the Ruck, they looked fairly adequate.

One sight of the woman made Slater forget his training for a long, breathless instant. She lay at one end of the line of beds, her close-cropped hair outlined by the white pillow. Her eyes were a strange shade, somewhere between yellow and brown, and she was quite small. The nose was square and short above the full lips and the rounded chin. Her skin was the typical Rucker beige, a faded olive, but a faint flush of rose was visible over the cheekbones. She met his gaze impassively and her eyes moved on to examine the others, then returned to him. For a moment he thought he saw something else in their depths, a question perhaps. Then they left him.

One of the men said something short, harsh, and savage to the others. Five sets of burning eyes settled on Thau Lang, who seemed as calm as ever. He in turn said something in a whisper to Colonel Muller. It was equally unintelligible to Slater. He must speak Rucker, thought the young officer. God, what a man Muller is!

The five captives lay in their cloth cocoons and stared at Thau Lang, who walked slowly along the line of beds staring serenely back. When he came to the girl, for she was obviously no more, he paused and said one word, a long rolling sound, which to Slater meant nothing. It sounded like "Kareeem." The old chief turned to the officers and this time spoke in Unit.

"Leave the room. I must speak with these people. You must not be here. Not even you, Louis."

Muller nodded. "Come on, you types. Captain Feng, all monitoring equipment turned off at once please. That's an order. This room is to be completely private, until we are asked back."

The Intelligence officer snapped an order to Lieutenant Dutt. Slater was pleased to see that she had lost her proverbial calm. She stepped out and gave some orders into a wall phone. Feng had meanwhile waved the armed guard out as well. Muller was the last out and closed the door behind him.

He said, "I hope that this succession of shocks is not more than you can stand, gentlemen. There are going to be lots more and I need all three of you. But use of the spy-eyes and recorders would be a clean breach of my agreement with Lang. And I stress, gentlemen, that he is more important than any of us in this matter. With him, we have a slender chance to seek out and destroy this damned conspiracy. Without him— none."

Nakamura had been silent and glum since the meeting had broken up. The big man took his hatred seriously, and suddenly being allied to "friendly" Ruckers did not seem to have done his feelings much good.

"What's the matter, Nakamura? The very idea of cooperating with one enemy against a far greater one too much for you?" The sarcasm left Colonel Muller's voice. "Look, boy, I'm counting on you and a few others. I can't do this job alone. But if you feel it's too much to ask, then say so now!" He spoke the last words slowly. "There won't be any hard feelings and it will never appear on your record—my word on it. But I want volunteers, even if I do pick them myself!"

The colonel so obviously meant the last statement that Nakamura's control broke as he realized what he had just heard. A slow grin stole across his face, followed by a rumbling laugh. The colonel stared up at his towering junior in surprise and then began to grin himself. The other three joined in the laughter.

"Sorry, Colonel, I'm over it." Nakamura's dark-brown eyes met Muller's gaze frankly. "I'm a little slow on the reflexes, I guess. Killing those bastards is all I've had in mind for too long. Moe here actually likes the Ruck, sir, while it just makes me jumpy. Maybe I'm not the right man for this job, and if you want to wash me out that's all right. But I'd like to stay."

"You'll do. That's the end of it. You may have qualities that you aren't aware of, Lieutenant." The colonel swung around abruptly as the door to the cell opened behind him. They stared at Thau Lang, who appeared as calm as ever. His right hand was bloodstained and he was cleaning his long dagger on a piece of torn sheet held in the left.

"Down your piece, Private!" Slater had been the only one to see the enlisted guard by the far door to the corridor raise his carbine. Even as Slater spoke, he was in motion, a Martian leap placing his body between the old Rucker and the gun. Time froze.

The I-Corps private lowered his weapon at once. "Sorry, sir," he said quietly. "I saw the blood and got jumpy, but that's no excuse." He appeared embarrassed.

"Forget it," the colonel said. "We're all jumpy. I haven't briefed everyone I should. Feng, fill your people in, and quickly; no one else. The general orders on Thau Lang are already on the boards upstairs." He looked hard at Slater and said, "Thanks. That fellow was out of my vision. Inexcusable on my part." He looked back at the konsel, who had never changed his expression or moved. "What now, old friend?"

"Come back in here. The people are all free, but they will not harm you. We must talk." He turned and led the way. Mohini Dutt had left with Feng, so only the two lieutenants were with the colonel.

The first view was a shock. Three figures were praying, or in the attitude of prayer, on the smooth, plastic floor. Before them lay two other shapes, covered from head to foot in bloody sheets ripped from the beds. As the three officers entered, the two men and the girl stood and turned to face them, standing proudly erect.

Slater was conscious of the same thrill again. Her eyes met his again almost involuntarily and locked on them. The faint rose color over the cheeks seemed to deepen. Then the long lashes drooped and her head turned away.

"You see Danna Strom, a Wise Woman of the True People." Lang's deep voice rolled out the formal introduction. "You see Arta Burg and Milla Breen, who are warmen Who Have Killed. They will help us; indeed, they were sent to help us." He turned and bowed to the two still shapes, then turned again and continued. "The dead are gone from us. They are Jon Sodo Kar and Kolai Grado. They would not help us. They accepted death rather than do so. They were brave men and they will be remembered in the Writings of the Dead. Their bodies will feed Marswood. Peace to them, warmen and kin."

The colonel stepped forward. "Do you wish them buried now? And do you want any help?"

"Let them lie. We will take them out tonight and we will go alone. Now we must talk, Louis. These three have much to tell us. If you think it best, let us go back up to your room, where the big maps are. We shall need them."

As they returned to the surface, Slater studied the three Ruckers as closely as he could without seeming to. The two men were young and wiry, less than his own height—five eleven and three-quarters—by some few inches. The taller, Breen, wore a round cap of fur over his cropped black hair. Burg wore no hat and his brown hair was long, held by an embroidered band. Both were dressed in the usual oiled leather suits, dappled in green and brown. On their feet, like Slater himself, they wore the supple, tough boots, knee high, which the Ruckers had developed and the UN forces had simply copied in a synthetic. Slater suspected the leather was better, being less rigid and less pervious to cold. The men were clean shaven. All Ruckers were, and the secret of the depilatory they used was eagerly sought by every pharmaceutical house on Earth.

Danna Strom wore the same supple leathers as the men. She was small, hardly over five feet, Slater guessed. Her curly hair was so short it needed no restraint. Around her neck was a heavy leather thong that disappeared into the collar of her suit. On her left hand she wore a heavy but worn gold ring that bore a great blue jewel in its center. Something about the ring drew Slater's curiosity, and he decided to ask for a look at it some time if the occasion presented itself.

When they were all seated around the long oval table in the conference room, Slater was still chuckling over the looks that they had received on the way. The orderly sergeant outside at the desk had almost gone into shock.

A husky voice speaking Unit with a curious accent broke in on his musings. He realized the girl was standing and brought his thoughts back to the present. She went straight to the subject without any introduction.

"We, the Wise Women of the Ferkat Clan, sent messages to the other Wise Women, to all we could reach. We sent messages also to some of the konsels such as Thau Lang, men we knew to be True People, unchanged and unready to give up our old ways. We sent warnings. We began to look about us and see that the clans were being torn apart. Strange men had appeared who would not listen to other speech, other thoughts, than their own. The True People have no way of making people listen, save by persuasion. The Wise Women and the konsels are only to advise, to counsel, to dream for the people. They cannot give orders. Only men in?—" She looked at Thau Lang, obviously not knowing the word in Unit that she wanted.

"Bond?" Colonel Muller said thoughtfully. "Men who were pledged, perhaps, Thau?"

"War pledge is good," the older man replied. "War pledge, Danna."

"Men in war pledge then, men who have sworn to follow a leader to the death, they can be commanded. But no others, unless a man and a woman make a oneness contract. Then they must follow each other forever.

"Two of our years ago, such men began to come from the South, from the bad country. They were men of a new clan, they said, a secret clan, one that had been hidden deliberately to wait for the day when the whole planet would rise against Terra. They were to be our leaders, they said. There were not many of them, but they were a kind of True People, to most appearances anyway. We had no clan feud with them and we showed them such of our secrets as we would men of any clan with which we were at peace. They invited some of our young men to see their own country. They lived down south in the Bad Country, they said.

"All this was some time ago. Nothing made us, the women, suspicious, and we even helped and sent these stranger men on to other clans, as they asked us to do.

"But then things began to change. When we asked to be put in touch with the Wise Women of their secret clan, they grew puzzled, these messengers. First they said what we now believe to be the truth, that they had no Wise Women. When they saw that they did not gain approval by telling us this, they changed the story. Now they said that they had Wise Women, but that these women *ruled* them and were so powerful and secret that no one was allowed to see them." She stared at each of them before going on.

"Thau Lang says I must tell you certain things, things known to our men. This is so you can understand us when you come out with us into the Ruck."

In the name of God the Omnipotent's camel's ass, *WHAT*! thought Slater.

"True Men and Women," she went on, "do not lie, unless a prisoner, taken in clan feud, is asked things like the place his clan hunts. A lie to protect the clan from an enemy is the only kind we can tell! Do you men understand?" Slater and Nakamura nodded, as did Feng, who had slipped silently into the room some minutes before.

"This meant," the girl went on, "one of two things. Either these men were lying about their clan and thus considered us their enemies, or something much worse, they were lying about *everything*, their whole story was a lie, and we, the Wise Women, were being tricked for some purpose we could not even understand. Either way, it seemed that we had a secret enemy. Now we are sure of it.

"Those two down in your cellar were True People also," she said. "But they simply could not believe that helping Greenies was the way to solve the problem. It is hard even for us," she added naively, "but since we felt such cooperation necessary, after listening to Thau Lang, we had to kill them. Had just one more of us decided the other way, we would have attacked you instead."

And I'd never have seen your pretty pearl-gray teeth, Slater thought. Wonder who threw the winning vote? And when we go into the Ruck? Into the Ruck *with* a party of warmen and one of their legendary Wise Women! Whow! Despite his outward calm, Slater could not help but feel a thrill at the thought.

"I have said that these strange men came from the bad country. I do not know what to say about that. It is a place we avoid. I do not know if I should say more. I will let Thau Lang talk now, since he is the elder among us and has much wisdom." She sat down but could not help looking at Slater as she did so, a demure quick glance.

Her eyes seemed to pierce his very flesh and he grew warm. What in hell is happening to me? he wondered to himself.

"Look at your map, soldiers." The konsel now stood before the big map that Colonel Muller had used earlier in the day. His horny forefinger moved down from the Ares Base at the North Pole to a point marked Mare Cimmerium.

"We keep our own records you know. Some are quite complex. Among them are maps, early ones and any new that we make ourselves. Our young men make new maps whenever we go into new territory. Also, we steal your maps when we can, since you have the spy-eyes, up in the high heavens, and can see things once in a while that we do not." His finger went back to the blot marked Cimmerium.

"We do not know this place. Men who have gone here—that is, young men seeking visions or new games areas, who *said* they were going here—have not ever returned. If any early expedition of your people, or perhaps far back, when they were *our* people, went here, it did not report either. For a long time we have avoided this place. On the maps kept by the Wise Women, which all clans have a right to use, this is bad country—'Bad Country One,' because it is the first one we found." His finger moved to another uncharted area, also in the south, a narrower one labeled Scamander. "This is a second such place, Bad Country Two. We have heard of others still, on the other side of the planet, but they are only rumors, and it is with this hemisphere that we have to deal.

"So, we have two bad countries. They are deep places, with what you call great canyons or rifts running down the center. And there are other things we know about them. Marswood is very strange there. The *old* Mars plants are large there as well as our new ones. In fact, they are very thick there. Also, there are some things you have never seen, and we—only far off.

Beasts of some size but not, we think, of old Earth." His quiet tones died without echo. His auditors had plenty to think about.

It had not surprised earlier scientists at all to find that Mars possessed a native plant life. Many were surprised, though, at its complexity. Save for a few thoughtful exobiologists, no one had realized that if Mars was truly a dying world, its oxygen locked up in its soil, any surviving forms of life would probably be extremely sophisticated, rather than the simple mosses or lichens of the earlier speculations. The plants of Mars were fantastic, both in appearance and in their methods of living.

And they were still around. The tremendous boost in the oxygen content of the atmosphere had probably eliminated a few species, but most of the others had adapted somehow. For one thing, with all the free oxygen they needed, they could colonize places that the Terran life-forms still found too barren. As a result, the poles were a veritable jungle of Mars plants. They also grew thickly on the barren rock plateaus and deep into the caves, wherever even a minute amount of light penetrated. Many were distinctly dangerous.

When still small — in the long eons before Terraforming — many of the latter had learned, like the bladderworts and pitcher plants of Earth, to trap the tiny "insects" that the first explorers found occasionally in the ground cover. In many cases now grown to large size, these same plants, the "old" plants as Thau Lang called them, were only too pleased with the introduced animal life, up to and including human beings. The time of greatest danger to unwary humans was the long Martian winter, when many of the introduced species died back, sporated, or simply hibernated. The Ruckers had learned to live with the plants of old Mars and even to make use of some, but a faint element of fear still shrouded everything not of Terran origin. For all their local knowledge, even the True People felt on occasion that they were only trespassers on an ancient and alien world.

"What animals? Only a couple have been recorded much larger than an Earth cat — the original ones I mean, not the ferkats." Feng was perhaps sharper than he meant to sound.

As an Intelligence officer, he was supposed to be the last word on Martian life-forms. On Mars I-Corps was the military's science section as well, and the tall Chinese was a skilled biologist. But Lang was unruffled.

# CHAPTER 4

# *What's Out There?*

"CAPTAIN, I DO NOT KNOW HOW TO ANSWER YOU," THAU Lang replied. "Men who have very carefully scouted the edges of these two forbidden areas claim to have seen large shapes, to have seen strange tracks, to have heard sounds unlike anything else we know. If we go into the Ruck together—as Louis and I plan—perhaps then you will be the first to learn more. Who knows?"

"Old Martians." In Nakamura's deep-chested tones, the phrase rang like a gong. "After all these years, are we really going out to look up some drunk prospector's tale? Granted, the weapon we just saw is a peculiar thing, but does it have to mean that an alien technology exists? I'd use Occam's Razor, sir, and postulate some kind of trick to make us believe just that—to take us off guard, so that the real enemy could be at our throats." Nakamura's glare of dislike swept the table but landed only on the four clanspeople. He had brought up something that they had all avoided, perhaps unconsciously.

When old friends with long service on Mars met for a relaxed evening in a secluded spot, a certain subject was very apt indeed to recur—perhaps a tale about the finding of an oddly carved

35

stone on a distant plateau. When the waitress brought drinks the conversation would stop, of course. But when she left, a second veteran might cap the first tale with one of his own, about the moving lights he had seen far off on a winter's night deep in the Ruck, lights of a strange violet shade, which seemed to rise in the air before fading out.

Every scrap of such information, including the maunderings of the few half-insane souls who still tried to find treasure out in the wilderness of Marswood, was said to be kept in a sealed vault at I-Corps Center on Earth. This too was probably a legend, thought Slater. At least no I-Corps man or woman could be made to confirm it. All it meant, if true, was that even the cold computers and their human children who ruled I-Corps were not immune to the magic of finding another intelligent race in the Solar System.

Yet innumerable books and space operas, the Tridee fare of young and old, resurrected the Old Martians each time they were buried by the tired voices of orthodox science. At least twice a year in the Parliament of Man, some delegate could be counted on to rise and "disclose new evidence of a native intelligent race on Mars," as well as to ask (or demand) that UN forces investigate, preferably within twenty-four hours. And high-echelon visitors always wanted to know what the "latest evidence" for intelligent Martian life was. They all seemed to feel that the UN Command had nothing better to do than run down the latest rumor on the subject. Since they all seemed to feel that the very same people had a great deal of information they were concealing, and made this belief plain, the exasperation of any Mars veteran about the subject of Old Martians was not hard to understand.

All this passed through Slater's mind in a flicker, then he listened, for Muller was answering Nakamura.

"Your theory may be right, Lieutenant. That is *half* right. I too am in favor of Occam's Razor. Let us eliminate the unnecessary from our calculations by all means. However. All the evidence says that the True People, our beloved enemies whom you regard with such proper suspicion, are not behind this drive for unity. They are being *used*." He crushed his cigarette in an ashtray of native jadeite.

"That artifact we examined may have been made on Earth, or it may have been made here. By whoever is leading this movement—by the 'U-Men,' let us say. Or it may have been made in neither place." He smiled slightly at the effect of his words.

"No, I am not seriously proposing that we have visitors from Pluto or the Crab Nebula. But let's assume that we have human enemies to deal with. People who dislike the present world government. Does any *other* place seem plausible as a headquarters? I address my officers, since this is their province rather than that of the True Men."

"The asteroid belt. A secret factory. It's the logical place, sir, with all the big-company mines having their plants out there. A secret base would be a cinch and it's nearer than Earth is in most of its trajectories." Feng coughed and even appeared a little embarrassed. "I, ugh, sometimes compose absurd theories of warfare for my own amusement, sir, and I have often thought that the belt was a logical spot to use as a base for an attack. I thought of Earth as the target, though, not Mars."

"Yes, the belt is not well policed and we know that the big corporations do not always comply with regulations. If one of them is implicated, the belt is a good place. So good that we are having it looked at in depth, as we sit here. But it will be a long search, out there and back on Earth as well. The only thing we can do *here* is to improve our surveillance satellites so that if a ship is dodging the ones now used, it may be caught. And a good spy, maybe a plant at H.Q., could even negate that move.

"So we are left with the Ruck. Gentlemen, I need three flexible men—good combat men—to work *in* the Ruck, with our friends here. In fact, I want you disguised as Ruckers. If you accept, I'll get on with it. Any questions?—Yes, Lieutenant Nakamura?"

"My size, sir. I've never seen a Rucker my size. I thought six feet was the absolute limit. I don't see how I fit in here."

"Very sound thinking. I'll let Danna Strom answer you."

The girl was not rude, simply terse. "These new strange men, the ones who say they belong to a secret clan: They are all as big as you, Lieutenant, at least the ones we have seen.

They know that many of our foolish young men think that great size is important in a man. The strangers say that all will be their size, the size of gods, when the Greenies are kicked off the planet."

"You mean that I'm supposed to impersonate one of these mystery men? But I can't even speak Rucker, let alone whatever these weird types talk. And are they brown-eyed? With my yellow hair?"

"Don't worry, we've thought of that one." Muller's tone was easy and relaxed. "You'll have dye on your skin and hair. Contacts too. As for language, nothing could teach you believable Rucker in less than a year, so you'll be under a vow of silence. It's a common thing among the younger warmen, teaches them discipline. And you'll be getting lessons from the True People with us as well, so that in a short time you can *understand* some of what's said. That's the most important thing."

"Despite—well, shall we say pronounced lack of cooperation from the Ruckers, there is a considerable body of material available on their social life. I can release any of it needed. And I shall welcome the chance to see how much of our data are accurate." Captain Feng was as close to being enthusiastic as he ever allowed himself. "How long to when we leave, sir?"

"Three days. That is so no possible leak can develop and also because we are desperate for quick results. Not much time."

They were to plunge into the Ruck, into Marswood, on a mission of extraordinary danger allied to four of their bitterest enemies, people who had by their own admission killed many UN men in battle. With these strange guides, the four officers were to penetrate utterly unknown country, going into areas deemed by the savages themselves too dangerous to trifle with. Apart from the known hazards of Marswood, which were lethal enough, the likelihood of encountering something unknown and inimical appeared excellent. In cold light of reason, the only sensible thing to do was to bolt from the room and ask to be hospitalized, choosing cowardice as the far less of two evils!

Since no one contemplated anything of the kind, it was

evident that the colonel knew his men. Actually, they were being given an opportunity for a secret mission into enemy country—the dream of any junior officer. Even the usually imperturbable Captain Feng could not conceal his excitement. Yes, Muller knew his men, Slater conceded ruefully to himself.

"I will instruct Feng on how to brief you two," the commander said. "There's a dance tonight and you might as well enjoy it. Keep your mouths shut and I'll see you in the morning. This is Wednesday. We leave at dawn on Saturday, before daylight. The True People will be quartered in the I-Corps Section, except for Thau Lang, who will share my quarters. I'll give separate orders about them."

As the Ruckers filed out behind the old konsel, Slater kept his eyes on the young Wise Woman. Was he mistaken, or had a wistful look come over her face at the mention of the dance? At the door she turned and looked back at him before going out with the others. What did they say, those tawny eyes, that made his skin tingle whenever they met his?

The weekly dance in the Free Lounge was usually good fun, and this one was no exception. The fort was buzzing with rumors, and the tight seal on outside communication had hardly damped them. Since it was known that Slater and Nakamura were in the inner circle, they were besieged with pleas for information.

"Come on, Lieutenant, give!" Private Bobbie Lee Wilcox, the post clown, was eager for any kind of information. "You can have my booze card for a month, honest!"

"Bobbie Lee," Slater said, before taking a judicious pull at his Old Marswood and soda, "your ration was pledged, the last time I checked, three years ahead to various lads and ladies. Otherwise I'd be glad to help out." There was a shout of laughter from the others around them. "The Prophet forbids me strong drink," he added impassively.

Eventually the crowd drifted off to pounce on Nakamura, who had just walked in. Slater was brooding over his next drink when dulcet tones inquired if he cared to dance. Looking up, he found Mohini Dutt smiling down at him. The Benares Bomber wore a few strategic wisps of green here and there that managed to make her magnificent brown body seem about three times nakeder than if she had been nude.

Out on the floor, her approach was about as subtle as that of a main battle tank. "What are you guys cooking up, you Pathan rat?" she purred into his ear. "Feng won't tell me, although I know everything else. You types are leaving the fort. I know that because I get to be I-Corps chief until Captain Inscrutable comes back." She rubbed softly against him and at the same time looked deep into his eyes. Several watching males felt their temperatures rise ten degrees.

"Ah, what am I bid for my secret, Helpless Hindu Passion Plant?"

"I might have known," she said with mock weariness. "But," she added, her voice hardening, "I want something besides words. You bums are going on some spree or other. I want in. Why should I stay here and knit? I can deck any one of you, including Nakamura—and I mean in hand-to-hand, so wipe that leer off your face."

"Well, I do have a certain amount of discretion, Mohini," Slater said, his face rigid. "But I can't talk about it here. Why don't we adjourn to—"

"My quarters? Well, I can always throw you out. Anyway, my boy is on leave at Orcus and we couldn't go together. He must be shacked up with at least three of those rapacious base bimbos by now, poor darling." Her current flame was Senior Warrant Palacios, whom Slater had always thought a near relative of a Mountain gorilla. However, he had the sense not to laugh. He enjoyed the glare he got from Nakamura as he followed Mohini from the big lounge, but missed the tears in the eyes of little Spec. 4 Bronwyn Carter, who had been eyeing his dashing leanness for the whole fortnight of her present assignment.

"Never mind, love," said Bronwyn's superior, Sergeant Palla Gluck. "Have a drink and relax. That big slob will wear him out and it's only a temporary arrangement anyway. Next week he'll be free again."

After a pleasant but totally enervating night, Slater reported to Captain Feng and soon discovered that he was not there for a rest cure. Classified hypnotapes of what was known to I-

Corps about the Ruckers began at once. To break the train of thought and keep one alert, a refresher on the life-forms of Mars, native and introduced, began the minute a segment of the other tape stopped. By noon, lieutenants Slater and Nakamura had the feeling that they had been carrying bricks up Mount Everest. Hypnotapes are not easy to digest, being high-pressure, subliminal teaching of the most advanced kind. A morning on the couch was followed by a long afternoon of the same. Slater and his friend had only the dubious comfort of seeing Feng put himself through most of the same tapes, with Mohini Dutt taking over the transmission machine. The colonel and Thau Lang remained in Muller's quarters and the three younger Ruckers stayed in a sealed-off section of the I-Corps basement. No one mentioned them, but Slater tried to burn into his mind every scrap of information he could extract about the Rucker Wise Women. Mohini Dutt would have been quite annoyed to learn that even in their moments of greatest passion, the curious amber gaze of Danna Strom had kept intruding into Slater's mind. Somehow he could not get the girl's face out of his head. Or her slim body. Even while tapes and pictures fed into his brain through the omniviewer, some-how the strange loveliness of the little wild woman kept ob-truding between his consciousness and the images he was supposed to be absorbing. *Damn! This is really incredible. It has to stop! Back to work, idiot!*

"The outstanding characteristics of the Mars plant we call *Neorhus* and the locals, giant ivy, are incredibly fast growth, adaption to considerable cold, and the refined vesicant poison of the leaf surfaces. The constituents of the latter, a mutated modification of the *urushiol* secreted by the ancestral plant, consist essentially of two complex vegetable proteins. Serums worked out on Earth, where the original plant is no more than a nuisance, are useless here on Mars, and the virulence of the mutated secretions must be combated by different measures. First, injections—"

The droning, supercilious voice on the tape he was listening to suddenly cut off and the mask of the viewscreen removed from his face. He found Mohini Dutt looking down at him. The others still lay under their headshields on nearby couches.

"I don't know about you, super stud" was her affectionate greeting. "I have orders to let the three new pets have whatever they want, within reason, that is. Guess what little Miss Maneater wants? You, lover boy, that's what. So shake loose and go hold her hand, or whatever she wants held. The colonel says you can have half an hour." She made an obscene gesture and went back to her machines.

Somewhat dazed from the omniviewer, Slater made no wisecracks as he went down the corridor. A guard, who had notice of his coming, admitted him to the quarters occupied by the three younger Ruckers.

Once inside the suite, he was conscious of a strange but not unpleasant odor. Then into the main room from a side door came Danna Strom. She carried two cups of something that steamed, the obvious source of the smell. There was no sign of the other two Ruckers.

"Sit down on this couch, please, Lieutenant Slater." As he did she extended one of the cups. The fragrance was sharp and yet pleasant, bittersweet and untamed, not unlike the girl herself. She sat next to him, still holding out one cup in invitation.

"I have made the Tea of Dreaming. You do not know yet what that is. As a Wise Woman, I cannot lie to myself. Our lives are mingled—at least, that is how I read it in my own dreams." The amber cat eyes stared into his from a foot away. "Drink. It will not harm you. I swear by my oath of guidance, by my medal of office." She drew the leather thong from out of her collar. From the end hung a flat medallion, apparently of hammered silver. With his right hand Slater reached for the cup. With his left he took the medal and held it up.

It showed one blank side, but on the other, much worn by time and use, a face. It was not human, but it might have been mammalian. The chin was very square and the large oval eyes wrapped around the round head to well on the sides. The ears, if that is what they were, were cones, set higher on the skull than those of humans, so that they were almost stubby horns. The forehead bulged. The thing was very, very old, Slater realized, and he knew that he was seeing something that probably no one not a Rucker had ever looked at before.

There was only one response to a gesture of trust such as

this. He tilted his cup and drank. He had been sitting erect, but as the hot liquid raced down his throat, its effect was instantaneous. Despite himself he clawed for his holstered gun even as he slid sideways. Yet his last thought was one of relief, for he saw with fading sight that the girl was slumping beside him, her drained cup also dropped to the floor. Then blackness closed in.

# CHAPTER 5

# *The Sea of Dreams*

$A$T FIRST THE DARKNESS WAS BROKEN ONLY BY VAGUE patches of light, as if Slater were in the ancient empty belly of space between the great galaxies, and the galaxies themselves were just distant blurs, the only breaks in the chaos of mindless night, the outer rim of eternity.

Then the light grew, the blurs increased, like ink spreading over a blotter, until suddenly it was day and Slater found himself looking out over an alien landscape. And beside him was the girl.

He knew, deep inside, that he was in the grip of the unreal, but he was quite incapable of doing anything about that. It was as if he and the Wise Woman were puppets being moved about the land by mighty and invisible fingers. Despite his awareness of the dream state, it was *real*, yet on another plane.

The sky overhead was green, and from it two suns flamed, one red and close, the other blazing white, twice the power of the red orb but much, much farther away. They sat in tall blue-green grass. In the middle distance tall trees swayed in the wind, their bronze trunks gleaming in the sunlight. Even as he thought this, the man realized that there was no wind. It was beautiful but quite unearthly. And un-Martian as well.

It was the immediate foreground that gripped him, however. The grass grew right down to the edge of water, brown still water that stretched out of sight, both before them and away on either hand. No beach was visible, just the sward reaching down to the sea. Somehow he knew that it was a sea, not a lake or river. Brown was its normal color, not soil or vegetational staining, this too he knew.

Now, far out, something broke the surface. Its details were beyond the range of vision, but it was coming toward them rapidly and soon its outlines could be made out. It was some kind of boat.

They stood up now and he noted that they were both nude. He felt as innocent as a child, and as lighthearted. She turned to him and smiled and held out a hand to take his. Together they walked down to the water, to await the boat, which was now very close to the land.

It was a small boat, high at bow and stern. In the stern was a tall figure, garbed in curious red wrappings, its head masked in a featureless round helm, also red, with no eyeholes. It was very thin, and as the vessel touched the shore it stood, holding a steering oar in bluish, bony claws, in an attitude of listening. Somehow, Slater knew, it could not see, but used another sense. For the first time he grew a little afraid, and he felt the girl shrink against his side. He noticed, almost in passing, a bulbous, glittering object protruding from the creature's scarlet belt, but caught no detail.

The compulsion to board the boat was overwhelming, and the strange helmsman and the dread he radiated were not enough to prevent it. The creature stood unmoving until they stepped aboard, and only then did it thrust with its oar and turn them from the bank. As the boat glided across the surface in the direction from which it had come, Slater realized that no means of propulsion was apparent and that the strange master of the craft steered it only with his oar.

So fast was the dream's pace! Already they were far out on

the waters and the land behind them had receded to a distant blur. All around them the brown and silent sea stretched, still, without wave or wind motion, without a ripple or a sign of life. On and on sailed the little boat. Hand in hand, like two frightened children, Slater and Danna sat silent in its center, ever conscious of the tall figure that towered behind them.

At last in the distance ahead another blur showed that once more they were approaching land. Like two numbed spectators of some shadow play, who cannot take part but are doomed forever to watch, the man and woman waited as the details of the land ahead grew out of the alien sea on which they floated.

It was not similar to that which they had left but higher, and as the details became clearer their blood grew chill, despite the warm and windless air.

Tall reddish things, slimy fronds limp in the dead air, rose above the dark soil of the landing place. Under these nightmare growths—for to call them trees was impossible—grew stunted, twisted shapes like deformed mushrooms, only far larger and with overlapping petals of a pallid yellow.

The boat came gently to rest on the marge, and still hand in hand, the two got out. Before them, up a gentle slope, led a path that they knew, despite their feeling an increasing dread, they must follow. As they began to walk, terror building slowly in their captive minds, behind them they heard the faint *swash* of their ferry craft's turning to retrace its track across the brown water.

Before they turned a high corner of the path, they paused to look back. Behind and below them, the half-moon boat was putting out to sea again, the red ball of the pilot's helm gleaming in the setting of the large red sun. The white sun had gone and now they realized that the light was fading. Far below, from the surface of the distant water, came a strange, echoing cry, high and mournful. It was the farewell of the nightmare boatman, a note somehow mocking and scornful as well as somber and menacing.

Now they turned once more and continued their enforced pilgrimage into the evening shadows of the strange wood. They were high on the shoulder of a hill, and before them the dark growths seemed to cluster closer still about the narrow path. The land leveled too, but they had felt no strain of climbing.

The sense of being *pulled* grew stronger yet, and as they advanced, for the first time, Slater tried feebly to fight back, as feeling grew that they were being lured to some unimaginable horror. The girl's pale body beside him, still gripping his hand, seemed to lend him strength. For the first time he managed to check his pace, as if the laws of the alien land of dreams were relaxing and might allow him—if he was strong enough—some control over his own body.

Then the pull strengthened and he was powerless to gainsay it. *Something* ahead was drawing them on, and no mere human strength would ever be enough to resist it. Lurching and stumbling, he and his helpless companion were led inexorably on into the deepening shade of the accursed tree things that by then actually grew over the path.

The red sun was on the horizon, and the gloom under the strange plant life was becoming hard to penetrate. The path still led on, though, and they had no trouble following it. Then the call began.

From the trees ahead there came a hideous sound. It was a wailing that rose and fell on the still air of the haunted wood. It was not loud, but it was curiously penetrating, seeming to permeate their very bones. Slater sensed a kinship to the cry of the eldritch boatman, even as he heard it. Despite the icy chill which warned them that only doom lay ahead, the two began to run. They were being called, called to some unknown end by some unimaginable horror and there was no way they could halt their progress, no way they could stop. Hand in hand they raced on, while the wailing grew in volume ahead of them. Now it was so close that a turn around the next corner would bring them to it. It had to be stopped, but there was no help, no help, no—

"No! No!" gasped Slater. He was half off the couch, his arms raised to ward something off. Beside him the Rucker girl was waking too, her eyes filled with the same terror as his, her mouth also open to cry out in defiance and despair.

They came truly awake and checked their cries at the same moment. Staggering to his feet, Slater leaned against a table on the side of the room and looked down at the girl who had come through the ghastly experience with him. For he had no doubt that she had somehow been with him, had shared whatever emotions and experiences he had. The mysterious drink they had taken had somehow linked their minds in a way he had not dreamed possible, but that he was nearly not sure existed. His breath came more evenly but it was still a moment before he could trust his voice.

"So much for your oath! I wonder why I believed you when you said nothing could happen to me!"

Her response was agonized. "No, no, you must believe me! Nothing like this ever happened before. On my life, Slater—on my life, I swear that nothing like this ever happened. We have been taken by something else that is not from us but outside! Please, I beg—" And here her glance grew proud and she sat erect. "I, Wise Woman of the True People, *beg* you to listen. You do not know what that means maybe, but since I became a woman, I have never begged anything. This is terribly important, what just happened to us."

He could not but believe her. Her sincerity was too transparent, and besides, the True People did not lie when they said, like children, that they would not. That much he had come to know from his most recent training. He sat down again and took her outstretched hand in his.

"All right, Danna. I'm sorry. I was too hasty. Tell me what you think happened. Better still, start by telling me what you think *ought* to have happened when we drank the stuff—it links minds, doesn't it?"

"Yes! The Dream Tea helps one to see the future, and it also ties the minds of those who—well, of friends, persons who trust one another together so that they sometimes can see part of the future together. Only the Wise Women know how to make it, and we alone have the right to give it out. But it is uncertain. You cannot always trust what it shows. It might show a hunt, with men being killed. Then the real hunt might have other, different men killed. Or it might show a man his father or mother when they were long dead." She made this latter announcement quite calmly, as if it was the most ordinary thing in the world.

She looked away and her voice grew slightly muffled. "I had a vision which said that you and I might be tied to one another in some way. It was a strong vision!" She looked back and her eyes grew larger as she continued. "But what happened to us, I never heard of anything like that! We were in a place that does not exist, being pulled by some awful power. I never believed such a thing possible. Those trees and whatever creature was in the boat, they were like things out of an evil dream, the kind you get when you eat bad food. That surely was no vision of the future!" Her voice was shaking with remembered disgust.

Slater was silent, thinking hard. He was deathly tired but he also felt that somehow, somewhere, the elements of the dream vision had a message for him. But the effort required to use his tired brain, already overtaxed by the forced learning of the hypnoptapes, was too much and he gave up trying. Perhaps it would make more sense later.

The girl eyed him in silence. She had recovered her self-control and now she sat on the plastic of the issue couch and waited for him to speak.

"I'm going to see the colonel and your boss, Thau Lang," he said, thinking out his problem slowly. "Maybe they can make some sense of this." A new thought came to him. "Where are the other two? They must have heard this, heard us cry out. How come they aren't here by now?"

A movement too small to be called a smile touched the corner of Danna's mouth. "They are asleep. They do not like the fort; they are like your Nakamura and cannot give up their hatred easily. I gave them a drug, to sleep until we go. Besides," she added, her voice perfectly frank, "I wanted to be alone with you. Our lives are linked. The dream showed that even if whatever else was there makes no sense. I think we are to love each other..." She looked down, as if a little startled by what she had said.

"Danna, Danna," Slater began. He could not immediately frame words, and paused, startled by the intensity of the emotion that swept over him. "Listen, I feel strongly toward you, but I am an officer on duty. I cannot talk of such things now, not until the mission is over. Do you understand?" Slater's words surfaced with an intensity that surprised him. Desperately, with a passion that one corner of his brain continued to regard with amazement, he wanted the girl to believe him.

She looked at him long and hard, the amber, slanted eyes seeming to weigh his very soul. Then she sighed, as a good child does when told that he only can go to the circus *next* week. "I understand," she said in her soft, husky voice. "I wish it were not so. But we may have a journey together; in fact, that is what is planned. Things may change."

As he left the room, shaken in body and spirit, she made no move toward him and his last glimpse was of her sitting, bemused, on the big divan. She could not have showed more plainly that she loved him. And he had been forced to reject her, a rejection that hurt him more than he would have believed possible. Extraordinary though it seemed, he apparently was falling in love with a member of a jungle race sworn to destroy everything he had been trained to uphold. Yet he did not seem to mind!

Slater returned to Mohini and explained that he had to see the colonel at once. She had no objection. The other two were still under their masks and the afternoon run of the lessons had some time to go yet.

There was no guard at Muller's quarters and Slater was admitted by the commandant himself. Though he had been invited in before, the room still held his interest. There were many loaded bookshelves, some of the volumes in languages that meant nothing to Slater. But there were also curious art pieces, many of primitive Earth art and, he had been told, valuable. A mask of wood, a Biafran antiquity, hung next to a painting of Martian hawks by Ferruco, the planet's best-known artist. The colonel had said that the curved throwing stick of polished wood that hung over the door was an ancient *woomera* of old Australia, a special kind called a *kirris*, used only for warfare and never for the hunt. Other mementos and curiosities were scattered about. The only visible weapon besides the boomerang was a very short, heavy Rucker bow. It was in the hands of Thau Lang, who sat at ease in a carved wooden chair, rubbing down the polished dark wood with a cloth and some oil. He nodded gravely as Slater came in.

Slater said quickly, "I need some advice, sir. And I think the konsel better hear it too."

He told the whole story, attempting to conceal nothing, but stumbled a bit when he came to the part that concerned his own feelings about Danna. Somehow he got through it all. The two older men listened in silence, occasionally glancing at one another but not interrupting.

"You were right to come to me," Muller said when Slater was through. "This is most important. I know a little bit about the Dream Tea and the konsel much more. I have never heard of this effect or any such dream, nothing remotely like it. What about you, Thau?"

"I have *heard* of it. But only—how do you say, Louis—secondhand. Such strange dreams have come occasionally, it is said, to men who have taken the Dream Tea when near one of the forbidden lands, the bad countries. Few care to speak of such things openly, and Danna is very, very young to be a Wise Woman. She probably has not heard of this, but there are older women of my clan who know about such dreams—they are meant as a warning by evil spirits, at least that is the explanation I have heard. I simply made a note of it in my secret files since I planned to go to the bad country some day myself—at least before I die."

Muller rose and began to pace the room, hands behind his back. "This sort of thing is a special study of mine. I've read about everything in five languages on it and a lot more that I got translated. I know the effects of most Terran and Martian hallucinogens, from the peyote buttons to the mutated *Rauwolfia* that makes up the main ingredient for that cup of tea you just had, Slater. But what I can't seem to learn anything about are the *temporal* effects, the distances covered in space and time by these happenings. Because there *is* an element of predictability and this sort of experience *does* show the future, however dimly—and the past, sometimes. But I have never dared ask what the I-Corps files on the subject have. Afraid of a reprimand, I guess."

He wheeled suddenly and glared at Slater. "How strong was this feeling that you had seen something familiar, something you recognized?"

"Well—it's hard to pin it down, sir, but it was strong enough to make me feel that it was important. I've never been that scared in my life, but still I knew I'd noticed something, maybe some *things*. I just can't seem to recall what it or they were."

"Hmph. And you're no chicken, either. Well, let it alone for now and try to sneak up on it mentally later. Otherwise, if you're anything like me, you'll never get it. That weird boatman of yours, now. Did he make you think of anything? I have an idea of my own, but it's one I'd rather mull over a long time before producing."

"No—nothing in particular, just something alien and malignant. Wait! I did have a feeling! That . . . if the creature's helmet had been removed, I might have seen the face that I saw on Danna's medal." The old konsel stiffened as Slater spoke and he realized belatedly that he had not mentioned the medal.

He backtracked and described the whole thing again. It was quickly obvious that Thau Lang was shocked.

"Louis," he said abruptly, "and you, too, young Slater, this is a terrible thing you tell me, if what you say is true. Louis, you know more of the True People than any other off-planet man. You and I have a plan to bring peace to Mars, one that we have shared for many years. But *this* is something that no outsider, not even a blooded warman or clanwoman, should know. The medals of the Wise Women and the ones that we konsels get, they are given at secret ceremonies that no one outside must hear of, on pain of death." He paused, his face a graven mask, the chevrons of the senior warmen standing out on his lined forehead.

"I do not ever mention my medal except to an equal. I will not show it now. It is here—" He tapped his breast. "But I will say to you both, under secrecy, that it resembles a smaller one like Danna's. Young Slater, do you know what you are saying about our most sacred emblem?" His voice was agonized and sweat beaded his forehead.

"Calm, calm, old friend." Muller's answering voice was deep and reassuring. "You are a konsel, a senior warman, not a child. You have a new thought, that the True People may have been in the grip of some alien force for many, many years. That your sacred secret was foisted on you by something that is using you and your people. It may be so and yet—it may be nothing of the kind. The Dream Tea tells many half-truths and not so infrequently a sheer fantasy, with no truth at all—only the ego wish of the one who dreams. So take heart. Even if—I say, *if*—there is a connection of some kind between your medals and the evil we seek, then you will need a man's full strength to untangle the evil web. This is no time to fall to bemoaning past mistakes. We must be alert, keep our eyes open, and watch for new things, new ideas, new interpretations. And you are no longer alone." He leaned over and lightly punched the sinewy shoulder of his friend. "Some day you will tell me, if you think it fit, how you got those medals."

# CHAPTER 6

# A Menacing Start

*T*HAU LANG WAS CHAGRINED.

"You are right, I cannot afford to be weak. Thank you, Louis. As you say, it is better not to be alone in a case like this. We had—" He paused, head cocked on one side. "A runner comes this way, Louis. Someone needs you, I think."

A peremptory knock brought them all to their feet. Muller opened the door and a breathless sergeant saluted and handed him a message flimsy. "Duty officer said this was marked Most Urgent, Colonel, so I ran."

"Thank you, Sergeant, you were quite right. Say nothing to anyone, and tell the duty officer and the communications man who took the message the same. Clear?"

"Yes, sir!" In a second the man was gone, striding up the passage. As his footsteps died away, Muller's impassive face relaxed a little and he sighed as he reread the flimsy.

"This would have to happen now! Of all the infernal damned luck! No, wait! I won't believe this is luck, by God! Too many coincidences make a pattern." He tossed the message to Slater. "Here. Read it aloud."

Slater read the eight-word message slowly, as much due to

tiredness as anything else. "Pelham escaped. Believed heading your way. More follows." It was signed by the governor of Mars, Slater noted.

Thau Lang sat up at this. Even the Ruck was not thick enough to keep out Pelham's story. No one needed to ask which Pelham. If there had been a thousand men of that name on the planet, the fact that the governor sent a personal comm would have made it plain who was meant. In an emergency there was only one Pelham.

"Junius Brutus Pelham is loose again. JayBee," Muller said. His tone was soft, musing, as if he was reminiscing to himself rather than talking to others. For five years, long *Martian* years, the most dangerous man on Mars had been securely caged. Clever attorneys, paid with much of the loot Pelham had secreted and which the government's best efforts had been unable to locate, had beaten the X Chamber. But they could do no more. Life imprisonment was the best they could get him, and the settlements had almost risen in revolt even so. For JayBee Pelham, as they called him, was no ordinary criminal, or even killer. He was a monster, a throwback to some age of Attila or Timur, or to use a somewhat more recent example, the warped animal who had created German Naziism. A murderer a dozen times over, Pelham was also a criminal genius. And more, for the man could attract adherents, men and women who were themselves no common thugs; people of great talent who believed Pelham to be their Messiah.

The People's Work Force, the political party he organized, had no real program beyond hazy utopianism and Free Everything, but it had JayBee and that made it a standing menace. Before he was exposed for a thief and murderer, the PWF had won many local elections and come very near to dominating the Martian Union, the planet's unicameral legislature. But the Planetary Security Service, working with I-Corps of the UN Command, learned of the criminal conspiracy Pelham headed, and it was they who finally hunted him down. His exposure wrecked the party beyond recall. The evidence was too clear, for all save the fanatics—and there were few of them. When they realized that they had come so close to electing a demogogue and spellbinder who was as dangerous as a plague bacillus, a vast wave of nausea swept over the older cities that held the majority of Mars' citizens.

Still, the police and military almost failed to get their man. Even while the net was closing, JayBee and his inner circle did the unexpected—they took to the Ruck and vanished. To most of the planet, they seemed to have committed suicide.

I-Corps and the high command on Mars were not so sanguine, however. They had come to respect Pelham's abilities and were unwilling to assume that he was dead until the body was on display. The thought ran around the council chambers like lightning. "What if Pelham somehow managed to join the Ruckers?" Pelham and the Ruckers in combination? The very idea was a nightmare!

The finest "bush" experts of the UN forces were consulted. Rewards for information from True People informants—there are always a few, though the information they would give was very limited—were doubled. And a number of hunting groups were formed. One was led by Muller, then a major, but already known to be the best man in the Ruck on the planet, at least in Terran uniform.

Two months later, acting on intuition, scraps of information, and computer forecasts, Muller found his man in an arid section of the great Elysium plain. Pelham had not been able to get outside help, and his extraordinary powers were gravely weakened away from the areas under civilized control. He and his little band of the faithful were ill, and they surrendered without a fight. Many people who knew nothing about the matter tended to discount the fabled Pelham ability after that, but Muller was not one of them, as he now explained.

"He talked quite freely to me on the way back to the copter LZ. We had a bit of a wait and he was a little delirious.

"Consider what he did. Knowing almost nothing of the Ruck, he managed to remain hidden and unkilled by the True People for two months. His group, five men and three women, were ill but not dying. I honestly think they were getting better! He never stopped experimenting, did JayBee—on people, plants, clothes, anything he could reach. Listen to what he told me, will you: 'I made a mistake, Major, a bad one. I never paid any real attention to the Ruck before. Next time I'll know better. This is where the action is, not in the Enclaves, and this is where the power is. Look for me next time and you'll have a little trouble.' He actually smiled at me. He has great charm, you know.

"Well, I laughed at him, which was my mistake. I was sure he could not escape the X Chamber. Now he's loose at the worst possible time and in the worst possible area. Add another factor to an already dubious equation."

"Could he be behind this, sir—I mean, the very thing we are investigating?"

"No, I don't see how that's possible, Slater. There's an active, guiding element involved, but one that just isn't Pelham. I'll tell you this—and I may even be wrong about what I said earlier—Pelham is now probably pretty much of a Ruck specialist. He gets books, and you can bet there's a leak, even in a MaxSec prison like Orcus Center. He still has followers, that we know. We didn't get them all, and some of them are still probably hidden in places where they can cause a lot of trouble. As well as seeing that JayBee got all the dope on whatever interested him. Oh yes, he's a Ruck expert now. And whatever is going on out there, he knows something about it, whether he actually started it or not. And he's going to be mixed up in it from now on too." Muller paused as if thinking.

"I'm going to talk to the High Command and the governor on my own set. There may be more information. Slater, go get some sleep. You have more tapes to audit tomorrow. Thau, you look tired too. Get some rest. We may not have too many chances in the days ahead." Despite Muller's gloomy words, he smiled as he spoke.

This gives him a charge, all this worry and excitement, mused Slater as he shuffled wearily back to his own quarters.

Friday morning found Slater back on his couch again and by noon the previous night's rest was spent. His brain seethed with newly acquired knowledge of the Ruck and its inhabitants: human, lower animal, and plant. Lunch break gave him a half hour of respite and then it was back to the taped pictures and voices. By late afternoon he and the other two looked as if they had been pulled through a vise. When the last tape ended he got up and stretched wearily. Feng and Nakamura had some minutes to go and he was about to head for his room and a shower when a sinewy brown arm encircled his neck from behind.

"What about our bargain, louse? I know you types leave tomorrow. I thought you were going to try and get me on to the strength." Two firm prominences pressed into the back of his sweat-soaked uniform, and he was aware that Mohini had on some musky scent that cut through his tiredness like a knife. Yet what Slater felt was a rising irritation.

"Now look, gorgeous, what can I really do? You know it would take I-Corps permission to get you taken along. By now you know pretty well what we're looking for, because the I-Corps dope has been issued to all you types. And you know about Pelham too, don't you?" He had turned in her grip and was holding her firmly by the waist, looking hard into the deep-brown eyes as he spoke.

"Yes," she admitted. "Intellicom told us about Pelham. No one else, though. The planet news services haven't got it yet and they aren't meant to either. The longer we have without outside attention the better. But what about me?"

"For God's sake, Mohini, be reasonable! What on Mars can I do about it?"

"You can speak to Muller, that's what, you jerk! He's the boss on this thing and he can do anything he wants to. And you're his fair-haired boy. If you ask him the right way, suggest that a woman operative, I-Corps type, could be useful—and I damned well could too—he might think it was a great idea."

Slater stood irresolute, holding her by the waist still. It was a shock to realize that the garrison thought Muller liked him that well. Was it true? Could he really ask such a favor? He did not hear the door open behind him, but he saw the startled look in Mohini's eyes and felt her pull away suddenly. He turned only in time to see the door slide into its recess.

"Who the Hell was that?"

Mohini smoothed her hair in the gesture of a woman who needs her confidence restored. "Only your cannibal from down the hall. Who cares what she thinks anyway? Hey!"

Slater ran but he could not make the length of the corridor in time. The guard was gone from the door, but it was shut, and although he pounded on it, it would not open. "Danna!" he called, trying to keep his voice down. "let me in!" He could hear no answer. After five minutes of futile effort, he gave up and went away. He had to get ready for a final briefing with the Old Man that evening and he badly needed even a few moments to rest to get his thoughts in some kind of order. But all he could think of was a sad, small figure sitting on the big couch. What had she thought when she had seen him with his hands on Mohini? Ten minutes later he was in his own quarters, in the depths of sleep, utterly dreamless, the slumber of total exhaustion.

His comm buzzer woke him in pitch darkness. His watch said two in the morning, and he had no sooner discovered that fact then Nakamura was pounding at his door.

"Come on, Lieutenant, Sir Pathan. We have a lot to do, or had you forgotten all the briefing yesterday?"

Slater shaved and dressed in seconds and headed for the I-Corps cellars at a run. He had forgotten nothing, but there was precious little time for all that had to be done. As he left the room, he clipped the flat impervium box to his belt. Grabbit was coming too, rules or no rules.

He found Thau Lang and a short, square Rucker warman he had never seen before deep in conversation with Danna Strom and her two male companions. To one side, Nakamura and Feng were being painted with dark stain by two I-Corps enlisted men. The short Rucker turned and glared at Slater as he came in.

"You going to be this late out in the bush, Lieutenant?"

Despite the familiar voice, Colonel Muller's disguise was so good that Slater had been completely taken in by it. The worn leathers and fur hood, the faded chevrons apparently cut deep into his forehead, the belt of ferkat hide, and the gaudy hand-carved grips on the issue lasgun, all were perfect.

Muller smiled at his expression. "You'll be this pretty too, but not if you stand around all day. Get over there and get into the juice with the others. Once that's done, we have a lot more junk to get ready."

Ten minutes later, skin still damp from the stain, the three younger officers were climbing into thermal underwear and then into handmade imitation warsuits of the Rat Clan, suits on which the fort's tailor and his assistant had been slaving for two days. Once in the suits, they began to conceal about themselves the devices that lay on the long table at one end of the room. Slater managed to shift Grabbit's box into his Rucker belt pouch without being detected.

"We'll each have a minicamera." Muller held one of the tiny things up to the light. "They fit into the hilt of your bushknife, and they can't be—the knives, I mean—opened except by a reverse twist and a push toward the blade. The big knob on the hilt of each knife is a tiny beacon with a two-hundred-mile range and a service life of one hour. Copters and satellites will be listening to get a fix on it all the time. It is for the direct emergency only, and I don't mean personal emergency either, but that of the mission." He tapped the big knife on the table.

"It takes a good hard blow to smash the fake plasteel knob, and that activates the homer. Now look here." He held up a small package swathed in cloth.

"This is concentrated rations, Rucker style. It's hypercompressed, freeze-dried meat, uncooked. What animal, it's better not to speculate, except it won't be human. We'll each have three. Inside each block is a tiny blast grenade, a miniature of the issue type you're used to. The meat is genuine and edible. You'd have to rip the block open to find the grenade."

Muller continued to spell out the equipment, down to I-Corps minitorches, ultra miniature radio compasses, night-vision goggles, captured bows, and rifles as Slater tried to catch Danna's eye. But she seemed fascinated by the colonel's lecture and paid the anxious young man not the slightest attention, even when he shifted his position to place himself nearer her.

"I said, Slater, can't you use a Rucker bow? Are you awake yet, man?" Suddenly aware that he was being addressed, Slater tried to pull his wits together.

"Sir, I—yes, I can. I've practiced a lot and even killed some small game."

"I know, but you're certain not to be warman standard. That makes four of the party who can use one. Feng and Nakamura can carry spears. A few of the warmen do because some men simply never make good bowmen, no matter how much they practice. We'll all have rifles, but the cartridges can't be replaced, of course, so we'll nurse them—like real Ruckers."

The immensely powerful little cartridges he referred to were not the various pellets or darts that both the handguns and the rifles actually fired.

Filled with compressed nitrogen under enormous pressure, the cartridges powered the different projectiles, however. Once they were exhausted, only a UN ordinance depot could reload them. Rucker artisans could make or duplicate almost anything in their hidden factories, but the precious propellant cylinders had to be stolen or done without. As a result they were the most precious form of loot to any of the True People and the one universal coinage of the Ruck. With cartridges one could buy almost anything except another human being or escape from a blood debt.

"Well, that's about it," Muller said. "Captain Feng, a private word with you." He took the I-Corps officer off into a corner, and they spoke in low tones for a minute. Slater noticed that Feng seemed agitated and angry, rare thing for a man who cultivated imperturbability as a matter of course.

"I'm sorry to have to make this statement," Colonel Muller said as he returned to the others.

"Briefly, Lieutenant Dutt would seem to have deserted. She came to my quarters last night and asked to speak to me privately. I was surprised at the intensity of her plea as well as its nature though the latter was perhaps understandable in a young and ambitious officer. She wished to be one of our group, and gave many reasons, none of which I found convincing. I refused. Here is where she was and, indeed, is needed. She has had no special training for the Ruck and, as a matter of fact, appears actually to have disliked it, from what I can learn since. She was chagrined at my refusal, but perfectly correct about it. I thought little of the matter until an hour ago, when the gate guard commander, Lieutenant Choibalsan, reported that he had let her out the gate. She had the password, of course, and also a 'verbal order' from me! To 'inspect' something or other." He turned and smiled at Feng, who was obviously unhappy. "Any other branch but I-Corps might have had a rough time pulling off that stunt, Captain. But your branch has its own rules. I've even heard rumors that line officers who make trouble for you don't get promoted. A reputation that opens doors, and gates, is sometimes embarrassing, eh?

"I had to tell Feng first, since it concerns his branch and because I-Corps occupies a special position in our plans and, of course, our defenses. Captain Feng says that he wishes you all to be made aware of this matter, and he has also offered to resign his position and remain here at the fort. I have refused his offer since Chief Warrant Le Sage is perfectly capable of handling the I-Corps work for the time being. I have already sent a comm to I-Corps Central asking for another experienced officer on a crash basis, to stay here until the present matter is settled." He looked around, his gaze cold.

He went on. "I don't know what this means, but I don't like it at all. However, I am leaving warman Arta Burg of the True People here at the fort. When information I have asked for comes in, he'll bring it to me. I thank him, and Danna Strom for asking him. Now, enough talk. You all look fit and ready. Let's be on our way." He led the way out the door and all the others followed, leaving Burg and the two enlisted men behind. Slater felt sorry for the young warman, who plainly hated the fort and all it stood for.

At the main gate, two figures appeared out of the icey dark and identified themselves as Major van Schouten and Captain M'kembe.

"All right, Major, I'm off," Muller said. "Now listen. You are in actual command. But you are not to give an order without consulting Captain M'kembe, do you understand? He has ten times your combat experience. I have cleared this with Ares and Orcus. If there is any doubt in your mind whatsoever, I'll have a written order drawn up." His voice was low but penetrating. Slater, who stood nearest to him, could hear clearly, but he was sure that at least a couple of the others could too. Knowing the colonel, this was unlikely to be an accident. He could not demote van Schouten, but he could take precautions. Now there were witnesses.

At van Schouten's murmured assent, Muller swung away and waved the others on past him and out the gate, which had been opened just wide enough for one to pass through at a time. Even so, Slater noted as he squeezed out, a squad of riflemen was deployed in the shadows behind them. Yes, Muller took few chances!

The little party ran at a lope across the frosted grass of the cleared areas, crouching as they did. No sound came from the fort. The sentries had been alerted, of course. A viewer on the battlements would have seen only a flitting patch of shadow, hardly darker than the surrounding night. Then Marswood swallowed them. Far away, the scream of an animal broke the silence. In the east, no glow appeared. It was still night and dawn was far off.

# CHAPTER 7

# *The Wayfarers*

*T*HE FOREST SEEMED SILENT AS WELL AS CHILL TO SLATER as he padded over the leaf mold. He had never been out in it at night. Save for Muller, who was notoriously a law unto himself, he knew of no one in the garrison who had. The Old Mars hands whom one met on leave, retired prospectors and whatnot, always claimed to have lived for weeks in the Ruck by themselves. Some had, there was no question of that, but most were liars. At any rate, regulations forbade night work except under direct orders and in extraordinary circumstances. In the Ruck odds against a man were tough enough during daylight hours, without adding to them.

They were moving along a narrow game trail quickly located by Muller and Thau Lang. Thau Lang was at point, Muller following. Behind them, in single file, were Nakamura, Danna, Feng, Slater, and, last, the young warman, Milla Breen. The Ruckers were thus interspersed through the little column to help the three greenhorns. Muller, it was obvious to everyone, did not fit that category.

As his first tenseness began to ebb away, Slater found himself drinking in the beauty of the night. Random perfumes and strange scents came from the half-frozen, tangled vegetation around them. Insects whose DNA-modifications had tailored them to survive the dank chill stridulated and something croaked regularly. There was even a song, a gentle rise and fall of melody, which died away behind them after a time, leaving the night the poorer. Slater had had no idea that a night-haunting bird existed, that it sang to the dark wood. Certainly he had never read of such a thing. Perhaps it was not a bird. The Ruck had many strange life-forms of its own, many native and very old. The catalogs were a long way from being complete.

Other noises abounded. Ferkats, those solitary prowlers, screamed their war and hunting cries. Once in the distance a series of echoing howls momentarily silenced the wood. Muller halted the column, and they did not move again until the howling came again from a much greater distance. Marswolves, the mutated offspring of early settlement dogs, were both cunning and ferocious. Like the canid ancestors from which they sprang, they were pack hunters, making them dangerous even to large parties.

As Slater's night sight grew better, he began to move with less hesitation. The party could not move really fast anyway, but there was a confidence in the steps of the three Ruckers and Muller that he envied and hoped to acquire.

So far as Slater could tell, they were angling to the east. The fort lay on a corner of the shallow plateau called Isidis Regio, the southern section of a larger plateau area. The fort had been designed to protect the cryolite mine that lay still farther to the south, on the edge of a deep valley called Thoth after the ibis-headed god of ancient Egypt. As well as he was able to judge from occasional glimpses of the stars through the tangled leaves, the track they were on seemed to parallel the broad trail from Fort Agnew to the Universal mine. He could see the reason for avoiding the actual trail easily enough. The Universal officials had their own police who were not above setting an ambush for Ruckers themselves, and the warmen might also be hoping to catch some late traffic.

Suddenly Muller signaled a halt. Slater could see his hand flung up against the far northern stars, where a racing blot of liminescence against the night horizon revealing the recession of Phobos, the larger and nearer moon of the Martian twins, hurtling along on its second journey of the twenty-four-and-a-half-hour day. But Muller had not halted them to look at the moon. Then, behind him, Slater heard Breen take a deep breath. He copied the warman's action. And down a gentle but icy breeze came the stench of decaying flesh.

In any wild area that scent attracts predators. In the Ruck, at night, there was simply no telling what might be drawn to it. Muller and Thau Lang spoke briefly, heads together, voices low. Slater simply watched the dark huddle and listened to the noises of the night. He could see Danna, a slight shape some few paces off, and had the urge to speak to her, but he was a trained officer and the discipline of the march was a thing one did not break lightly. Instead he rested, leaning on his rifle. He carried the short bow slung over his back, since there was no point in his even thinking of using it at night. A blotch of shadow he identified as Lang moved off and so he settled down. Evidently Muller thought a one-man scout party would be in order.

The old konsel was back in no time and the group hurried on at Muller's wave. In a few moments they were standing under the source of the smell, now so strong it made Slater gag. Yet he saw that Muller's face in the dying moonlight was quite serene as it looked up to the things above them.

They stood in a little clearing, and the light was three times that which they had been using in the dark thickets. Most Terran trees adapted to Martian conditions did not grow tall, despite one-third Earth gravity. The incredibly violent winds of the smaller planet, and the temperature extremes, did not encourage great height as a survival characteristic. But here, in a slight depression in the forest, two or three had managed to reach a respectable height. One of them was the tree under which they now stood trying to ignore the stench. It looked to Slater something like a beech, but he was no botanist. From an outstretched branch, like a crooked arm, two shapes hung at least fifteen feet off the ground. Once human, they were now very dead. Milla Breen made a grating noise in his throat and Danna touched his arm. He was silent but Slater saw the glitter of his eyes. He felt a touch on his own arm and saw that Muller had come over and was holding a knife out to him.

Slater estimated the distance, laid his weapons down, and jumped. It was about twenty feet, a good jump even at Mars weight and for a well-trained Earthman. He caught the body he had aimed for in one gloved hand, praying to himself the thing was not so decomposed that it would come apart under his weight. A human body is tougher than it looks. This one held. Open-mouthed, for he simply could not use his nose, Slater swarmed up it and onto the limb from which it hung. There it was a simple matter to cut both down and follow in one leap, bringing with him a section of the rope.

He handed this to Muller then trotted over to a corner of the clearing and was quietly sick.

He almost jumped when Muller spoke from close beside his ear. The way the colonel moved was simply inhuman. "Thanks" came the frosty breath. "They were Ferkat Clan. Hanging them up that way for the birds to play with is the worst thing an enemy could have done. No Rucker would have done it. Not even to one of us, let alone one of themselves. They always bury their dead out in the wood, under a tree or other big plant. This rope is Terran, or a good imitation. Someone is trying to make trouble." He ignored the reason that Slater was off by himself and went on.

"Whoever did this is either a mining company halfwit or serious about raising all the clans at once. Against us. I think the latter, personally, and so does Thau. I wish I hadn't had you jump though. It saved time, but it also emphasized that a Terran could do it easily." He left and went back to the others. The big knives cut a rude grave under the tree and the two poor husks were shoved into them. Thau Lang spread his arms and said a few words in his native tongue, then half-frozen soil was scraped over the bodies and tamped down. Quickly they were off again, padding over the cold, dead leaves and tangled grass, breath steaming from their hoods as they loped along.

They had gone a few miles and Slater was beginning to feel the strain in his calf muscles when they halted again, this time in response to a signal from Lang. Phobos had set and the night had the same predawn black that comes to Earth at the same hour. Slater crouched under a giant thistle, careful not to touch the leaves, then noticed that the others were holding their rifles at the ready. His came off his back in a second and he leaned back and signed "what?" to Breen, who was right next to him. Breen cupped one hand to his hooded head where an ear would have been. Slater nodded and listened.

At first there was nothing, save for the usual night sounds. Faint animal cries came from far away and the insects still chirped feebly here and there. Then he heard it. The howl of a Marswolf pack, somewhere off in the night, a rising chorus of sound. It might even have been the same one they had heard earlier.

Slater wondered later on how Lang could have known that the beasts were on their track. Certainly the pack was not close. The ability was, he decided eventually, one of those little things that made you one of the True People. You just knew. Again the cry came, welling through the frosty air. The very faintest shade of gray was lifting some of night's shroud. Dawn was not far away.

Muller made a signal and they all began to run, ignoring noise and going as hard as they were able. Strung out on the narrow path, they could not come up with a defense that had any chance of success. To make use of their weapons, they needed room. Behind them, about a half kilometer off, were the oncoming wolves. Slater's heart began to pound, but there was no sign of a slow-up from the leaders. Self-discipline was the only answer to Slater's pain. If you had a leader, he was the man to give the orders. Without warning, the cover broke and they ran into the open, automatically spreading out to give each one a field of fire. It was lighter now, and visibility was spreading as one watched.

Lang had found them another round clearing, larger than the one where the dead warmen had been hung up to rot. The floor of this one was stone or sand, and little grew there but long, gray moss. When Slater saw Muller and the old Rucker wheel and fall, he did the same, rifle at the ready. Lang had not left them much time, but just enough.

Fog was already beginning to rise from the ground in patches.

The cold, heavy fog of a summer morning would not burn off until 10 A.M. or so. Through it now, hungry and lean, came the Marswolves.

In two hundred years, the inexorable rules of natural selection had produced a new canid, far removed from the beloved pets of human beings. Lighter gravity had given the wolves longer legs and the cruel winters of Mars—minus 40°C. in places, despite the warming ability of the new atmosphere— had given them really thick fur. The stupid and the weak were gone, rigorously pruned by the harsh conditions. What remained were big-chested, hundred-pound demons with mottled pelts all the colors of a brown-gray-black spectrum, able to run down and devour just about anything that moved. A dozen of these burst into the clearing at a dead run and fanned out as had the humans whom they were hunting.

Slater switched the rifle lever past NARCOTIC and EXPLOSIVE, to POISON. He quickly shot two wolves and saw one die in midair, so quick was the action of the hybrid cyanide mixture in the needles. A metallic sound made him look to the right and he saw Danna wrestling with her rifle. A Jam! And a yellow-fanged, mostly black monster was charging her from the side. Slater fired as Danna disappeared under the weight of the brute.

Totally unconscious that the seconds-long battle was over, he ran over to her, stumbling as he ran, and frantically tore at the heavy carcass. Suddenly the wolf's body seemed to heave of its own volition, and Danna pushed it away, sat up, and glared at him. He reached down to help her up but she angrily struck his hand away. She said nothing because the wind had been knocked out of her. Feeble though she might be for the moment, it was plain she wanted no assistance from Slater. He turned away, not angry, simply relieved that she was all right. He caught Breen watching him with a curious expression and wondered if the young warman was jealous. Without a word, Slater reloaded the rifle from his belt pouch.

Danna was walked about for a moment by Thau Lang, who seemed to be talking to her, though no one could hear what was said. In the full light of morning, even with the constantly growing fog, she seemed perfectly sound.

The eight dead wolves were simply left lying. The rest of the pack had fled. Scavengers—plant, animal, and a couple of local oddities that were really neither—would deal with the bodies.

For some two hours they marched without a break. Occasionally Muller would consult with Lang. Magnetic compasses were useless on Mars, which has low magnetism of any kind, so the military used a type that fixed on a radio beacon at Ares Base. But their present disguise precluded carrying such things. The stars and bush training had to be their substitute.

As on much of the old planet, the ground thereabouts was fairly level, with few rises and most of those gentle. But the second birth of ancient Mars made Marswood anything but old and tired. When the warmth and light of the new day hit the plant growth, it seemed to burgeon and curl into fresh life as one watched, and as the travelers passed through each wisp of fog, new shapes reached out at them—not literally in most cases, but by virtue of their sudden emergence from the shrouding mists.

Once, however, a green tendril struck at Lang, who happened to be in the lead. The Mars bloodsucker was one of the few native plants that competed with the imported stock on even terms. Most of the older planet's original life-forms were apt to do better at night, when the imports of Earth were dormant. And they tended to like the more barren areas and the poles, where even mutated Terran vegetation had too hard a time.

The bloodsucker was an important exception. Its green color owed nothing to chlorophyll, but was nothing more than a chameleon pigment it used to lurk undetected in the mass of imported plant life. As to whether the bloodsucker was a plant itself, the zoologists were still battling with the botanists. It resembled a very large, dirty sofa cushion, with six twisting arms, one of which had just swung at Lang and missed. He leaped aside while ducking as Muller sprang back then whipped up his short bow and fired an arrow into the brush. There was a wheezing hiss, as if a very large snake were speaking. Muller laughed, a short bark, and Thau Lang clapped him on the back.

"They don't die easily," Muller said to Slater, who was still staring off the trail to where the sound came from. "I gauged where the body would be and let go. The brutes store gas, mostly oxygen and carbon monoxide, under pressure. That's how they move the tentacles, gas pressure. I popped the balloon and it will take the thing a few days to mend the hole and build up pressure again. Meanwhile it's dangerous as a toy loofah."

Slater could only marvel at his commander's skill. He himself had known everything about the bloodsucker that he just had been told, but knowing it and putting the knowledge to use in an emergency were very different things.

They stopped twice a day for food, using the tough jerked meat and hard bitter bread made from a root found in the Ruck. Water was no problem; pools were common, some of them large enough to require a detour. They were apt to be shallow and have soft bottoms. Vast, low, sprawling willows, many with trunks a meter and a half across, grew around them, the descendants of a dwarf species from Earth's Arctic. At one small lake Breen speared a black frog the length of his arm that had foolishly goggled at them from the water's edge for a moment too many. In camp that night, Muller and the three Ruckers ate the legs raw. Breen got the eyes as well for snaring the creature. Slater, Nakamura, and Feng abstained.

By the next day, Slater had decided that it would take quite a while to get to enjoy the Ruck or the mission. Danna spoke to him when addressed, but in terms of utter indifference. Nakamura was silent and morose, and the two older men and Feng spoke little and then mainly to one another. Only Breen seemed friendly. It came out finally that he had been favorably impressed by Slater's killing the Marswolf.

"We all would die to protect a Wise Woman, Slater," he said earnestly. "One reason that I and Arta joined with you and not the two who are Gone Down is that these new men from the South seem to despise the Wise Women. This is madness and worse. They do not say so openly, of course, but one gathers hints from what they say when alone with us young men. Someone who has the chance to save a Wise Woman is lucky too, a good person to be with. My aunt was a Wise

Woman but I do not have her power. I will never be a konsel and I am glad. They have to learn too much."

Slater tried to store away everything he heard for future reference. He knew that Rucker clans were matriarchal, but the details were obscure and much of the information he had seen conflicting. No one spoke while on the march, but once the party had stopped and posted a guard, Breen was willing enough to speak. Slater learned that the offices of konsel and war chief were not synonymous, it being most rare for one person to combine them as did Thau Lang. As a result he was held in tremendous respect. A konsel was like a male equivalent of the Wise Women, but he was also a permanent delegate to the only supraclan government the True People recognized— a kind of informal parliament that seldom met in the body, but nevertheless managed to keep members informed and even to vote on matters of common interest. The body had no name, or at least not one Breen was willing to give.

By the third day Slater found himself toughening. He began to sleep better at night, instead of tossing and turning in the bitter chill. He had been fit anyway, but fitness for garrison duty and fitness for the Ruck were different things. Now his muscles were hardening. Even the cold-adapted insects were not so bad, he found.

The fleas and lice of Earth had managed to survive on Mars and in most places were far too abundant. During the day gnats and mosquitoes existed in dense swarms, particularly near water. Fortunately the night cold kept most of them immobilized, though once in a while one would find the heat of a sleeping body sufficient to awake it. Slater killed one crawling thing— a kind of crab louse, he suspected—at least an inch long after it had brought him out of a sound sleep with a savage bite. He saw spiders ten times as large, but they seemed as eager to stay out of the humans' way as were the latter to avoid them. No snappers were seen, and Grabbit was quiescent in its box.

Breen, when queried, tended to minimize the spiders. He admitted they could bite and that many were poisonous, but most, he said, sought smaller prey, chiefly rabbits, rats, mice, and birds. He warned Slater that the giant scorpions were another matter, and that they were irritable and frightfully venomous. Fortunately they were not common. Other things to avoid were the bloodsuckers and a nasty form of burrowing armored slug, a heat seeker and native of the planet, which haunted the plateaus and rocky cliffs in the higher elevations. Though small, the slug could tunnel into the body in seconds when hungry. Then there were the sand crawlers. Like most native Martian life, they had been rather small, no more than a half meter long or so to begin with. Terraforming had changed that; now they could be bigger than a bulgote. They looked like bulbous armored fish, perhaps of the flounder variety, and were all sorts of bright colors. Cruising about on small jointed legs buried under a fat body, sand crawlers mined pockets of soil for worthwhile minerals. But their mineral-detecting organs functioned equally well on living things, which are, after all, equally well stocked with interesting substances. Slater did not care for Breen's description of what a man looked like after a crawler was through feeding. They were apt to be haunters of the night.

Between the stories of the Ruck and its inhabitants and being marched to the point of exhaustion every day, Slater managed to make do. He envied Nakamura the special lessons he got from Danna, but there was nothing he could do to put himself in the big man's place. Danna was teaching Nakamura how to act like a member of the strange clan from the South. She was patient and, Nakamura admitted privately, very good at what she was doing. "She must have perfect recall, damn it. If I miss even a shade of accent, in just one word, or pick my nose the wrong way, back we go and do it all over again. Reminds me of Year One at the Academy, only worse!" But he seemed less sullen, and Slater had the feeling that he no longer thought of the Rucker girl as merely a variety of dangerous animal that ought to be exterminated.

Ten days out from the fort, they were filing down a gentle slope through moderately thick cover, when Muller used the hand signal "down!"

Slater had long since ceased trying to guess where they were or what exactly it was they were to do whenever they got to wherever they were headed. Enduring the hard conditions so unsure of the details of the mission was difficult, but at least he had the training that only long discipline gives.

Flat on his stomach under a cactus, rifle forward, he peered up the slope in the same direction as the others. Next to him Breen cocked one eye at him and winked. A swarm of minute bugs crawled over both their faces after their sweat. Slater could sense nothing but the usual noises of the Ruck during midafternoon, but he knew he was no judge.

Suddenly he saw that Danna was standing, rifle by her side, looking up the tangled gradient. As he watched, she cupped her hands and called, a gentle quavering sound, "ooh, aaahh, ooh," which ran up and down until it died away. From not far off an answer came, the exact same cry. At the crest of the rise, a man stood up, rifle held over his head in both arms.

"Arta," Breen said from beside Slater's ear. "He moves quiet, that one. But not quiet enough for your chief or Danna. She and he worked out that call together. It's an animal, what you call a one that hunts by, well, *singing*. You know it?"

As Arta Burg jogged down the slope and was welcomed by the others, Slater admitted to his new friend that he knew nothing about any animal that hunted by singing. Presumably it was yet one more example of Martian life that had not yet got into the books.

Burg headed straight for Muller and passed him a small cylinder, which he took from a pouch at his waist. He carried the bow and rifle and a small backpack. To look at him, one would think he had been for a walk around the block in a Terran apartment city. Slater was supremely conscious of feeling dirty and looking it, although the males were all using the Rucker depilatory, which at least kept them from being shaggy as well. Not for the first time, he wondered sourly what Unilever-Gradco or the Supaharto Trust would give him for a tube of the stuff.

"I should like everyone to come over here at once please," Muller said after conferring briefly with Thau Lang. When they were seated around him, minus the old konsel who took the guard position uphill, he began without any preamble.

"Warman Burg brings us a message confirming certain suspicions I had. There are several points, and I will take them in order.

"One, Lieutenant Mohini Dutt is a deeply planted traitor. She is of Indian descent, all right, but born on Mars and then taken back to Earth. Her parents were fanatical followers of JayBee Pelham. The mother is dead. The father, whose name is not Dutt at all but Medawar, is believed to be one of the men who arranged Pelham's escape. He is probably with him now. Very probably Lieutenant Dutt is on the way to meet them at some rendezvous. She may know more about living in the Ruck than she led us to believe. Also, it is obvious why she tried so hard to be one of this party. She wished to be able to warn Pelham of any countermeasures. And she knows much—not just about Pelham but our other business, the U-Men." His voice grew even gentler. "A pretty girl, but I rather wish she were dead. If any of you get the chance, see that she *is* dead." He grew brisk again.

"JayBee has found a guide, I'm afraid. An old Marsrat named Deimos Smith. I've heard of him, though he usually operates on the other side of the planet. The True People like him, and he seems to move quite freely among them. He's said to be not a bad sort, but he has a kink—he's one of the last of the old White Supremacy crowd. Seems Pelham hooked him with some wild tale about the master race taking over Mars. Even Pelham is not that crazy, and anyway, he's an eighth Melanesian and three-quarters Hawaiian mix himself.

"Back to us. *We* are going to a big meeting, one of several clans. We hope to arrive after the delegates from the new Clan of the Giants." He bowed to Nakamura, who saluted back, deadpan. "The new clan people have gone back to wherever they came from. We will appear with our own giant and, quite reasonably, follow them. Their headquarters has to be found very quickly. Any questions?"

"On behalf of my corps, I wish to say—" Feng began. He looked as though he had just been hit by a rocket shell.

"My dear fellow," Muller said quickly, "how could anyone blame you for Dutt? This has been planned for many years. The I-Corps security checks were made too late. Miss Medawar was a 'sleeper,' an agent buried in place since she was young.

So. Now, let's be off. There are two hours of good daylight left."

Feng still looked miserable, but he was a very good man. It was obvious that what Muller said made sense. But Slater did not think he would care to be in Mohini Dutt-Medawar's shoes if Feng happened to lay hands on her. What a ghastly waste of fantastic bed material, Slater thought ruefully.

He found himself near Arta Burg in that evening's campsite. Burg quietly thanked him for saving Danna. Breen had filled him in and he seemed deeply grateful. Slater decided to trade on the gratitude for purely selfish reasons. "I'm afraid she's annoyed at me for some reason," he said mendaciously. "Frankly, Burg, anything you can do to make us friends again would be a real favor to me."

Burg said in surprised tones, "This is not like a nice girl, not like Danna. She could have come to your bed if we were in camp—real camp, not on a trip. Of course," he added in confidential tones, "the Wise Women are funny. They have their own rules about things. Maybe you got in the way of one of those. I will ask Milla what he thinks. Since Danna is the responsibility of us two, she can at least be polite." He went off, leaving Slater wondering what the last sentence meant. By Earth standards the Ruckers were very casual and, at the same time, very finicky about sex, following complex customs of their own devising. But he dared not risk giving offense by asking for too many particulars.

Late that night, while he had the watch under the cold distant shine of Phobos, he heard a small noise, like a muffled cough, and whirled. Danna looked at him soberly from a yard away, her hood thrown back, the moonglimmer showing her short, curly hair.

"Milla and Arta told me I was not a nice girl," she said in a sad little voice. "They were right, Slater. Even if you had not shot the wolf, I had no right to be nasty." Her eyes narrowed momentarily. "But I wanted to kill that big woman you had your hands on."

She sat on a rock next to his knee and gently took one of his gloved hands in hers. She looked up at him fondly and he dropped down beside her, caught by the expression in her eyes.

Then he remembered he was on duty and started to rise. She pulled him back down. "Milla will watch," she said demurely. "He is by the big stone on the other slope. I asked him." She took his face in her cold hide mittens and pulled it down to hers. The world vanished from his mind leaving only the sweet intoxication of the kiss, the warm perfume of her breath, and the delightful musk of her body, rising from her clothes through the opening at her neck. Eventually they came up for air and stared at one another with startled eyes. A feeling of mutual surrender had overpowered them and as normally strong, self-contained people, the sensation had made them nervous. Danna pulled off her right glove and smoothed her hair.

"I have wanted to do that ever since I first saw you," she said quietly. "I knew it would be wonderful." The great ring on her hand gleamed in the faint moonlight and Slater took her hand to look at it, the blue stone in the middle stirring his memory. She slipped the ring off and handed it to him. He took a pencil flash from his pocket and, shielding it with his body, examined the ring.

There, worn but plain to a student of military history, was the galley of the long-gone United States Naval Academy, flanked by half-effaced seahorses and surmounted by a trident. On the other side, the spread eagle hovered over the propeller. The class number was too battered to be made out.

"Do you know what this is?"

"Yes, I think so. It came from my mother and from her mother and from hers again, and hers too. It comes from Earth, and it means that among my ancestors was a warrior who went upon the water, which we cannot do here."

He returned the ring and patted her hand. What an end for the ring of an ancient American naval officer! Probably a pure white, if his memory of the racial customs of that period was accurate.

"Danna, that ring is from a school for—well, soldiers like me, back on Earth, as you know. Whoever the man was, he is your link to Earth and to what Earth stands for." He smiled. "You're just an Earth girl a long way from home. We two are natural allies."

She bent over him and kissed him gently and briefly. "Perhaps we are, Slater. Perhaps the wild woman of the woods is your natural ally." Her eyes surveyed him calmly. "Some day we will have more time together. Now we are at war." She added as she rose and slipped away, "And you have not yet told me what you were doing with your hands on that fat-rumped woman who has betrayed us all!" He heard a faint giggle as Danna disappeared into the dark.

The next day the group moved more slowly because they were getting close to the big Rucker encampment one of the two younger warmen was to enter. The others would wait, polishing their roles as Rucker clansmen from the other side of the planet, ready to appear if the strange giants and their allies had left. They had moved off the Aetheopis highlands and were now approaching the edge of the Sinus Gomen valley. Not too far beyond it, to the south and west, lay the unknown deeps of the great Cimmerium rift that the Ruckers called the bad country.

That night Breen and Burg slipped out of camp while Feng, Slater, and Colonel Muller tested each other's masquerade as members of the remote Bulgote Clan. Muller had to be perfect since he was the one who would talk while the other two pretended to a vow of silence. At the same time, Nakamura was getting a last review of his attitude and appearance from Danna. Over and over in the dark they rehearsed their mission, until even Muller and Danna, both stern judges, were satisfied.

As he curled up, Slater heard a wild bulgote, the emblem of his new clan, bellow far off in the frozen dark. It seemed a good omen, and he wondered if he was developing a Rucker mentality. A strange fate for the descendant of Afghan chieftains. Or perhaps not strange at all. He fell asleep trying to resolve the question.

They lay low through the following day while a strong, damp wind carrying a promise of bad weather grew and moaned among the jumble of great boulders where they lay concealed.

Muller cocked an eye skyward. "This is going to be a wild night. I hope the boys come back with good news first. If not, we'll simply have to last it out somehow. Anyway, it's good training."

Despite Muller's carefree words, Slater saw that he was

concerned. As the wind rose, Muller roamed the area, popping up and down like a jack-in-the-box. Eventually he found what he was seeking. With a wave of his hand he summoned the others to the lee of a vast, rounded stone. At its base grew three tough thornbushes, which Muller parted to display a dark opening about three feet high.

"Get in here. It gets a lot bigger inside. I've been inside and there's no danger I could detect. The storm that is coming is going to be a very bad one. Lang says so too, and he doesn't exaggerate."

Overhead the gray cloud rack raced past and the first drops of a freezing rain began to fall. With Muller last, they dove, one by one, into the hole at the rock's base.

After a few meters, the passage became roomy enough to stand up. When they flashed their torches around, they found they were in a chamber about twelve meters across by eighteen long. The roof was fairly lofty, rising to a peak in the center of the chamber of perhaps nine meters. The floor was stone, and boulders of various sizes lay scattered about. Some large openings gaped blankly in the light of the beams, back against the inner wall of the cavern. It was not too comforting a place to look at, but it seemed both warm and dry. The wind's shriek was only a distant whine deep under the rock.

Then Feng called to Muller. "What do you make of this?" His torch illumined a section of the wall near him, and the long, regular gouges in the dense rock were obvious to everyone.

"That's the mark of a pick, or something very like one," Muller said. "What do you say, Thau?"

"I don't know, but I have seen them in other places. This whole big rock is a hollow dome. It is a shelter, I think, maybe also an observation post. I have found them more than once in the past. I think it was a shelter against the great sandstorms of the old days, not the kind we have now. . . . Ruckers never made it." His words hung in the silence, and they listened to the distant sound of the wind echoing through the entrance tunnel.

"Against the sandstorms, eh?" Nakamura did not sound so sarcastic, not the way he had back at the post. There were no more giant sandstorms on Mars. But before the Terraforming there had been no other kind. For countless ages, the thin dust of the surface, the limonite powder and the motley sands, had swirled high into the thin atmosphere, as the great winds of the seasonal gales had blasted and ground down the very skin of the fourth planet. No one said the words, but out here in the night of the Ruck, *they* were on everyone's mind. Old Martians.

"I don't much care for these tunnel openings behind us, whether unused for centuries—or never used," the colonel said. "Let's move some of those big rocks and block them. Then we can post a guard at the entrance and get some sleep."

Muller took the first watch and the others settled down to an uneasy sleep. Slater would have liked to sit with Danna for a while but he saw that she was deep in low-voiced talk with Thau Lang, so he curled up in his sleeping bag next to Nakamura, who was already snoring. The floor was hard, but it was the best rest stop they had yet had.

A light touch on his eyelids brought Slater awake on the instant. He sat up and saw the giant Norse-Japanese grinning down at him. Weak light filtered through the tunnel entrance so that he could see perfectly well. Feng's legs were disappearing through the hole as he sat up, so Slater hurried to catch up.

Once outside, he saw that the storm had been a bad one. Huge chunks of rock lay about, torn from their beds by the force of the terrible wind. The ground was sodden from the rain and sleet, and dense fog was rising from the many new pools of water. Trees, some of them very old, lay in fragments. The cold dawn air was fresh and clean, but few animals or birds called and not many insects.

"I'm worried about the two young men." Lang was uneasy, and his normal iron reserve was missing for once. "I have seldom heard of a night this angry. I trust that they were not caught without shelter." He gazed around him. "No one could live through this, save by the spirits." As he spoke, he made a peculiar gesture on his breast with his right arm.

As they looked about, Slater noticed that Danna was trying to hold back tears. He moved over to her and tried to put a hand on her arm. He was shocked to see two Ruckers in such a state of nerves.

"Danna, don't be too alarmed. They're competent men, both of them. We'll see them pretty soon, bouncing over the rocks." His words rang hollow, even in his own ears. She did not shrug off his hand, but she looked up at him and despair was on her face. Her cheeks looked sunken.

"They were all the family I have, Slater. I had no brothers and sisters. All I had was my two husbands. And now I think they are dead."

# CHAPTER 8

# JayBee's Council

S LATER KEPT HOLDING DANNA'S HAND, BUT HE STARED over the curly head, his eyes blank and unseeing. Little was known of the Wise Women. Their duties, rank, and status in the web of rumor and myth assembled on Rucker society had not stressed any special attitudes or modes of sexual practice. *Every bit of knowledge is useful*, a small icy corner of his mind said, *and should be assimilated and conveyed to the most logical and useful section of the Ares Command*. The mind was repeating what the hypnotapes had emphasized. Everything learned about the Ruck was of the utmost value, and everything learned should be considered the property of the Central Computer Bank at Ares.

Including the fact that the woman he loved had two husbands already.

The mores of Earth in the Twenty-third Century were casual enough. You could find any sort of living arrangement you wanted. No one cared how others arranged their lives. But units of two people still made up the vast majority of those who chose to live together on a permanent basis. And he was in *love*! With a woman who had *two* husbands and yet apparently loved him in return!

Danna looked up at him and blinked through her tears. "You are very quiet, Slater. Do you have some idea, perhaps, of how we can find them?"

He cursed himself and returned to reality. He loved Danna and now she was in pain. He had no right to brood over her private living arrangements.

"I was thinking that maybe Colonel Muller and the konsel have some plan. This sort of situation can't be entirely new to them. Don't lose heart." He put all the confidence he could manage into the words, and he squeezed her hand in attempted reassurance.

"We'll have to move on the big encampment without them," said Muller, after he had conferred with the old Rucker chieftain. "They could be dead, could be lost, captured even. But we can't wait. I'm sorry, Danna. This is too important."

She nodded in silence.

The wreckage of the storm met them continually as they marched. The litter of the terrible wind had been laid indiscriminately over everything, and no clear path existed wherever it had been. Tangled, broken rock and pieces of thorn tree and cactus scrub were everywhere, and the party was forced to scramble slowly over the debris, no matter which way they turned. As the sun rose, sweat beaded their faces. Muller allowed little rest and drove them relentlessly until dark made the journey too hazardous even for him. They spent a bad, silent night, exhausted but unable to sleep. The next day was little better. Danna and the colonel conferred frequently with Thau Lang. The way had been lost, and they were now behind schedule.

At the start of his watch that night, Slater was pacing to and fro, when he heard a sound. Signs of animals had been few in the broken land they were traversing, as if the implacable gale had destroyed them or driven them away. Even the insects were subdued. Now he heard something that sounded like the faraway hum of a giant bee.

He refrained from jumping as Muller, who should have been lying quietly asleep in his robe, spoke from beside him.

"That's a ramjet. Not one of ours either. The hum is too high pitched." The noise died away in the frosty night and was heard no more. Muller left, his thoughts his own, and curled up once more. For the rest of the night nothing was heard but the occasional cry of a faraway animal.

About one hour before noon the next morning, they emerged suddenly from a wadi choked with broken stones and found a broad, well-beaten trail before them. Thau Lang, who had been leading, motioned them all back and they retreated out of sight of anyone who might pass.

"This is the main trail to the new camp," the old man hissed. "I was far off the track, and we are coming to the camp from the wrong direction. We must be very close to the camp for the trail to be so plain. We were lucky not to be seen before this. We must plan what to do next."

They had rehearsed their parts so many times they were sick of them. But the remorseless Muller put them all through a brief check once more before he allowed them to proceed. Apparently the unrelenting practice had paid off; satisfied at last, Muller motioned to Thau Lang and they set off down the trail.

They had hardly gone two kilometers when they were challenged. A shrill whistle sounded from a low mound of scrub and boulders on their left. They were expecting this and halted, holding their weapons high in the air, in a position from which it would be almost impossible to fire.

Thau Lang, who had been in the lead, called out a long sentence, of which Slater could understand only the konsel's name, and then waited. Two whistles replied, and with no more hesitation, Lang dropped his arms, as did the others. They had never seen their challengers. That the wrong answer would have brought something besides whistles, they all knew well.

In a short time Slater could hear the sounds of the big camp. In territory they considered beyond the reach of the hated government, the Ruckers were not so cautious about noise though just as vigilant in other ways.

They rounded another bend in the trail and the entrance to the camp lay before them.

A shallow declivity led down to a large pool of water at the bottom of a long slope, whose actual length was masked by the gentleness of the grade. The far side of the long pool was overhung by the lip of a great gray, beetling rock, which thus created a vast shallow cave almost five hundred meters wide. It led so far back into darkness that the lights of fires were visible as flares deep in the black inner recesses. As a hideaway to avoid aerial observation, it was hard to beat.

Hundreds of shelters pitched outside were exposed to the air, domes fashioned of the universally available plastic cloth, the cheapest and most widely exploited material human science had produced. Each was stained in mottled browns, grays, and greens. Hordes of children ran and played before the entrances to the shelters, which stretched out of sight into the cave. Only their quiet voices, unbroken by any loud yells, betrayed the fact that the Ruck's training was a savage one that began early. Around and with them romped many large dogs, partially domesticated Marswolves. These made no sound at all and not by choice. Rucker dogs had their vocal cords removed during puppyhood. They were the guards of the children, the home, and the domestic stock. Hunters on Mars moved with stealth and very few dogs are as quiet as a well-trained man.

The women were much in evidence also. Older ones chatted as they went about various tasks, younger girls in tight breeches or short skirts strolled about in groups, eyeing equally casual groups of young men, whose wanderings seemed somehow to bring them near. Off to one side, herds of domesticated bulgotes, the descendants of the original dwarf stock, grazed and browsed in hulking flocks. Some weighed 450 kilos, and the big bucks stood over two meters at the shoulder. Children and dogs watched the flocks, keeping the leaders from fighting. Mostly light gray, with a black stripe running down the spine, the herd beasts were hardly less savage than their wild congeners. But Slater knew that they were clever and adaptable. Experiments at Ares Base were aimed at producing a strain that could be used as draft and riding animals.

Thau Lang halted suddenly and gave a long, echoing call. Then he sat down and folded his arms. The others followed suit. The Ruckers nearest them paid no attention, but in a short time a group of men walked around the nearest cluster of domed tents and advanced upon them. As the strangers approached, Lang rose to his feet, but the others stayed seated.

The Ruckers were eight elderly men, in ordinary leather suits, the assembled konsels of the five clans that were meeting there. They had come to greet their equal. They looked calm and dignified, and bore no weapons except for belt knives and holstered lasguns, the Ruck equivalent of going unarmed. It was obvious that someone had forewarned the camp, for they had been waiting close by.

Each one stepped forward in turn and embraced Thau Lang, muttering words in his ear as they did, words of secret greeting that none else must hear. When all had done so, Lang turned and, in a courteous gesture, lifted Danna to her feet. Each greeted her the same way, acting as if he had never seen her before, though one at least must be the konsel of her own tribe.

Then Lang waved a hand over the others of his party and said a few words. The other elders nodded, in apparent disinterest. But Slater was conscious of their examination and wondered if his disguise was holding. One did not become a konsel by taking things for granted. Finally Lang turned and beckoned to them to follow him. Only then did Muller rise, the others copying him, and set off in the wake of the older men.

Half an hour later they were in a large empty tent, under a shadowed angle of the cliff but not too far from the edge of the pool. After seeing Lang's party to it, the elders had bade the konsel a dignified and affectionate farewell. Once the elders left, it was possible for them to speak Unit, but Muller persuaded Lang that he or Danna should walk about outside occasionally, just in case.

"I agree that we should take no chances, old friend," Lang said. "But I think you will find that a konsel's tent will be given a wide berth. And too, we have a Wise Woman. These are not matters that the True People care to interfere with."

"You forget things." Muller was unusually curt. "We have the so-called new clan from the South, plus whoever they have suborned among your people. Have you forgotten the assassin? Konsels are not subject to casual assassination, remember? And now there's JayBee. Who knows what his contacts are? Please, don't make things harder."

The tent was furnished with cushions and skin rugs. Hooks had been provided for hanging utensils and weapons, and the rest of the surroundings, too, were those of almost any nomad culture. Slater ransacked his memory for tales of the tribal, anti-Russian raids of his ancestors that had been related by an ancient grandmother from near Giltraza when he was a child. He felt a thrill at the realization that he was reliving the past of his own people, on another world.

Danna left them without a word and Lang said nothing. Slater guessed she had gone to inquire after her husbands. She returned, quietly and suddenly, while they were eating a simple meal cooked over a small charcoal brazier. She slipped through the flap like a small ghost.

"I've seen Milla! He was not with the people from the South. They've left already. These are others. And they have Terrans with them, Terrans *with guns!* They are to speak to the people tonight. Milla signed me not to speak to him. But there are plenty of my people here. They'll be sure to notice if he and I ignore each other. Oh, what shall we do?"

*I imagine there will be certain folk who will notice if a wife ignores her husband. Even if she has a spare or two missing somewhere about.* As the thought crossed his mind, driven by undiluted jealousy, Slater tried to bury it. He simply could not let his emotions disrupt their mission!

Muller caught the key part of the girl's speech at once. "Terrans allowed to have guns! That has to mean JayBee. No one else would be permitted here armed. He must have cultivated closer contacts with the tribes than we suspected. Did you see or hear of Lieutenant Dutt?"

"No."

"A small mercy. Then they have no way of learning about us. I was planning to leave as soon as we found out when and in what direction the giants had gone. Now we better stay at least until tonight and try to find out what JayBee is up to."

"Should I go with you to this shindig? It might look odd." Nakamura was quite conscious of his role as a giant from the

South. They had all noticed the looks that he drew from the konsels and every other Rucker who crossed their path.

"Good point, Nakamura. You stay in the tent. Your clan is so mysterious that nothing you do would be considered odd."

As darkness fell and the cold grew, the fires were allowed to die out and they made ready to depart. On Muller's advice, Thau Lang had got a good supply of travel rations laid in from the local intertribal council, a group that seemed to control the actual daily workings of the big camp. Whatever a konsel wanted was brought at once. They carried all their weapons and gear with them so they could leave as soon as the public business was over, under cover of darkness.

Muller's party followed Danna and the old konsel into the crowd of Ruckers streaming into the great cave. Even as the lights near the entrance were guttering and going out, more were springing up far ahead. A line of torches appeared in the distance, and looking back for a moment, Slater saw that the paler hint of the evening sky was quite far behind them. The cave was enormous! He wondered what Milla was doing and how he had been able to mix with JayBee's renegades. And where was Arta Burg?

When a small hand slipped into his, Slater flinched momentarily. Then he realized that Danna had taken advantage of the dark to reassure him and let him know of her presence. He squeezed back, wondering if he was ever going to get out of the mad business.

The crowd was slowing down, but there was no pushing and all the talk was muted and low. Rucker politeness was proverbial, as proverbial as their readiness to kill. An anthropologist had once described Rucker manners as a blend of Eskimo gentleness, Muslim fanaticism, and the quick-draw psychology of the American West in the late-Nineteenth Century.

The lights were brighter now. Great wooden torches flared from stone sconces set in the walls of the narrowing passage. Fluors might have been cheaper, but a Rucker's instinct was always to use what was available and to save what might be needed for emergencies for just that—emergencies. As the light grew, Slater saw that his party was mingling with many others and that the cave opened out once more ahead of them. In a few more steps, the amphitheater lay before the group. A sloping, lofty chamber seemingly hewn from the rock of the planet, it had tiers of rude wooden benches set in a semi-circle around the area. A platform of rough-hewn logs was raised at the empty end, against the rock wall, and more large torches flared from metal cressets around its edge.

The Ruckers, still chatting in low tones, ebbed and flowed about the ample floor space, seating themselves when ready, and more and more streamed in behind them. Acting on Muller's instructions, the group tried to keep fairly close to the entrance, save for Thau Lang, who left them and headed for the platform. At a gathering of this sort, a konsel sat with his peers.

Just as those in the group were about to seat themselves, there was an eddy in the ranks immediately in front of them. A bent figure limped past and took station next to Danna. One side of the oldster's dark, lined face was covered with white weals from some encounter, and a heavy stick of dark wood aided his limping gait. An unpleasant smell came from his direction, and Danna pointedly moved away from him and nearer Slater. The old man paid no attention, except to scratch himself with vigor. If his habits matched his appearance, thought Slater, he was certainly lousy.

He forgot the old derelict, for a sudden hush fell over the assembly. A man was mounting the platform. Behind him came eight more and Slater saw that they were the konsels. Lang marched last, perhaps by accident, but he also remained the one nearest the steps leading up.

The leading elder moved to the front of the platform, the others ranked behind him, and began what was obviously an invocation. His voice was strong and resonant, his words few. He lifted his hand on finishing and joined to the others. Now another stepped forth, and this time the remaining eight sat down on a low bench at the back of the platform.

The new man was Albar Jonzin, a stocky and bullet-headed fellow. He spoke in sharp, bitter phrases. Though Slater could not make out his words, he was obviously exhorting the Ruckers to do something, and the manner was inflammatory and brutal. When Jonzin finished his speech, he waved a hand to the steps. He was clearly introducing the next speaker. The crowd leaned forward and drew in its breath. A Terran mounted the platform. He wore two lasguns in trim cross belts, one under each arm.

JayBee Pelham drew attention just by appearing. It was nothing so simple as physical good looks, although with his white hair and high cheekbones, he was a fine-looking man. Rather an aura of almost electric force emanated from him, a vibration in sympathy with almost every person he encountered. Slater had never seen him live, but he understood instantly how Pelham had seduced half a planet and might do so again if given a chance. He dominated the crowd of Ruckers, perhaps the toughest variant of humanity ever to appear, as easily as he had done with the farmers and technicians of the domed cities. He made no concession to Rucker dress but wore a splendid bush suit, obviously tailored for him, of some expensive deep-blue synthetic trimmed with white fur at collar and sleeves. His face was calm, his eyes thoughtful and considering as they moved slowly around the cavern. He might have been about to address a convocation of religious leaders after lunch at a good Ares restaurant. When he first spoke, Slater was startled.

"Friends!" Though the voice was marvelous, the deep vibrant tones of a great orator, it was the fact that JayBee was using Unit that surprised the officer so. And from the look on the faces of his neighbors, they were as amazed as he. No doubt the enemy language had never been used at a solemn assemblage of this sort in recent history. But the magic of JayBee was strong enough to overcome even that prejudice.

"I speak to you in a language that you can all understand. It is a language you hate. And rightly so. But I do not apologize. For as a friend to all the True People, here and elsewhere, I must use the tools I have, and not those I hope some day to acquire. I know that each child of the free clans learns Unit as soon as he can be taught it. I shall some day speak to you in your own language. And each child on the Mars of the future will learn the language of the True People, not first but only! For it will *be* the language of Mars, and Unit will be the language of banished Earth, of the dirt grubbers and the ruins of the domes, the wreckage of the forts, the empty memories of the departed and the dead, the enemies of the True People, obliterated and expelled from the planet on which they have no place!"

And he had caught them. In only a few burning words, he had made the ancient magic possible between people and a natural leader who was an orator. Forgotten was the alien speech, the enemy garb, the hereditary dislike of the foreigner. Slater knew that if he were to live two centuries, he would not see a greater orator in action. The Rucker crowd was on its feet. They were not shouting, that was not the custom, but their intense murmur was combined with the snapping of fingers, the ultimate in Rucker applause. Slater found himself joining in, and not entirely from a wish to maintain his disguise! Beside him, Danna was snapping her fingers with equal enthusiasm. A wink from the grinning Muller brought Slater back to earth.

Pelham continued to speak, his theme a justification for the destruction of Mars Command and the concomitant total shattering of the domed cities, agricultural enclaves, and the mines. All non-Ruckers of any age were to be offered three choices: mingling with a Rucker clan, repatriation to Earth, or death. The simple program delighted his auditors and the finger clicking increased in volume. Slater wondered how JayBee was going to sell his supporters in the cities on the idea of living in the Ruck, but the man was cynical enough to try to sell anyone anything, that was the only answer he knew. Promises made to his supporters in the domes would have no relation to what was said in the Ruck. As the promises grew wilder, Slater's contempt for Pelham grew along with them. But the Ruckers loved it.

At one point Pelham beckoned to a group of men, Ruckers and Terrans, who stood near the base of the platform. A young Rucker warman mounted the stage and handed him a shrouded pole. Was the choice of a Rucker rather than a Terran accidental? Slater wondered. He thought not. JayBee did little that was accidental.

It was a flag, by God! The Ruckers did not use such things,

and even the clan emblems were little used in battle, but once again Pelham had struck a right note. The flag was reddish brown, the color of much of Mars' soil, and bore a black circle flanked by two smaller circles of unequal size. Deimos and Phobos, and the planet itself.

"Here is a new thought I offer you—the flag of the free clans, the banner under which the True People will destroy their enemies and cleanse Mars of the pollution of the domes and of the scum who wish the men of Earth to spread over the planet's entire surface." No one in authority wished this, of course, and the land area of Mars was so large that it might have taken five hundred years even if they had wished it. But JayBee's appeal was not to reality. Nor did he make the mistake of explaining how he proposed to create any of his contradictory wonders, such as the self-contained society of peasant-technologists and totally free nomad–hunter–agronomists. His spell needed no second thoughts. The finger snapping was so violent Slater wondered about the possibility of dislocated knuckles.

His attention suddenly became riveted on what JayBee was saying. He was introducing the members of his entourage. The first three were Ruckers, one of them a chief who smiled grimly at the tribesmen and women below, his gray teeth flashing in the flickering torchlight. The fourth was a tall, lean Terran, with a wispy black beard and a rigid face. His name rang across the cave. Medawar! Then this was Mohini "Dutt's" father!

"This man," JayBee shouted, "has given his daughter—his only child—to the cause, *our* cause! She has been spying on the enemy soldiers for years, from inside, as one of them, and has only recently escaped! Honor this man and listen to him. He will tell you things you need to know about some of those who pretend to lead you."

A familiar figure was mounting the platform. Mohini! She must have been hidden or disguised as a man. But now, her long hair flowing over her combat uniform, she stood with her father at the front of the platform. And she was looking in their direction!

"Spies sit among us!" Medawar said, his voice hoarse and rasping. "They must be exposed, they must be destroyed! My daughter knows them. They are in hiding, they are in disguise, but she knows them. She has left the enemy fort to smell them out for you. Trust her! She is a faithful servant of JayBee and of free Mars, the Mars of the True People! Let her unmask the traitors and the spies who are with them!"

The silence was suddenly profound. The crowd waited, each man looking at his neighbor, each woman at her sister, all wondering what was up. Only the breathing of the crowd could be heard. The limping old man turned to look at Slater, and it crossed the lieutenant's mind that the creature's rheumy eyes were somehow familiar. His hand felt for his belt gun and he moved closer to Danna.

"Those men in the back of the cave, with the Wise Woman of the Ferkat Clan, they are Greenie officers led by Muller himself. You know who *he* is!" A sigh rose from many throats. Muller was known to all, the Greenie they could not trick, the man who always outthought them. A thousand sharp eyes glared at them, waiting for the word.

"The Wise Woman is a traitor too. Don't let them escape. There are still other traitors who must be unmasked after they are taken. Take them alive. Make them talk!" Mohini's high-pitched tones rose until they were a scream.

It was only at this point that Slater noticed something. Muller was gone! Somehow, even before Mohini had started speaking, he had slipped out! He had simply vanished! Slater, Feng, and Danna were alone. On the platform, Lang could be seen conferring gravely with his fellow konsels. Obviously Mohini had either not dared to denounce him or been instructed not to.

The Ruckers in front of the three turned and began to move quietly forward, their faces set with hatred. They must have hesitated a little over Danna, but a Wise Woman's being a traitor would in the end make them angrier and less inclined to ask questions. Slater got ready to die, since he did not intend to be taken alive and interrogated.

A great voice bellowed something from behind him, something unintelligible. Whatever it was, it froze the enraged Ruckers who faced them in their tracks. The voice roared out again. On the platform, everyone froze, Mohini still leaning forward, her hand extended in menace.

Someone whispered in Unit. With a start, Slater realized it

was their bent old neighbor. "Move slowly toward the door. Don't crouch; Stand straight. Walk as if you have been insulted. Let Danna go last. Whatever you do, don't shoot!"

They stood up and backed unconcernedly toward the passageway to the camp. From the corner of his eye, Slater saw that a giant figure, hands outstretched as if in warning, stood at the tunnel mouth. It was Nakamura. His disguise as one of the clan of giant wizards from the south was perfect. Such was the awe surrounding *them* that the mass of Ruckers was hesitant. It was enough to hold the furious mob of True People in check, at least for the moment.

Mohini broke the spell. "He's one of them," she screamed. "I know him! He's an officer from the fort, not a true Opener of the Way. Don't listen to him! Take them all!"

It was the fact that she spoke in Unit, perhaps allied to her uniform as well, which prevented total disaster. The conflicting emotions that JayBee had stirred up, the accusations against a Wise Woman, the hated uniform, the alien tongue, all had thrown the True People into confusion. Nakamura added to it now.

He bellowed a string of mysterious syllables in his great voice and held up an object, glittering in the light of the torches. It was the strange poison weapon they had all examined back at the fort. And it was more. It was the thing Slater had seen in the belt of the mysterious hooded boatman in the dream he had shared with Danna! That was what had jogged his memory at the time, the thing he could not recall. All this raced through his mind while he felt for his lasgun under his cloak and eyed the nearby Ruckers who were staring at the group with anger and fear.

Slowly but steadily they shifted through the loose groups toward the tunnel exit. On the dais, heated argument was apparent. Mohini was arguing with her father and Pelham, but her voice was inaudible. Close to them, the konsels seemed engaged in a separate debate, ignoring the Terran delegation. Nakamura's great voice grew louder as Slater and the others approached him. Slater watched his friend caper about, waving the strange weapon in mystic passes as he did so. The True People at whom the object was pointed moved nervously farther away from it. A hum of angry and confused voices underlay the bellowings of the disguised UN officer as the crowd swayed to and fro, confused and frightened at the unprecedented happenings in their midst.

The crouched and evil-scented oldster swung his staff in mystic passes before them now, muttering as he did so. The Ruckers revered the aged, for few of them attained long years. They backed away from the old man, though their eyes were angry as they glared at Slater and the others. Danna stared coldly back and walked as if she had a right to go anywhere, while the men tried to copy her insouciance. Slater felt as if a thousand missiles were about to bury themselves in his body, but he was still more concerned about the girl.

Now they were next to Nakamura. He ignored them, jumping about oddly and yelling discordantly until they passed. As they did, he fell in behind. Still walking, despite the impulse to run, the little party passed into the great tunnel and the light dimmed at once, for the torches that had lit it on their arrival were out or dying.

"Run, all of you" came a hiss from the gloom ahead. "They will break into anger in a moment." It was the old man, now standing straight in the gloom ahead.

"Yes, hurry!" Danna said, clutching Slater's arm. "Listen to Arta. He knows what to do!"

Slater gulped and swallowed in silence. So that was where Arta Burg had been! Danna's second husband. Not dead, not lost in the storm, but disguised, waiting to surface when needed! He felt stupid, since the others seemed to have penetrated the disguise at once.

They ran openly now, Danna and Burg in front, the others following. They had not gone far when the swell of voices behind them rose into a great roar. Ahead they saw the light of the outside world. Behind lay certain death. Would there be guards, Slater wondered as he sprinted, or would the way be clear? And what would happen to Thau Lang, whom everyone seemed to have forgotten?

Behind them, mingled with the roar of the assembly, came the vibration of running feet, but none of them looked back. At least, Slater thought, they aren't shooting. If Pelham and

Company had carried the day completely, we'd be targets by now.

The entrance loomed before them and they raced out, weapons drawn. But there were no guards. In the near distance a few children and women stared at them, open-mouthed the herds of bulgotes fed peacefully.

To their right, deep in the shadow of the overhanging arch, though, stood a figure. It was Muller, and with him another man, a younger Rucker whom Slater had not seen before. They were holding the reins of two huge buck bulgotes, the backs of which supported laden pack harnesses. Suddenly he realized the new Rucker was Milla Breen!

"This way," Muller called. "No time for talk. Follow me, all of you—and hurry! We've an ally in camp who will know what to do. Don't waste time!" He led off at once, and Slater found himself leading one of the bulgotes at a rapid lope. They were not heading away from the cave but parallel to it, farther back in the shadows of the great overhang, down a path that led between rock shapes and grew rapidly narrower until they were going single file. The man who had been with Muller at the cave mouth had never moved and as they rounded a sharp curve, his stolid shape was lost to sight. No one of their pursuers had yet come into view either, and as they turned the corner of a right angle, all noise from behind was lost to the ear.

The gray-black basalt grew closer overhead with each stride, as the ceiling and the walls of their passage drew together. The light was very dim. The bulgote Slater led snorted and checked briefly. The young officer wondered desperately what he would do if the great brute reared and began to fight in earnest.

As if he could read minds, Muller was beside the animal in an instant, fastening a dirty cloth bandage over the animal's eyes, crooning to it in a low monotone as he did so. In a second the job was done.

"He'll do," he said quietly. "Talk to him if he shies. He's a lot smarter than a horse." With that, he was gone again, eeling his way past Feng, who was in front of Slater.

The dirt floor of the path changed to hard rock, and they

were in another equally narrow black tunnel. When the passage straightened, Slater could see that someone up front was using a pocket beamlight. It was all that was needed so long as the passage kept narrow and straight. The other bulgote, apparently led by Muller or someone right behind him, blocked much of the light. There was little talk, only an occasional whisper, the sound of the animals' hooves, and the padding of human feet. The quiet procession seemed to go on for hours, and Slater felt himself growing numb with fatigue. It was cold too, though not damp. The tunnel bored on and on, only now and then taking a gentle curve. But always it sloped very gently down. The rock walls felt quite smooth to the hand, and he wondered who had carved the shaft and when. He had never thought of the Ruckers as miners, and this seemed expert work.

They had marched four hours without a break when the light up ahead suddenly grew brighter. It hurt Slater's eyes and he blinked and squinted for a moment, before he saw that it was only a wooden torch set alight and that he had emerged into a cavern, or a greatly heightened and widened segment of the tunnel. Behind him the others came, and he smelled Danna's wild fragrance for a second as she walked by him, to where Muller held the torch. The air was moist, dark, and cool, and the walls glimpsed in the torchlight were wet though the tunnel floor was not.

"We'll take a break, but not too long," the colonel said. "Feed and water the animals while I talk. We can't stay here long. Too dangerous. You'll find water bags and grain in the lefthand pack on each animal. Hurry it up, now. By the way, Milla was JayBee's flagman. Fun, eh?"

Suddenly Danna was beside Slater as he fumbled with the lashings of the unfamiliar pack. "Let me, you clumsy Terran, or Strombok will bite you." Her voice was gay, and he wondered at it even as he fought back an almost overpowering desire to hold her tight in his arms.

"He's my own baby," Danna said happily. "I raised him from a kid. Isn't he pretty?" She crooned to the huge mutated goat, as if to a child, and Slater was jealous while he listened to the brute crunch its feed.

"I wanted him to be led by you," she went on in a low

voice. "He might need to know you later if there's trouble. They won't let just anyone handle them. They are very... sensible? No—sensitive, that's the word. And I wanted him to like you too."

"He's lovely," Slater said, watching one of the bulgote's amber eyes roll at him in the torchlight. He hoped he sounded sincere. An uglier beast had never existed, he thought. Strombok looked as if it ate babies for breakfast. The great knobbed horns had needle tips; the Ruckers never polled their herds. The horns were needed for fighting off the wild dogpacks and such, but Ruckers admired strength and ferocity anyway, hating the clipped and fatted stock of the Terrans. Suddenly Slater realized that Muller was talking.

"A fellow named Gunsmit is on our side. He's a camp chief and a good man. He can lay a false scent and be believed. At least for a while. This tunnel and lots of others are things known to the Wise Women and a few, not all, of the older men.

"Before someone asks, Thau Lang is in no danger. A konsel is usually above attack, unless he declares a feud, and Thau Lang can only be condemned by his own clan, which is a long way off and wouldn't do it anyway. He's a great war leader as well, and famous far beyond his own borders. Neither JayBee nor the U-Men would dare attack him openly, and he's too wise to the danger now to be taken by deceit. He will move out tonight and catch up to us when he can. Milla slipped out while Mohini Dutt was raving at us.

"Finally, we are on our way to the South—the area the U-Men, or their allies, come from—by a shortcut. This network of tunnels may save us as much as thirty miles or more still, before we surface. But we have to move fast. There is only a remote chance that we'll be followed, which would mean that JayBee, the U-Men or both have suborned a konsel or Wise Woman. But not much is known about these caves and tunnels. Certain routes have been charted through them. I have a rough map of ours. But no one stays in them longer than necessary. Many of the first explorers from the clans never came out. Sometimes they were found, or what was left of them. Sometimes there was nothing, just the Long Silence. Save for a few of the shortest and most open, like the big council cavern, they are used only in dire emergencies. So we rest now for half an hour, we guard our perimeter constantly, and then we move out."

A shape moved next to Slater, and a hand touched his shoulder. He could just make out the ragged suit that covered Arta Burg in the flicker of the torchlight.

"Half of the Scorpion Clan, who live over to the west of us, were lost this way many years ago." His voice rang even louder than had Muller's in the silence. "They sheltered deep down from a great wind, much worse than the one two days ago. Only a few bones were found by the ones who looked, a few bones and many long tunnels going back into the hills beyond light and knowledge."

"Hear that, everyone?" Muller asked. "Relax now and try to get some rest. Burg and I will take first watch, he at the way we came in, I up ahead here."

Slater found himself sitting between Danna and Nakamura. Feng and Milla had gone to sleep, each taking a bag from the nearest bulgote. The torch had been extinguished and they sat in the dark, talking in low tones. Occasionally a light flickered at the entrance to the cave or back beyond where Muller and Burg played their pocket beamlights at random. Otherwise it was night in the depths.

"I'm delighted that Arta and Milla were not lost," Slater said. He was, he found, not lying, though he still hated the thought that Danna had two husbands. Arta and Milla were good comrades, decent fellows. It was not Arta's fault that an alien had fallen in love with his wife! A wife he shared with another man anyway!

"It's wonderful," she answered. "Here we are all together. If only my grandfather would come, it would be perfect."

"Your grandfather?" Nakamura was no more puzzled than Slater, but he spoke first.

"Oh, we did not tell you. Thau Lang is my mother's father. Many of the True People still do not bother with much record keeping, who is related and all such things. But the Wise Women know what genetics are. We are not such savages as you Greenies think." She laughed and poked the big lieutenant.

"Besides, it is important to know who the ancestors of a Wise Woman are. We can speak to those gone down at times, and also we wish to be able to breed and transmit our power to the daughters to come. But anyone would want to be related to Thau Lang. He is a wonderful man, a konsel and one of the greatest warriors as well. Usually konsels are only middling fair as fighters. They have to think too much. But he has killed over forty men and many terrible beasts. A wonderful man!"

The combination of superstition and pride at having the most murderous warrior around as a kinsman caused Slater to wince in the dark. But he felt rueful a moment later. Who was he to flinch at his savage love and her pride, he who had been raised on tales of war against the Russians, ancient British, the Sikhs, and the other Afghan and Pathan tribes? Danna's pride was honest, like everything else about her.

She was sitting close enough to Slater so that he could feel her muscles quiver, all in an instant. At the same time her voice cried out, "Back here to the others, Muller and Arta. Something comes!"

Each man reached for his pocket light while Feng and Milla Breen uncoiled from sleepbags only a fraction of a second behind the others. With a rush of racing feet, the two outer men joined them and in seconds they were all seven in a circle, lights and weapons facing outward, the two blindfolded pack beasts in the center.

"I can *feel* it," Danna murmured, her voice low and unsteady. "It is out there . . . watching."

Her outstretched arm was pointing toward the blackness in the direction in which they had been heading.

## CHAPTER 9

# *Through the Long Silence*

THE BEAMS OF THE SMALL FLASHLIGHTS DIED PERHAPS A hundred or so yards away and were swallowed up by the moist dark beyond. The smooth damp walls of the tunnel, even though far wider than their original track, were still visible on either side. Only the roof above lay out of sight. Slater felt a ghost of an acrid scent in his nostrils and wondered if he were imagining it.

"Listen!" Muller said. "I heard something! And I can smell it!"

Now Slater heard it too. It was a curious sliding noise, as if something damp was brushing gently against a smooth surface. They strained eyes and ears, but they could not pinpoint the sound. Nevertheless, it slowly grew louder, though somehow more diffuse, as if a number of different objects were involved. Then they saw something.

At the farthest limit of their beams, something shining came in view, white and featureless, glistening. It seemed small at first, but as it advanced, it grew in girth. Behind it came another and yet another, weaving, twisting, and almost oozing over the basalt floor of the tunnel, yet always approaching. The tips were soft-looking, eyeless and shapeless. But the bulk of whatever the things' length represented grew constantly as they emerged into the light. At the back, the limit of the humans' vision, they were now as thick as cables. And still they came. At least eight of the horrid things were in view, and even as they watched, another appeared. In fascination, the seven watched the inexorable advance.

"It is old," Danna said in a strained voice. "Old and hungry. And also it hates us, for we can see."

As usual, the colonel had not been idle. He broke the spell. "Get down!" he shouted, and threw something far and straight, back into the dark where the living ropes bulked thickest. As he hurled the object he fell forward.

Slater had thrown one arm over Danna as they fell, and now he felt the floor of the cave heave to the blast of the explosion while his ears went numb at the same time. When he opened his eyes, the white glare of the tiny bomb had died but there was sufficient afterglow to see the shambles it had created. Great torn coils of twisting, living, pallid substance writhed in agony, blocking the tunnel as far as they could see, snapping and beating with soft but massive thuds against the walls, reaching and grasping far up out of sight into the dark above. At the same time a pain, a thrilling vibrato cut into his head as if something was screaming on a note that humanity was never meant to hear. His eyes shut again with the agony. He felt Danna choke under his hand and knew that she and the others were having the same experience. The acrid, piercing scent had become a fierce reek.

As suddenly as it had come, the pain died and was gone, leaving only a feeling of stretched nerves and overstrained muscles. One by one the ghastly ropes ceased their movement and slowly settled to the cavern's floor. A foul stench rose from them like steam, and as the party slowly rose, weapons and lights at the ready, the bulgotes snorted and began to rear, straining at their reins. Danna, Milla, and Arta ran to them and soothed them with pats and caresses, crooning until the fear subsided.

"It has gone," Danna said, turning to Slater. "I can feel the hate still, but far away, down deep in the cold water and the dark. It is not dead, but badly hurt."

Muller and Feng had cautiously gone out and were examining the closest of the now-motionless things. They held their free hands over their noses as they peered and probed with lights and booted feet. After a moment they came back, faces drawn.

"You are a great warrior, Muller," Danna said warmly. "None of the True People—no, not even Thau Lang—ever fought such a creature as this!"

He brushed aside the praise. "You warned us about them, or 'it,' as you call it, Danna. How did you know it was coming? We all felt the supersonic cry when it was hurt. Yet you gave us a full minute's warning. And you seem to know something about it. What?"

Surprisingly, it was Burg who answered. "You have lived with the clans, Muller. Thau Lang told us that much back in your fort. You know the True People better than any Greenie on the planet. Haven't you learned anything about a Wise Woman yet? They see and feel the *unseen* in ways no other can. They can tell when the great storms will come, when water will fail, when the volcanoes come from the rock. They speak with those who have gone down. Why should Danna not know the thing was coming?"

"You're right, Arta. I must be getting old. I have seen enough in the past. There was someone, a woman, once..." He cut himself off in midspeech, an odd thing for Muller. "What do you think it was, Danna? Is it intelligent?"

In the beamlight, Danna grew thoughtful. "These feelings come, Muller, and they go. I *felt* rather than *knew*, do you understand? Now there is nothing beyond a vague sense of hurt, which is far away and growing farther. But it was one thing, I know that, and those were its...hands. It must be big, very big. It lives mostly in water, and there has not been any water on the top of Mars, until we made it—we humans—for many millions of years. So it lives below. But I felt that once it lived up on top, long long ago, beyond the memory of man. Or maybe its fathers did." She paused. "You asked, 'Is it intelligent?' I don't know how to explain. I feel that it is perhaps, but not the same way we are, if that is something that makes sense. Also"—and her voice dropped a little—"I got a feeling it might have been *sent*, yet that is not right either. Maybe told, or, what's the Greenie word—alerted. That's closer. But it is all feeling, not something I know with my brain. I hope that helps." She looked at Slater and smiled, as if she were a child who could not repeat a lesson correctly. His heart went out to her at the same time his brain reeled.

Muller had been conferring with Arta, Milla, and Captain Feng. Now he summoned them all to the center of the open space. He took a wooden torch from Strobok's pack and lit it.

"Let's get out of here. The bulgotes come behind, with Arta and Danna leading them, Slater and Milla last. Keep your eyes open, son, and warman Breen. We could still be hit by something from behind. Nakamura, come up here. I need those big muscles of yours to lift this muck. Watch it carefully. Some of those things may have reserve nervous action, even if their owner isn't attached any longer."

Rags were tied over the gotes' muzzles, since the stink of the dead limb segments was overpowering. Slater went to dampen a cloth on one of the dripping walls and made an interesting discovery. Narrow gutters running along the sides of the tunnel, only an inch or so wide, served to carry the moisture away, so that the main tunnel floor remained dry. He reported this when he came back, and Muller looked thoughtful. "Whoever built this knew what they were doing."

"Whoever or whatever," Nakamura muttered. He and Feng carefully cleared a path through the torn mass of white and slimy tentacles, hurling the loathsome things aside and wiping their hands on rags as quickly as possible. Slater touched one in passing and shuddered at the feel, which was both gelatinous and rubbery at the same time. Mars clung to many secrets, and knowledge of the dweller in the deep caves was one the old planet could keep indefinitely as far as he was concerned.

The party passed through the gap thus created, the gotes snorting only a little, and they soon came to a place where the foul remains abruptly ended. The tunnel was narrowing again but still sloped gently down. Before them now, clear in the torchlight, was a broad smear, several yards wide, of glistening slime and ichor. The odor was still overpowering, but the way was clear.

Muller led and the others followed cautiously. In the light, the foul track led straight on, but suddenly Muller halted and held his torch high. To their right, a huge vaulted opening loomed in the tunnel wall, its base even with the floor. Into this led the awful trail of the monster, and beyond it, in front of them, the path was dry once more.

They hurried past, weapons ready, wondering if a mass of the things would rise through the black arch and assault them again, but nothing happened. In a few moments they were far beyond the hole, and Muller put out his torch, once more switching to the pocket beamlight.

As they went on, the damp in the air increased, until it was positively humid. The temperature, however, remained constant. The tunnel was narrow again, but never so much as it had been before the cave of the monster, and two could walk abreast easily. Once Muller checked for a moment and shone his light on the floor by the narrow gutter. A pile of some dark rubbish lay there, but the light caught on a glint of metal.

"Somebody drew this map and came back afterward, or there wouldn't be any map. Looks like someone stayed behind too."

The air remained fresh and moist. They encountered tunnel openings with increased frequency, and always passed them as quickly as possible. Their own road had stopped descending some time back.

After about five hours, Muller called another halt. "We ought to get some rest. Nakamura and Feng take the first watch. Danna and Slater next. We'll come, Milla, Arta and I, last. Two hours a watch. That should give us enough to go on."

Exhausted, those not on watch lay down at once. Slater felt he had hardly had a chance to close his eyes, when Nakamura shook him awake.

"Go see the Rucker's Revenge," the giant whispered, pointing to Danna, who stood a little distance off, her torch illu-

minating her face. "Wish I had your luck. Even the godddamn
gotes don't like me." He added, almost as an afterthought,
"Nice girl, Moe. Never thought I'd feel that way about one of
them." In an instant he was curled up and asleep in his bag.

Slater smiled to himself as he walked to Danna. If someone
who hated the Ruckers as much as Nakamura could change,
maybe there was hope for an eventual peace after all.

Though the two were supposed to be patrolling opposite
ends of the tunnel, they quickly found each other and Danna
came into his arms. "We should not be doing this on watch,"
she said finally, her curly head buried against his chest. When
he started to pull away, two strong little arms tightened around
him, and he could see the glint of her smile in the torchglow.

"Those who spurn a Wise Woman are said to die unpleas-
antly, Greenie. And besides, we get so few chances to be
alone."

"My friends call me Moe," he mumbled. Then, before he
could catch himself, the one thing that had been on his mind
for the last three days came out. "Besides—what about your
two husbands?"

She pushed him away and looked up at his face. "That
bothers you? Ah, I understand. You Greenies!" She shook him
gently by the front of his leather jacket. "You thought I was
making love to them both!" He heard her choked laughter in
the moist gloom.

After the soft laughter had died, she said, "Moe, you know
little about us, though that is not surprising. We steal your
records, your vid-tapes, your books, your newsheets, and we
leave little for you to find in return. Thus we know much of
you, but you, only bits and snatches of our lives."

Her voice grew sober as she explained. "Let us walk together
in a circle, and we can talk as we do, so that the guard is kept.
I will tell you about the Wise Women. My mother was one
and she died long ago. My father I never knew. No one speaks
of him, not even Thau Lang. He once told me my father was
a great warrior of a far-distant clan and that he had to leave
me as a baby. Thau Lang told me that some day he would tell
me more."

They walked the cave in silence for a moment, circling the

sleeping men and the cud-chewing bulgotes at a distance, flashing their lights about at random. Slater's heart was beating harder than he thought it could. Danna was *not* sleeping with Burg and Breen! For the moment, that was all he needed to make him happy.

"Moe, I was raised by the two other Wise Women in our clan, wonderful old women. It was hoped I had the power too, but it does not always come to the same blood, though it sometimes comes from families that had none in the past. When I was a small child and it was realized that I could see things far off, the clan married me to two boys. They are my brothers and more, and they must always protect me, all their lives, until they die or I should decide to give them leave to marry, I mean *really* marry." She laughed again, a low gurgle. "Moe, they are the only two men I must *not* sleep with! They are my teachers, about men's things—how men think—and they are my guards. When Thau Lang told me to be captured and come to help him at your fort, they had to go along. They can never leave me, until I formally dismiss them before the clan." She paused and looked up at him. "I have slept with a few boys, Moe. I was supposed to, to know how men think, you see, which I must know as a Wise Woman. I enjoyed it, but it was only . . . fun, nothing more. Does that make you angry?"

"Now that I know you have no husbands, nothing could make me angry, Danna." He paused too. "I think I love you, as we know the thing on Earth. Are you allowed to love me, I mean, after this is over?"

"I can love anyone I want. No one tells a Wise Woman what to do, except our own council, which meets seldom, and then only on the gravest of matters. It will be hard—if we are to stay together, I mean—but I will think of something. I cannot leave my people. It will be hard."

She spoke further about the life in her clan, and he wondered again at the fate that had made him her enemy and that he had ever thought the Ruckers savage. Among themselves, they were kind and open-hearted, laughing a lot and full of fun. She had been on many trips into the wild with only her two guardian "husbands" and they had encountered every kind of danger, had fought shoulder to shoulder against Marswolves and other menaces. Being a Wise Woman had not excluded her from work when younger, and she had had to learn to herd bulgotes, to sew and clean hides, to make ammunition, and to weave the wonderful Rucker blankets that they sold at the Truce Fairs for fabulous prices. Indeed, it seemed that she had to work twice as hard as other girls, for the arduous training of a Wise Woman, about which she would not speak, was simply piled on top of all her other duties. He felt very lucky that such a being had chosen him, and also a little humble.

For him, the two hours went by like seconds, and he did not realize how tired he was until the last three on watch, the colonel, Breen, and Burg, had taken up their posts and he had finally lain down again.

After a quick bite of cold rations and some water from skins on the gotes, they had not marched for more than an hour when Danna called out.

"There is something ahead, Muller, though what I cannot tell. But it is life of some kind. I can feel it. It does not feel bad, or dangerous, just strange somehow. And there is more room, I think. I sense a great open space."

The slope was still level, and Muller crouched and began to examine the Rucker map in the beam of his pocket beamlight. "Nothing marked on here, except a lot of forks and branches to be careful of. I'll go with the map in my hand. Behind Burg and Breen. They're the best shots. Keep your guns at the ready, boys. Danna, Nakamura, and Feng lead the animals and you, Slater, bring up the rear. Everybody need to be told to stay alert? Good, let's move out."

For almost half an hour they marched slowly forward, every sense on the alert. Then a low call from Danna halted them once more.

"There are many things, so many I can't count them. They feel us too, and they are frightened. Should we go on, Muller?"

"We have to, Danna. Watch it everybody. Let's go."

They had gone only a half kilometer more, when the tunnel suddenly widened. They switched on their beamlights, keeping one hand free for weapons, but the powerful beams were lost in the immensity before them. They had entered a cavern so enormous that it simply ate the light, in every direction save down, for the floor stretched level as far as they could see. Here and there rock outcroppings broke the flat expanse and there were viscid-looking piles of some substance staining them and the floor as well, which gleamed in the light. Slater felt a musky and unfamiliar scent in his nostrils. He had the feeling he was being observed too. Then, even as they drew close together, it came.

They heard the sound of the wind suddenly, far overhead; a wind in the echoing bowels of the planet, where no breeze ever blew. A vast soughing wail, it rose from nothing and then—down it came with hurricane force and in an instant was upon them.

"Lie down—get the gotes down flat," Muller screamed above the howl of the storm. There was no time for more.

Slater saw the blackness, a living, pulsating blackness strike the beams of their upheld lights and then he was down on his face as things, countless soft things, flapping beating things, a living blanket of dark life, poured at and just over them, in a tide of matter, moving as one down the tunnel from which they had just emerged. He caught a glimpse of one individual as the wave of creatures hit them and saw the blunt eyeless head, toothless red mouth, the arch of shiny wings, and then nothing more as the gale force of the living wave flew past and through them. The noise of the countless pinions beating was actually deafening to his ears.

As it had come, so it was gone. The whole thing was over in a matter of seconds. The silence seemed deafening as they raised their heads and stared at each other. The gotes were snorting and trying to rise, and Danna gave them their heads and stroked them until they subsided while the others checked their weapons and examined them and each other for damage. Amazingly, beyond a few bruises, no one was hurt or even scratched.

"I ought to be shot," Muller said suddenly. "Quick, all of you except Danna, use your lights. I was holding the map and the rush of those bloody animals tore it out of my hand. I kept the light and my gun and the map's gone. We have to have that map!"

But the map had vanished. They searched far back down the tunnel and far out into the great cave, whose limits they could not even guess, but found nothing except the long-dead body of one of the creatures that had assaulted them and piles of what they surmised must be the things' excrement, the shiny goop they had first glimpsed in their lights.

The usually silent Feng was almost rhapsodic about the dead animal. "Fascinating! Observe the wings are neither a bat's nor a bird's, but more akin to the ancient flying reptiles of the Jurassic age back on Earth."

The thing was not too large, the body light and vaguely mammalian in appearance, jet black all over. The earless head was also eyeless. It might have spanned a man's outstretched arms with its strange wings, of which it possessed two pair. There were small claws on the wings and two hook-clawed feet near the rump. The total weight, allowing for dessication of the specimen they held, was no more than two kilograms, about that of a small chicken.

"What can they feed on, and where do they find it?" Feng mused. "There are no teeth. And yet there must have been many thousands of them to overwhelm us the way they did." He carefully stowed the strange carcass in one of the bulgote packs and then joined the others.

"This place is a real maze," Muller said. "Without the map, I have no idea how to proceed. But we have a hidden asset, which has saved us before, and I hope will again. Danna, can you lead us out of here or sense the most direct way to the surface?"

"Let me think for a moment, Muller. Those creatures, which did not hurt us and were very frightened, must have lived far up on the roof of this cave. There are stories among my people of things that fly at night, in great clouds, at certain seasons of the year, though no one has ever been close enough to see what they were. I think these strange things also once had eyes and lived up on the surface, just as I think that devil thing you bombed once did. But they have no thoughts and it did, at least a hate of others. They were only scared.

"Anyway, I think there is a way out up top, far above us. But it will probably be concealed and very small. And we have no way of getting there. I am not happy about this. I cannot sense the surface, not down this deep. In the wild, the Ruck, I can use animals when I am lost. The bulgotes know direction if one tells them what is wanted. Even certain of the wild things will come to a Wise Woman and will not attack, if they are told what to do. But I cannot use the gotes this deep underground. Their direction finding is useless here. If only I could get hold of some other creature, even a ferkat, or something that lives here. But alone, I fear that I can do nothing. Do you suppose we could catch a flier, one of those things that hit us?"

"Don't see how," the colonel said. "Anyone else have any ideas?"

"I surmise they have all gone, perhaps to another cavern that connects to the tunnel," Feng said. "Do you sense any life, Danna?"

She shook her head. Even Muller could think of nothing to say, and they all stood in silence, racking their brains for a way out of this unpleasant impasse. Were they doomed to wander at random in the endless tunnels and caverns until their food and water gave out? It was not a cheery thought, and even the tough soldiers and their hardened foes of the Ruck found it hard to maintain their poise. The Long Silence cast its pall.

At this point Slater had an inspiration. "Danna, how big does the animal have to be? Could it be small? Very small?"

The others crowded around, caught up by the excitement in his voice.

"What do you have in mind, Slater?" the colonel asked. "Got some bright idea?"

"Well, sir, it's Grabbit," Slater said, fumbling for the tiny impervium box at his belt. "I took him along and I forgot him, we've been so preoccupied. But he's alive, and I just remembered he was there." He opened the box and the little snapper waved his claws in greeting, his stumpy legs clawing for a foothold on the smooth surface.

"Jesu Christi!" Nakamura exclaimed. "I thought you left that little horror back at the fort. What the Hell did you bring it along for?"

The snapper clicked and hummed audibly as they watched it in silence, trying to climb from its box in vain.

"Moe," Danna breathed, "that is a terrible thing you carry. We kill them whenever we find them. Not even a Wise Woman would have one around. They get into tents and attack children once in a while, or even bite the leg off a bulgote, the bigger ones. You must be very brave." Her admiration was not lost on Nakamura.

"Or very crazy," he snapped. "What-in-hell good is that vermin now?"

"At ease, Lieutenant," Muller said. He turned to Danna. "What do you think, Danna? Can you use Slater's pet? It lives on the surface. I assume it wants to get back there. And it seems to like Slater, which is why I've let him keep it in the past. Want to try your luck with it?" He did not add that they had very little choice.

"I don't know." Danna examined Grabbit at close range with her beamlight. "I never heard of anyone trying to get close to one of these things. Even a rockscorp or one of the big spiders is said to have more feeling to get hold of. But I can feel that you are right. It does like Moe, and it will not attack us. Maybe we can do something. Could we rest, while I look at it more closely and talk to Moe about it?"

Nakamura said nothing as Slater and the girl walked a little apart, but Slater had no trouble guessing at the ribald comment in his friend's mind. But Danna was bent strictly on business. She sat down and held the box on her lap, motioning to Slater to sit beside her. For a long time she stared at Grabbit in silence, as if trying to see through its very armor. To Slater's surprise, the creature had stopped trying to escape and lay quiescent in the container, as if somehow the girl had calmed it. All at once, before he could even protest, she reached down and tipped Grabbit out onto her palm. Slater almost reached over to seize the snapper. It had had no food since they left the fort. But there was an air of authority about Danna that stopped him from moving. He was watching a Wise Woman at work and he felt her power and authority. Grabbit waved its small chelae once and then lay quiet once again, while she lifted him to her eyes and held him only millimeters away. At last she seemed satisfied and gently replaced the odd little creature in its box.

"It really likes you, Moe," she said, patting his hand. "The small mind is very strange, harder to reach even then the things we have seen here in the dark of the world, the flying things and the other. And its kind is very old too, as old as they, but different again. I feel that *they* grew, as part of Mars, but the snappers, if this one is like the others, are stranger in other ways. They give me a feeling, or maybe this one alone gives it, as if it were a creature that had lost its masters. It's like a tame bulgote that one recaptures after it has run away and joined a wild herd, maybe. But I get the thought that it thinks of you as its master, and it knows enough to leave people and things you like alone and eat only what you give it. Is that so?"

"He never bothers anyone around me. I give him the free run of my quarters, and he catches roaches and things. I keep the door locked when he's not in his box, of course, and I feed him now and then. The scientists I've talked to at Orcus say they can go without food almost indefinitely. No one seems to know how long they live or how big they can get. No one's seen any bigger than a ferkat, unless your people have. I leave wooden stuff lying around and he never chews on it, and the same with cloth."

"How did you get it? What *made* you get it, I mean?"

"Well, he or it, I guess, found me. I was on a stalk for a wild bulgote with some others and I got separated. I took a little nap under a thornbush and when I woke up, there he was, sitting on my belt buckle, cheeping away. I was a little scared, but somehow, damned if I know how, I knew he was friendly. So . . . I gave him some of my ration chocolate. He ate it and I put him in my pocket. When I found out how dangerous they can be, I took him to Colonel Muller. He said I could keep him, and to watch if he did anything interesting or new, so that we could put it in the files. I've had him a Marsyear or more."

Again she fell silent, staring at Grabbit. At length, she picked up the box, rose to her feet again, and they walked back to where the others were eating, the torches laid on the rocks casting a subdued light.

"It may not work, but I can try, Muller," she said.

"I'm afraid it's you or nothing, Danna," Muller said.

They assembled their things and the two warmen took the leads of the pack animals. Then, with Danna and Muller in the fore, they set off.

"I have tried to tell it what I want," Danna said. She held the box, lid raised, in one hand and her light was focused on Grabbit. "We are going to have much luck, if it understands. Now—watch."

As they looked, Grabbit began to move slowly. It crawled to one corner of the box and stopped. The claws were retracted and the blunt prow, for one could hardly call it a head, stayed fixed, pointing in one direction. At the same time, something else happened that made even Muller catch his breath. From behind the turret of Grabbit's one great eye a minute hole appeared. Out of it came a shiny plume, of a dark-blue tint, like an enameled feather from some tiny bird. This grew to about twenty millimeters in height, then bent halfway, at a right angle. The direction in which it pointed was the same as that in which Grabbit faced. Nothing could have been plainer.

"My God," said Nakamura. "The little bastard has his own compass radar set! How about that!"

"When they are dissected," Feng added, "all the internal organs dissolve in some acid. Nothing like this has ever been noted before."

"From the standpoint of military affairs," Muller said in dry tones, "I'd like my officers to reflect on this creature. It eats anything, lives for an unknown period, is very well armed, and possesses compass-radar or the equivalent. And also it owns an effective self-destruct mechanism that forbids tampering. Any ideas come to your mind?"

"It, or they, were *built*." The words hung in the silence even as Slater said them. Instinctively, they all looked around at the great dark that lay about them. The fact of Grabbit's abilities had brought the same thought to all their minds. Who or what had dug the tunnels, and who or what had made the snappers, or bred them, and turned them loose?

"The idea is quite logical, especially after all we have seen in these caves," Muller said. "Something we can continue to call Old Martians, for want of a better term, was a bioengineer of fantastic ability. I should not be surprised to learn that the other two life-forms we encountered here, as well as numerous others on the surface, had certain interesting applications. The tunnel system was not dug—nor were the water gutters arranged—by Ruckers. We are in a place built long ago, and for purposes not ours. Be watchful."

In silence they resumed their march, with Danna in the lead, holding her animated compass before her eyes. The others kept their lights on and flashed them from side to side as they walked.

The cave was indeed vast. For a long hour or more they tramped across its floor, finding it quite level except for occasional chunks of rubble that must have fallen from the lofty ceiling. Danna kept steadily on, her eye never leaving the snapper's compass-needle plume.

As he marched Slater found himself stroking the big blindfolded gote he was leading. He realized it only when he stopped for a moment and Strombok nuzzled his ear, the soft lips an obvious caress, and an appeal for more.

*Be damned if he doesn't like me. Who would have thought it?* He patted the soft nose and kept one hand on the gote's neck after that. At least he had tamed one of the Ruckers' own beasts, and that was quite a thrill too.

At last a great wall loomed before them. In its base were five wide tunnels mouths, set some distance apart from one another. Again they came to a halt around Danna.

"Here's his first big test, Danna," Muller said. "What does he say?"

The plume turned slowly as they all watched, their breaths held in nervous anticipation. After a moment it stopped. It pointed to their left, and they walked slowly in that direction. After a bit, Danna stopped.

"It moves no more," she said. "Look, Muller, now it is straight, pointing to that hole, there." Before them a tunnel opened, the second from the left in the line of five. As they went on Grabbit's strange antenna never wavered, its tip angled always to the black mouth they were approaching. In a few moments they were in the tunnel and marching on.

It might have been the mirror image of the one that had led them into the fliers' cave. At once apparent was that the floor of the new tunnel led *up* ever so gently. Shallow gutters conducted the damp trickle from the walls, and once again the central walkway was dry.

"Where in Hell does this water end up?" Slater mused. "It has to go somewhere."

"There are striated layers of frozen water in much of the deepest subsoil," Feng said didactically. "It comes down here as melt, I presume. That cave we were in, who knows how large it really was? There could have been a most sizable lake in it or even below it. And no doubt there are many other caves of equal magnitude elsewhere. I am beginning to suspect that the builders of these tunnels led water down to permanent basins."

They marched for four more hours and always the upward slope of the floor continued. Twice they passed tunnel mouths opening into theirs at right angles and once they came to a fork. Grabbit's antenna led them straight to the lefthand one of the two and they had no choice but to follow. They were no longer so depressed, but the monotony of the dark, the echoing damp walls, and the featureless surroundings were wearisome. Yet all were disciplined veterans and no one grumbled.

They halted for half an hour, fed themselves and watered and fed the bulgotes. They were tired, but no one argued when Muller gave the word to go on. The dark and the perpetual silence, broken only by their movements and occasional voices, were so dispiriting that they were all prepared to march until they dropped if it meant getting out of the caves. And Muller never forgot for a moment why they had come. His driving anxiety to make up time infected them all, and they tramped on in his and Danna's path, even though all were weary and suppressing the ache of overtaxed muscles and nerves.

Eventually even Muller had to call another long rest period. They had reached another widening of the tunnel, and again there was a fork. This time it lay behind them, since they had emerged from one entrance to discover another alongside and only one path before.

Slater had the first watch with the colonel this time, and found the latter willing to talk.

"I think that beast of yours will get us out, Slater," he said. "Plus our Wise Woman, of course. But I'm worried about Thau Lang. The map I had made no reference to any danger, nothing about that thing with the tentacles, nothing about the fliers or that vast cavern. Yet it was a Rucker map and he may be following us on it. Also, now that we're relying on the snapper, we may come out nowhere near where I had planned to meet him. This means we may end up nowhere near either JayBee or the U-Men, and/or the new clan from the bad country." He fell silent for a moment. "I can't think what I could have done, besides losing the map, that I haven't."

"We'd all have been dead a dozen times over, Colonel, if you hadn't been with us." Slater was abashed that the legendary Muller could even have a second of self doubt. "Really, sir—"

"I'm not apologizing, young man." His sharp eyes glinted and he looked hard at his young subordinate. "But I am human, you know; I eat, breathe, and relieve myself, just like the rest of you. I even have feelings. Now, get over to the other side. I want to think. And one more thing, boy. Don't hurt Danna. I'm rather fond of her." He turned and left Slater wondering at his last words.

At the end of the rest period, they set out once more. For two hours the trail led on. Side tunnels had ceased, and only the gradually increasing gradient of their own brought any hope. They were silent, all desire to talk having been lost.

Then Danna halted them. "I can smell something. Life is ahead, life that sees the sun!"

Muller quickly arranged them in battle order, Danna leading the two gotes again, and this time put Nakamura up front with the two young warmen and himself. Slater was happy to have the rear. He had come to feel that his Wise Woman was the only thing worth protecting, and he wanted to be the closest to her.

They had advanced cautiously for another kilometer, when

a spitting screech, a sound they all knew well, echoed down the tunnel from up ahead.

"Ferkat!" the girl hissed. "Maybe we are coming to a den."

The thought was sobering. The savage feral wildcats of Mars could grow to the size of a leopard.

Light! They all saw it at the same time, as they rounded a gentle bend in the tunnel. A diffused, dim-gray light, but it was coming from some external source. It made them blink, gentle as it was. They halted, switched off beamlights, and waited for their eyes to adjust. After a pause they moved forward. The light grew stronger, but there was no further sound, beyond distant insect noises.

"I can smell the cat," Milla said. "I hear nothing and there must have been only one."

Even Slater caught the ammonia reek of the den, and soon they saw piles of litter, dead leaves and sticks that the animal had dragged in for a bed. They rounded another shoulder of rock, all at once rough and broken, and saw they were in a low cave. Light glared in through a jagged crack at the far end, and once more they had to stop and blink until their eyes could adjust. The floor of the den was covered with rubble, and through it they cautiously picked their way.

"Must have been a land slip at this end," Muller said. "The tunnel builders never ended their work this way."

A dense thorn vine grew over the entrance and they hacked it aside, trying to make as little noise as possible. The hole grew and soon they had a passage large enough for the gotes to follow. Muller went first and then the others. Eventually the entire party was standing on a broad shelf, and the view opened up before them. It was dawn and the growing light showed a strange landscape.

Before them unrolled a scene of unparalleled beauty. They were looking down from one wall of a mighty and fantastic gorge. Clouds of mist swirled about them and hid the depths far beneath. Matted vegetation clung to every vantage, save where a few bare rock pinnacles had resisted any growth. Many of the plants were familiar, such as the massive twisted cedars and deodars, but many were alien and new, such as a barrel-shaped monster like a giant, red, up-ended, pine cone, which towered many meters tall on their right near a spine of shrouded basalt. At their very feet, great ferns sprouted head high. All the Earth plants were far larger than any they had ever seen.

The far side of the gorge was out of sight, and they could not tell whether they were on the side of a vast crater or of a giant canyon. Strange hooting calls echoed out of the mist far below, and once a shrill scream reminded them of the ferkat they had dispossessed. Insects buzzed all about them.

Muller sat down and beckoned the others to join him. "Any thoughts on where we might be?"

The Ruckers shook their heads. "We have never seen a place like this," Danna said. "Most of these Marsplants are new to us."

Captain Feng's voice broke the ensuing silence. "Are we not on target, as it were, Colonel? I see no other explanation."

"I agree, Feng. We've come through the wilds by going under them. This can only be one place. I'm damned if I can escape the feeling that Slater's little pet knew we wanted to come here, somehow. This is the bad country. And we have got here right in the middle of it."

# CHAPTER 10

# *The Abyss of Cimmerium*

$F$ AR AWAY, IN THE BURIED CENTRAL CONTROL ROOM AT Orcus Prime, the military commander of Mars turned to his executive, a man grown as gray in the UN service as himself. "It's not like Muller to have failed to report somehow, even if by a Rucker message shot into a fort with an arrow. I don't like this at all. We can't wait too much longer, Bob."

General Robert Vivian Campbell Scott, otherwise his Grace the Duke of Buccleugh, smiled at his superior. It had always seemed amusing and appropriate to him that centuries of service had brought his family, through accident, skill, and brains, once more into the service of a king. He looked at his friend's broad, swart face, the crisp white curls, and reflected that even stripped of any ancient powers, Philip Mutesa, the last Kabaka of what was once Buganda, had proved by his rise through sheer merit to UN Marshal that royal blood might still have its uses.

"Our people are rounding up the network of copters and their bases that Medawar had set up, sir. JayBee is quickly going to find himself a little short of supplies and reinforcements. And Earth Command and I-Corps are closing in on United Minerals at home and their hidden bases in the belt, pinching them off at both ends. They were behind JayBee, we now know. This has cooled things a little, you'll agree?"

"Agreed. But what about the U-Men? If they aren't part of this, who are they? And JayBee still has the Ruck, and he knows a hell of a lot more about it this time. Suppose he gets together with them?"

"If Muller's anywhere near that Cimmerium area, Marshal—and he's supposed to be—the spy-eyes are going to pick up very little. The canyons and craters are immense and deep. We've never penetrated that region on foot or even with jet choppers. And we've tried. Atmospherics are terrible, while the fogs are heavy and seldom lift. The planet forces are on full alert. What more can one do, Phil? Except wait, that is. Satellites tell us nothing about those deeper rifts, or almost."

"You're right, as usual," the marshal grumbled. "I just wish I were out there *doing* something, not stuck in this office with a lot of old fogeys like you who couldn't march three feet without a cane and a cold beer."

"I trimmed your ass in the last squash match without drawing breath," his subordinate said equably. "But the beer sounds good. Let's go have one and I'll show you the latest additions to my Tridee collection, just in from Earth. There's one with five girls and four guys, imitating a frieze from the Black Temple at Konarak. The girls are painted gold, the guys silver. Fantastic!"

"I thought Scots were supposed to be Puritans," the marshal said. But he allowed himself to be led off, still muttering. His fine-honed mind knew that he had done all he could. There *was* nothing to do but wait. And pray for Louis Muller. *Where was the man, goddamnit!*

The seven had eaten and were relaxing and observing the landscape of the great rift that spread out before them, pointing out new sights to one another as the mists swirled and thinned, each time revealing new scenes. The three Ruckers were as excited as the four UN men, for this was a part of their own world, hitherto unexplored and wrapped in strange legends. Behind them the two bulgotes, their blindfolds off at last, fed eagerly on any and all of the vegetation that curled about the broad ledge, their snorts of satisfaction punctuating the conversation.

"We'll have to do some cutting," Muller said, "but the slope here doesn't look too bad so far. We may hit a sheer face lower down and have to come back though."

"It's certainly hopeless above," Feng added. "I've prowled the edge and it's all naked rock that way, with pronounced overhangs. We can go down or sideways, but not up."

"Listen!" Danna called from the edge a little distance away. They all fell silent. High above came a sound they all knew well, the whine of a turbo-jet at low speed, rising and falling as it circled and came back again.

"That's a Greenie," the usually silent Milla Breen said. "I guess they are friends, no?"

The doubt in the young warman's voice made them all laugh, including Arta Burg. "For once we don't duck, Milla, or shoot at it. Maybe later, eh, but for now they are helping."

Muller was already hammering the butt of his big Rucker bush knife on a convenient rock. As the cap broke, he peeled away the shreds and revealed two tiny bulbs set in an impervium base. One glowed red in the morning light, but the other, a yellow bulb, was dim and lifeless. While they watched quietly, he stared alternately at the bulbs and the thick clouds that hid them from their ally far above.

"This be damned," he finally said in disgust. "The red means the homer is going out. But the yellow should light up too, which means the signal is being received by that ship up there. It isn't, that's all. Something is blanketing the signal, as if there were a dead zone encapsulating this place." He opened a belt pouch and removed a sealed lump of plasticene. In a few seconds he had molded a replacement cap for the knife and the stuff was setting solidly.

"It may, of course, be something natural that's doing this. We've always encountered atmospheric trouble in certain areas of Mars, and on Earth too, for that matter. But somehow, I don't think so in this case. I wish Thau Lang were here. He's explored closer in to some of these dead spots than anyone else on the planet."

"Haven't any of our people ever tried to find out about these unknown areas, sir?" Nakamura asked. "After all, we've been here quite a while."

It was Captain Feng who answered. "It's in the I-Corps files, Lieutenant. But I suppose you are entitled to the information. Especially since my exsubordinate, Miss Dutt, had full access to them. In the last fifty years, there have been three attempts, by scientists who had received full combat and ranger training. Two groups were sent by copter to a similar area, not this one. They landed below the mist and there was . . . silence. Nothing ever came back, no messages, no anything. The third group tried this very area, five years ago. It was the best-equipped and trained of the three, and each of the six men had three months bush training in the Ruck. Contact, bad but still contact, was maintained for about one-half hour. The team leader spoke of mysterious structures and said the team had detected signs of large life-forms though they had seen nothing. Their pack radar was functioning very badly, it seems. They had the feeling they were being observed, he said. Then he left his speaker, saying he would be right back. Nothing was heard but the hum of the speaker, according to the men in the command copter overhead. This lasted for about ten minutes, and came to an abrupt end with a sound. The sound, and I quote from the report, 'resembled more than anything else that of a small child's crying; *that* was cut off by a crunching noise, as if the set itself had been crushed.'" In the silence that followed his recital, he added, "The set had a self-destruct mechanism, as did all their technical and heavy equipment. None of it appears to have activated."

"How did they land in the first place?" asked Slater.

"The first two teams, in the other area, by parachute. This last one, the one here, by an armored copter. No malfunction of the vehicle was noted, and it was able to land with apparent ease."

Nakamura whistled. "So there is more than just old Marsrat tales to the Old Martians." He turned to Colonel Muller as he spoke. "Why so secret? I would have thought the Parliament of Man's appropriations for Mars would have been doubled if that had been aired, I mean."

"Probably you're right, Nakamura," Muller said. "But let's consider a few other possibilities, which we have in our laps as of right now, by the way. If there are strange devices of unknown power down here, whose hands do you want them to fall into? Would the inevitable rush of lunatics, adventurers, treasure hunters, and whatnot help? If the original owners still control these areas, what are their purposes and, above all, their *powers*? Assuming they exist, are they capable of losing their tempers? And what happens to this planet if they do? No, son, there are far too many imponderables, including the effect of this knowledge on our friends here." He smiled at the three young Ruckers, who were listening intently. "Thau Lang and I don't want them or any of the True People involved with these unknowns. And they have been, we now know, by means of the mysterious new 'clan,'—the giants who come out of this region with their talk of sweeping all non-Ruckers off the planet. And, as if this were not enough, we have JayBee and Company stirred into the soup."

He used his monocular to survey the gorge for a moment and then lowered it and turned back to his audience. "This is what I see, as of now. We are almost certainly ahead of JayBee and possibly the 'new clan' party that preceded him. We are coming down *on foot*—a method I argued for in vain when the last expedition tried this area. I hope we will be under or inside the blanketing force, whatever it is, that shrouds this place. I hope to look around, get an idea of what goes on here, and, if possible, prepare a reception for JayBee that he won't be expecting. Since we have been out about three days, the cave journey has saved us more time than I dared hope for. I don't see how the others could make it in less than five or maybe a full week. We're cut off from Thau Lang and whatever help he might bring with him, but that's the worst of it, aside from not having any contact with our own forces. But the latter, as I just pointed out, may mean we are actually inside the enemy's defenses, if they are defenses and there is any enemy besides the planet itself. Is that clear?"

At the nods of the others, he continued, "So . . . we leave a message on this ledge for Thau Lang, should he be following on our tracks. And we load up and go down, right now. Any questions?"

Muller wrote a short note on a piece of cloth and anchored it with one section sticking out, under a prominent rock.

The others were ready to leave when he had finished, and with Milla leading, they began to cut away the tangled growth at the right end of the ledge. Here they had help, for the well-worn though narrow track of the ferkat gave them a guide to follow. It was hard work even so, and the path had to be made wide enough for the two gotes. They came placidly down, however, still snatching bites from every plant within reach.

Danna was ecstatic about the new things they found and she kept pointing them out to Slater, who stayed close to her. There was a tiny version of the giant red pine cone, which had a tentacle and caught buzzing midges with it. Captain Feng noticed this too and looked thoughtful. Another thing no one could remember seeing before was a snakelike thing—whether plant or animal, they could not tell—but black and shiny. It had no visible head, but many minute stumpy legs, and was over two meters long. As they watched, it slid into the tangle of growth and vanished. The Earth plants made Slater homesick. Some of the cedars were as tall as any on the home planet, though their needles had taken on a bluish tint. Once the group rested under the shade of a willow that blanketed a vast area of the slope like a huge tent. Evidently a combination of rich soil and freedom from the terrible storms that swept the less sheltered reaches of the planet had caused the plant life to grow in ways it could never have done over most of the rest of Mars. Insects, some of them huge, buzzed and occasionally bit. Most were recognizable as mutants adapted from the original seed rockets, but some were clearly not, especially a conical object with two leathery wings and four grasping legs, which appeared at intervals and hovered over them. They watched one catch a large moth and carry it off with ease, though the moth was the size of an Earth crow, if a lot lighter.

"Goddamn it all," Feng kept lamenting. "No one's ever

seen half these things. I could spend a year collecting and not do anything but scratch the surface!"

The third time he came out with a similar utterance, the colonel called back, "Remember, Feng, that something collected three previous expeditions, a lot better armed than we are. Our first job is not to join them." The grim reminder sobered the group, and they peered about into the heavy growth with renewed vigilance.

By noon they had made a useful trail down about four kilometers of the great slope. Everyone had taken turns at cutting trail, and all could feel it in their arms. Muller had vetoed a suggestion by Slater that they burn some of the stuff with their lasguns.

"Bad thinking, Slater. One, we want no energy discharges if it can be helped. Two, we may need all our reserve charges. Just keep cutting, son, and pray this place has a bottom."

Danna poked him in the ribs and called him a soft Greenie, which made Slater momentarily angry, since he had been thinking of speed, rather than ease of movement. He wondered to himself as he hacked away whether he would ever reach a stage in which his own thinking anticipated all contingencies, and decided gloomily that he would never make it. Then he reflected that the colonel had probably felt the same way at some time in the past. Suddenly Slater felt more cheerful again.

Their next and last rest stop came in the late afternoon. The light was growing dim again through the fog and cloud cover, and Muller decided that they had better call a halt.

"We have enough hazards, known and unknown, without showing any lights. In a few minutes we'll need them to follow this trail, let alone cut it. We'll have a cold camp, stand watches, and start again at first light. I'm just guessing, but we must be close to halfway down, unless this hole goes into the core of the planet. Feng, have you noticed anything about the air?"

"Yes, sir. Once we stop sweating from movement, it's apparent that it's considerably damper. And new growth, better adapted to the moisture, like heavier mosses and softer, more fragile ferns, are replacing some of the things that grew higher up."

As he spoke, up through the damp fog came the long-drawn

hooting cry that they had first heard on the high ledge at dawn. It was now far louder and deeper, and gave a strong impression of size and volume. While they listened, the colonel said, "There are frogs a millimeter or so long back on Earth that one can hear ten kilometers away on a quiet night. Whatever makes that noise could be Grabbit's size, though I admit it doesn't sound much like it."

They listened again, but the sound was not repeated. As the night drew on, the screech and wail of ferkats showed that some Terran life-forms haunted the slopes. Once, far away, a bulgote bellowed its whinnying blare, which made Strombok and his fellow, Breenbull (he was Milla's property), stir restlessly at their tethers.

The great night moths flew by through the mist, the faint flutter of their wings clearly audible in the quiet, and something that sounded like a bird squawked restlessly in a nearby thicket as if it were having trouble settling down for the night. Biting gnats were not absent, but no worse than on any windless night in the Ruck far above. The Terrans used repellent and the Ruckers turned out to have the same tubes, no doubt looted from UN supplies.

Slater and Danna drew the second watch, but when he was awakened, he felt sure that they would have too much on guard to do more than exchange a few words. Danna, however, had other ideas. He had barely taken up his post on the upper trail and gotten settled comfortably in an elbow root of a vast shrub, when he felt a stir in the dark beside him and her warm, sweet scent rose out of the night into his nostrils.

Before he could say anything, she murmured, "Milla and Arta will take our places."

Slater still felt guilty at deserting his post. *What would Muller say? The cave was bad enough, but out here in the wild?*

He learned that Wise Women had mental tricks too. "Muller cares nothing except that the watch be kept," she whispered, tugging at him. "Come *on*, you great stupid Greenie! We may die tomorrow!"

She had located a bed of leafmold and moss just off the trail higher up, around a short curve. She also had brought her sleep bag rolled under one arm and now spread it on the ground. Under her leather suit she was naked, and Mohammed Slater, man of many conquests, watched the white shape appear in the night with his breath held and his mouth dry as any boy's with his first love. He had no time to ponder this, for then she was in his arms and he could think of nothing, feel nothing but her hands tearing at his leather jacket.

Much later a whistle, low and clear, brought her out of his embrace with the motion of a greased ferkat. They were at their proper posts and well separated when the two young Ruckers "relieved" them in silence. Slater managed to murmur "thanks," to Burg and felt a friendly squeeze on his shoulder in response. He remembered nothing more until Nakamura's toe prodded him gently awake.

The big lieutenant said nothing, but an eye closed in one large wink before he turned away. A good officer, Slater reflected ruefully, misses nothing! That makes Nak a good officer! He reflected more soberly that he was fully and passionately committed to Danna and allowed himself a second's wonder at what would happen in the unlikely event of their coming out of this jaunt alive. Then Muller's low call summoned them to eat and listen.

It was gray again, but the light was good enough to see ten meters before the dripping mists cut off vision. Though not so loud as earlier, animal noises still came from the distance on all sides. From very far off, a snatch of something like a trill of bird song sounded, and Slater wondered what sort of throat had produced it.

"The copter was back last night, and I tried again to contact it," the colonel said. "No luck, just as I suspected. Marshal Mutesa will be worried. In fact, if I know him, he'll be frothing." The thought seemed to amuse him, but he did not dwell on it. "The thing that hoots like an old Earth train called later, but from a long way off, unless, as is quite possible, there are more of them. Beyond that, did any of you notice anything?"

Slater felt relieved that neither Breen nor Burg did more than shake their heads and hoped the flush over his cheekbones would escape anyone's eye. Danna, he noted, looked as blank, childlike, and innocent as the dawn itself, and he wondered what she was thinking.

"Then let's march. I'll cut trail first. Burg, you guard me, the rest of you come as usual. Maybe today we'll see something besides new plants and animals!"

By midmorning they estimated that they had descended over ten kilometers from the starting point at the tunnel's exit high above. The path was easier then, for the growths and trees were positively enormous and the vines and scrub growing under them seemed stunted from lack of light and nourishment. Dense mosses were everywhere. It was possible to go around many clumps of vegetation in short detours, and the slope was growing steadily less steep, so that the constant strain in their calf muscles was reduced. All around them, it was now like a jungle in the Terran sense. A hush seemed to have come over the fog-wrapped slopes. Insects were fewer and quieter, and the sound of water dripping from leaves and roots was much louder. Due to fog and the shadows cast by giant trees and other strange growths, vision was not so good. There was no more talking at all, as they stole from one deep shadow to another like ghosts, one pair going first, then signaling the next. The bulgotes caught the mood and came obediently and silently at the merest tug on their halters.

The noise of rushing water suddenly burst upon them as they were about to enter the gloom of one of the monster pine-cone things, this one over seven meters around in girth. Indeed, the water saved them, for it made them halt. It was the first they had come near, and Slater saw Feng, Burg, and Breen, who were leading at that point, waving the others back. They had caught the glimpse of a large body moving through a rift in the mist ahead.

The mist thinned further, and they saw that they were look-ing across a small but rapid stream whose dark waters poured down from their right, through beds of rank ferns and huge mushroom-like fungi then vanished into the darkness to the left. On the bank of this rivulet, for it was little more, a pair of bulgotes grazed on the succulent mosses. The buck, as big as either of theirs, kept glancing nervously about, as if some-thing had alerted him. While the humans watched, a random shaft of far sunlight parted the mists on high, and the two animals were illuminated by it, their gray coats gleaming against the soft greens and ochres of the moss.

Suddenly a swish was heard in the damp air as it was cut by the movement of a monster whip. From far over the heads of the awe-struck group, a flexible cable of red bronze, almost a meter in diameter, slashed down through the haze, curled about the female gote, and, in one reflex snap, drew the bawling animal out of sight. The buck, *baa*ing in terror, fled down the streambank and was gone in seconds. From the murk high above, there was only silence.

"Quick!" Feng whispered to the huddled humans. "Danna, keep those gotes quiet! We've got to get back near the base of that thing and then go around it. I should have spoken sooner, but it seemed crazy. That pine-cone thing is either a relative or the adult of the tiny ones we saw catching flies higher up. It's not a plant at all as we know them. If we hurry, the gote may keep it busy for a moment."

Following the I-Corps captain and making as little noise as possible, they stole back into the shade they had almost left and angled cautiously away from the great cone thing. The gotes fortunately had not spooked at the sounds of their wild relatives' cries and allowed themselves to be led along in silence. Only when the terrible growth was completely out of sight did the team dare relax, and even Muller said nothing as they spontaneously sat down and mopped their foreheads.

"I take the blame for bringing us into this," Feng said to the colonel. "I wondered about the little bugcatcher Danna found and how much it looked like those giant cones. But they were so damned *big*! I just couldn't believe they worked the same way."

"Forget it, Captain," Muller said. "No one knows what's here, and you did get us out fast, which is what counts." He looked around keenly. "Anyone need any more lessons in being careful? That was only a plant or animal, after all. We're looking for much worse things—things with brains, human or otherwise. Let's get moving. We're close to level ground, I think, and we ought to be seeing lots more interesting things."

"I hear something," Danna said suddenly, bringing them all to their feet. "I hear it with my mind, not my ears. It sounds like something singing, a funny song, over and over, the same little song. It is not close, but not a long way off. Ah, now it has stopped." They all looked at one another and at her in bafflement.

"Could it have been something like a radio, a machine noise of some sort, on a higher band than most of us can hear?" Slater asked.

"No, it felt alive. It was not a machine. But what it was I don't know."

"We can't waste time on speculation," Muller said. "We have to get on with our work. Let's move out."

The colonel's prediction had been correct. They crossed the little brook lower down and in a short time found themselves on almost level ground. But there the going began to get really rough. There were wide black pools of water between great wrinkled tree roots, and masses of fallen wood and rotting vegetable matter as well. Huge logs, all covered with a riot of fungus growth in every hue of red, brown, and yellow, barred their path at every turn. Dripping fronds trailed down from the mist above and struck them in the face when they tried to move forward. In a short time their pace had been reduced to a crawl as they sloshed through muck and rotting vegetable matter and tried to avoid the obstacles of the dead limb and root tangles. New types of bug appeared too, and stung and buzzed around their sweaty faces. Muller said they should seek the lowest level in the hope of finding more solid ground and, perhaps, a path or game trail.

They had been wandering in the bogs and shadows for a couple of hours, seeking a more or less dry spot to rest, when Breen, who was leading, held up one hand, stopping them in their tracks.

"I see more light ahead. Danna, come up here and listen, with your head as well as your ears."

She sloshed to the front, pinching Slater's rump as she passed. A merry smile was visible through the dirt and muck on her face. When she peered ahead in the direction Milla indicated, she listened intently, her eyes shut.

"There is no life I can hear but the small things that creep and fly," she said, turning to the colonel. "But—remember, I could not sense that big plant thing that almost caught us. There is so much life here that it is hard for me to pick out one mind unless I concentrate for a long time. But Milla is right; I can see light, or less dark, up there, in front to our left."

They slowly stole forward in the direction Breen was leading. Now they could all see the lighter zone he had spotted, even through the mist. It ran across their path like a fence as far as they could see.

"Slater, you and Arta go up and take a look," Muller said. "Keep your gun handy, Slater, but, Arta, use your bow. If something has to be killed, do it quietly." He turned to the others. "That's a good rule for all of you from now on. No guns or energy emissions except in dire emergencies!"

Slater and Burg crept forward, their eyes hunting every spot of darkness as they sought for danger. All at once they could make out something solid rising ahead, a darker shadow under the light. It was a bank of higher ground that rose like a spine above the mud and water of the level they were on. As they drew closer, they could see more clearly that nothing seemed to grow upon it, save for moss and tiny creeping things, which was why the light filtering down through the constant fog was so much brighter there. At length both of them slid up the side of the mound, or whatever it was, and slowly raised their heads to examine the surroundings. The dirt under the close-growing moss and crawlers seemed dense and firm.

Stretching away on either side, as far as they could see, a close-packed road of beaten soil and crushed moss ran into the mists. That it was a road and not an animal trail was obvious at once, for a section just to their right was timbered, in a place where the road had collapsed in the past. Short logs had been fitted into the hole and dirt and rocks rammed on top, but the butt ends of the logs, with obvious tool marks, stuck over the side of the bank on which the road had been laid.

"Men have passed here, not lately, but not so long ago, either," Milla said. "And they were big men, Slater, as big as your friend Nakamura. Muller must know this. Watch the track while I go back and tell him."

In seconds, Burg was back, the colonel beside him. Slater had been trying to pick individual footprints out of the marks on the road, but beyond seeing that something had passed, he could do no better. The skills bred in the Ruck were not his, he realized.

After a minute of study, Muller made up his mind. "This is where the alleged 'new clan' comes from, the giants. Milla, go back and bring up the others. We'll follow the track, down to the right. One way may be as good as another, but I think that the center of things lies that way. There's still a tiny drift of this swamp water in that direction, and it just *feels* right, anyway."

When the others crept up, Muller explained what he wanted. "This dike or whatnot is obviously to keep the road above water."

Danna had been studying the tiny mosses that sprouted over most of the road, and now she held up her hand. "Wait, Muller. What keeps the plants from growing here? Right up to the edge of this thing and even over it, they are not just short, they are *cut*." She held up a few thicker stems to show the trimmed-off tops. "That is not all. Under the footmarks and the moss, Milla, you missed something. This road is pushed down— flat. Something comes along here and it weighs more than a Greenie tank. We have to be very careful, I think."

The colonel scratched his head. "Glad we have a Wise Woman along to show us scouts what to look for, eh, boys?"

Milla Breen looked up, his dark face darker than usual. "I am stupid. I don't deserve to be one of Danna's husbands."

"Forget it," Muller said. "I've spent more time tracking than anyone, except maybe Thau Lang, and I missed it. But thanks, Danna. We'll have to be more careful. If that's possible."

# CHAPTER 11

# *The Road to Time's Attic*

*T*HE GROUP ONCE MORE TOOK UP THEIR MARCH INTO THE unknown. The two Rucker warmen led as points, one on either side of the raised road. Then came Muller, Danna and the two beasts, while Slater and Nakamura brought up the rear, with Feng coming last. Around them swirled the pearly mists, which often cleared for sudden moments to the right, left, or front, then shut down and sealed the view as quickly as they had lifted. The surface they walked remained level, as smooth as if some colossal lawnmower had passed.

From the fogs and shaded swirls on either side came the sounds of Mars they all knew, the buzz of insects, the calls of birds, and some they had never heard. A bulgote bellowed far off and in the silence that came after it, they all strained their ears but caught nothing but the drip of water and the whine of insect life.

They had gone a mile or so when an alert whistle from Burg brought them to a halt, weapons raised. Now they could hear it. From far off came the hooting they had heard from higher in the great rift. After a brief silence it came again. This time it was louder and deeper. Another pause, and again it came, closer yet, as if in the misty depths of the fourth planet, an archaic tugboat from Earth's past was steaming down upon them. But there was somehow an animal undertone to the hooting that no steam whistle ever produced.

Muller was quite ready. He whistled himself, low and clear, and they all left the broad ramp and slid a little down the sloping sides, half going to right, half to left. Each party took one gote and made the animal crouch as it did. Then they waited, as they had planned when they first took up the new section of their march. The hooting cry was very close, and in the next pause they heard other sounds, those of ponderous weight and a massive tread. Whatever it was, was advancing straight at them. With his eyes bravely over the lip of the ramp, Slater stared like all the others at the curling white mists, straining to see what was bearing down upon them.

Then the mists parted as some vagrant riffle of air from far above, some ghost of a wind of the outer surface, thrust a last finger into the planet's depths.

Advancing out of the opalescent fog came a giant bulk, its armor shimmering in the subdued light in a strange, coppery way like that of an enormous tank.

The one great eye gave a reddish gleam as it swiveled in its turret atop the mighty prow. The two great forelimbs, their ends, like colossal, flat lobster claws, clicked and hissed as they swept steadily back and forth before the immense bulk, scissoring the plant growth neatly and as smoothly as any machine could have done. Like giant pistons, the side legs clumped and thumped on the surface of the ramp road, thrusting up and to the sides of the great sloping body. And Slater stared, frozen in disbelief, while one hand clutched at the tiny metal box in his belt pocket.

Vast and inconceivable, a thousand times or more greater in bulk and its armored majesty a thing of many tons—it was Grabbit!

One of the enormous, pillarlike legs smashed down no more than an arm's length from his nose. That bellowing hoot deafened him as the thing called again from close overhead. Did he hear a tiny answer from close to his heart? His veins seemed to freeze as the second great, stumplike leg crashed down, the blunt spike that terminated it sending bits of moss and dirt up in a small cloud before his eyes. He stared fascinated at the domed bumps that protruded from the carapace of glittering skin/shell above him. Each was twice the size of his own head and each, he knew, had a lidded photoreceptor. As Grabbit drew energy from the UV of the faroff Sun, so could this behemoth, which was a monster simulacrum of the tiny form in his belt pouch.

And it passed. He saw the blunt, spiky pointed end of the body disappear in the swirling shrouds of mist to his left. And now before him the sward was clipped evenly down to a two-inch height where the great claws had passed.

A voice, low and amused, broke in on his stunned silence. He spun his head and there crouched Muller a few feet away.

"How do you like having a miniature of the world's most efficient lawnmower tucked in your belt, eh?"

"I could only remember our chat a few kilometers up, sir. I mean that Grabbit had been designed for efficiency and had not just grown that way due to evolution."

"Quite so. And who designed it, if that's true? We are at or close to the bottom of the Great Rift of Cimmerium. I think we shall have a few answers to that and many other questions before too long. Mars still has a few surprises in store, I think." A faint smile glimmered at the corner of the colonel's iron mouth. Then he whistled sharply, and it was assembly time again. As his whistle ended, the hooting of the incredible bulk that had passed them sounded again, but a long distance back on the ramp, the way they had come.

They assembled again, gotes and all, and Muller gave them their orders.

They would proceed, in the same way, with the same care, and on the backtrack of Grabbit's giant twin. First, though, Slater had to remove Grabbit and look at him so that they could all see if he was doing anything odd. He appeared not to be and Slater shook him out on his palm. The three Ruckers winced at the thought of what those tiny claws could do to flesh.

But the Martian lucky piece seemed quite indifferent. Slater heard a minute clicking from him and dropped a shred of dried meat on his hand, which was carefully gathered and stuffed into the mouth under the tiny Martian's pointed prow. He was put back in his box and they went on as before.

The noises from the mists on either side had resumed as soon as the giant creature had disappeared, and they could hear the distant cries of ferkats and other familiar sounds. Where does this road go—and to what end are we going on it? Slater could only wonder and keep alert, and he knew the others were in the same position.

Slater soon noticed that the ramp was no longer level, but felt no need of mentioning the fact. Muller and the three Ruckers would have noticed also, to say nothing of Nakamura and Feng.

Deep as they were in the planet's crust, apparently there were deeper levels. The ramp was slowly tilting on the path before them and the tilt was downward.

They had gone only a little way on their resumed march when they all suddenly halted, weapons ready. It was the Ruckers and Muller, of course, who had caught the sound first, and somehow, Slater knew, they had caught a meaning that he did not in that eerie, piercing whistle. It seemed to come from behind them and yet to one side.

The air was clear enough at this point so that he could see Danna's face. To his amazement, he saw his Wise Woman was smiling, her face lit up in a blazing grin. Before this fact had registered, he got another shock. For she puckered up and blew a good strong answer, a whistle that quavered and trilled up and down the scale.

A soft chuckle suddenly sounded from beside him; he saw that the colonel had slid up in his usual manner. "I think we have company, my boy, and God bless the company. I have been very worried."

From the bog that lay to their rear there were some squishing sounds and then the thump of a firmer step. A shape emerged out of a patch of mist, a human shape, with one arm aloft and

rifle held flat in greeting. The broad, lined face was clear in
the soft light, the forehead chevrons plain to see, and a smile
as broad as Danna's lit the strong old face. It was their own
konsel, Thau Lang!

They crowded about him and the grins were universal, but
Muller coughed after a moment and ordered Milla and Arta to
take sentry to front and rear. Even Strombok and Breenbull
seemed pleased; Slater got a lavish lick on his left ear from
the former. Muller gripped hands hard with the old chief, and
the two of them smiled into one another's eyes.

"Took all my ability to find you, comrade," the Rucker said
at last. "Those caves and tunnels might have got me, except
for the things you left. Once out of them, it was not too bad,
though."

"Couldn't leave much," the colonel said, examining his
open free palm, which he had just taken from a pocket. Slater
felt another small palm steal into one of his and he knew that
just as he was staring, entranced, so were Danna and the others.

"Tiny foil balls, from candy wrappers!" Feng yelled. "Have
you been dropping those all the way, sir?"

"Only when I felt puzzled myself," Muller said. "At the
mouths of those tunnels, for example. The konsel did not have
that direction-finding pet of yours, Slater."

Thau Lang looked interested at this remark, and they had
to explain to him about Grabbit and his strange little "plume
of direction."

"Useful" was his terse reaction. "We must have more of
these when we go back. The True People could use such a
thing." His wise eyes looked hard at Slater and then shifted
visibly to Danna, at Slater's side. "Maybe a Wise Woman of
some variety could coax the secret from an unwary Greenie.
If she did, perhaps you would have them both shot, eh, Colonel?"

Slater looked at Danna and behold—his Wise Woman was
blushing in the pearly light!

The I-Corps saved his pride by breaking into the chuckles
of the konsel and Muller. "Better tell the konsel about Grabbit's
big brother, whom we just avoided meeting." Feng's crisp
tones killed laughter at once. Thau Lang listened as Muller

told him of the monster replica of Slater's pet that had just lumbered past along the dike.

"Hah, hmm," he said when the tale was told. "Let us move then, lest this other return. Let us go on, now we are together once more. We can talk later at length, when we are camped in a safe place, if there is one such on this road."

Within a few moments they were on the march once again, the only difference being that the colonel and the konsel now led the bulgotes in the center of the little column, Danna with them; and Feng, Slater, and Nakamura made up the rearguard, while the two young warmen once more scouted a little to the front.

Eventually the darkening mist told them that the day was ending. Noises from the swamp told them that it was time to rest again. No one wanted to continue in full dark on this strange path and even less did they want to meet Grabbit's large simulacrum in the night. One sight of that armored behemoth in what passed for daylight down there was more than enough.

Milla and Arta settled the problem of a campsite when they came loping back. "We saw a higher place," Arta said, "a little over on the left side. It was rocky and should be easy to get to, if we hurry and the dark holds a minute more away."

He was quite right. They had to go a little forward and then down the ramp and into mud and towering reeds, but mud no deeper than their knees. A kilometer of this brought them to craggy spines of stone that projected from the muck. That they easily scrambled up, for the pitch was not too bad. Strombok and Breenbull seemed to make nothing of it all and kept up the pace with no effort.

On inspection, their refuge seemed to be a little spine of rock, an island rising out of the muck about them. The top was mostly flat but four little crags stuck above the generally level surface at one end, and between them was a little bay in the rocks which made an excellent place to fort up for the night.

They had just begun to unload the bulgotes and to get things sorted out when they heard it.

A long way off, back the way they had come, there sounded

an echoing series of hoots. All crouched silent and, at a touch, the bulgotes dropped to their knees and even stopped cud chewing, to listen like the other mammals. Again the hooting came, and as before, it was louder and nearer.

Slater found Lang next to him and was intrigued to notice that the old war chief's eyes were alive with excitement. "So this is a real snapper, my young friend?" the konsel said under his breath. "Maybe it is the mother of your little one, eh, or the father? What think you?"

"Damn if I know, sir," Slater purred back. He knew when he was being kidded. "Might be the mother of all the snappers that ever were. It's more then big enough for the job."

He got a gentle dig in the ribs for his pains, and they all listened as the giant thing approached. That they were not the only ones listening was quite apparent. Aside from the hum of insects, the night or evening noises had ceased. No ferkat squalled nor bulgote bellowed. They knew when the lumbering supersnapper was right opposite them on the ramp road, for they could all hear its great chelae click as it scissored the moss and the thud and crunch as the giant legs slammed down.

As they waited in patient stillness, the hooting and the other sounds faded off to their left flank, as steadily and as regularly as they had come. The regular night noises of the Ruck remade their appearance as the hooting cry of the giant snapper faded in the night of the depths and the little party continued making camp, placing bedrolls and settling down.

"We can tether the gotes down near the edge," Milla Breen said. "They can be watched from up here by whoever is on guard. There is plenty for them to eat here, and if anything comes from the mud and water, they will hear it and so will the guard."

"We have at least four pair of night goggles," the colonel said. "And in the pack of one of the gotes, you will find a small-unit detector. I don't want to use any equipment not necessary, but that one can be set for short range, say a half klick. Then, if anything moves that is not heard, it can be detected. I don't think a low-level device on so small a scale as that could be detected by anything that was not already on top of us."

After a minute's debate, the colonel and the konsel even allowed a tiny fire set back in a rock recess and fed with dry reed stems.

Once watches had been arranged, other ideas crept out of hiding. Slater, who was to go on watch just before dawn, found himself roped into a party that one of his long-dead English ancestors might have called "huntin', fishin', shootin'," if he had thought it worth a name. The two older men seemed to see no harm in it and, save for warning all involved to be careful, did not forbid them to try. It was Slater's quasi-brother-in-law, Arta Burg, who put the idea into words as they had crouched about the tiny fire.

"We should save our trail rations," he said blandly. "Anyway, I hate the damned things. There must be fresh meat of some kind down here in this biggest of Rucks. Let's take some tonight. We are all pretty good hunters, are we not?"

None were very tired and all wanted to try to get something. They drew straws, and Captain Feng scowled at his short one.

"All right, I get first sentry go, but it's unfair. You will all be devoured by life-forms that only I should want to or would be able to classify."

The other, younger folk went in a party to the edge of the rock farthest from the ramp. On a low rock spine they slapped at insects and discussed what to do next. Danna had the first idea or at least gave it voice first.

She pulled a long coil of light paulon plastic line from her belt pouch and fixed a heavy, vicious-looking hook to it. On the hook she placed a very large slug she had found in the mud and also a chunk of dried gote meat from her ration. She whirled this about her head, nearly smacking Nakamura in the eye as she did so, and threw it far out into the reeds. Then she sat firmly down and grinned at the others. "You go and get muddy. A woman will get the best and be comfortable as well." The dark was so thick, Slater could barely see the gleam of those pearl-gray teeth.

The other four went a little farther down the shore of the islet and waded in. The idea was to herd whatever they might encounter back toward the rock. They all had spears, and Danna was to watch the shore side while she fished.

Slater was last in line going out and it was his role not to go too far out. Nakamura, his bulk dimly visible in the dark and fog, was the next one out, and the two warmen were in front of him. When Arta, who was farthest out, gave a whistle, they would walk toward the rocky shore.

The night goggles kept the bugs out of one's eyes, Slater realized as he spat a particularly large one out of his open mouth. He was damp, hot, and feeling immobilized by the thick muck through which he was wading. Ah, there came the whistle from out in the fog. Watching his footing carefully as he advanced, he turned left and began to angle back. He had only found one deep spot so far but had no desire to vanish over his head in a sea of ooze. He pushed through clumps of tall reeds and kept his mouth shut against the reed tops and the bugs, working his way slowly and with great care as he tested for firm footing under the muck before his advancing feet. Then he heard it, a sudden noise in the dank and fog of the dark before him.

A sudden splattering sounded ahead and to the left, and something heaved muck as it broke through the reeds. He could see nothing but he could hear well, and he heard something that lent fury to his movements. It was Danna's voice in a low cry, a cry in which he read horror.

He charged forward, keeping his Rucker spear leveled in the direction of the cry. One part of his mind registered the fact that his friends were following, for he could hear the *splosh* of their feet out in the dark. Ahead was a dim patch of light and movement.

He churned up on to firmer footing and saw the konsel and the colonel with belt lamps on before him, focusing on Danna and on her battle, for she was indeed engaged in one.

Her feet braced against a boulder, the girl was holding off a pair of shining, black mandibles, their full gape over a yard in breadth. They clacked and snapped as they tried to close on her body, and jerked about so that it was hard for her to keep her footing. Her spear was imbedded in the great mandibles of the thing that tried to reach her.

Slater noted with one eye that the two older men held leveled rifles, but he raced along the short stretch of rock and passed before them with his own spear, which he drove under a spiny leg and into the body just below where its shoulder could be said to be. As he fell, panting, to the rock of the shore, another spear buried itself next to his and Thau Lang's body brushed his own as the konsel drove that one home.

The monster snapped and wrestled for some time, but the main fight was over. Slater, his arm around Danna, watched the end of the fight. Nakamura, Breen, and Burg were all in it, and it was they who finally killed the creature and dragged the body, shining, black, and ten feet or so long, up on the rock to the top where it could be examined by the light of the tiny fire.

It had six legs, three to a side up near the head, which seemed small for the great jaws. The long body was rather slender and tapered.

"Can't blame this on dear old Mars, I fear." Feng, who had been relieved from sentinel and walked over to study their catch, exclaimed. "I should say a Martian version of *Dysticus*, one of our more predaceous water beetles—and in the larval stage at that. Let's see—I seem to remember looking at one long ago in school. About an inch and a half long, if I recall correctly. The rifts do seem to put bulk on our import and the native stock as well. Still, that giant snapper could use this for a snack."

The Ruckers wanted to know if the thing was edible. Usability was the keynote in Rucker life and the first thing they always asked about. Feng pursed his lips and finally nodded.

"Why on Mars not? Might even be good. One can eat most Earth bugs. Try it and see. That fellow ought to be a lot of meat. He would have eaten *us* if he could have sunk those mandibles in—or, perhaps, *drunk* us since I think he pumps in a dissolvant first." This silenced all of them, but they soon got over that and began to hack large chunks of whitish meat out of the chitinous armor. These they toasted on sticks over the fire. To Slater's surprise, he found them excellent. He told Danna she looked smug and pointed out the snapped plastic line that still hung from the small mouth below the creature's hypodermic jaws.

She winked at him, her mouth stuffed with the crisp meat,

burned on the outside and semiliquid on the inside. "A Wise Woman always gets her catch, Greenie," finally emerged around her mouthful. "Watch yourself or I'll have you for breakfast for a change."

The next morning they crossed the marsh and regained the ramp, in the same formation as the previous day. They had had a decent rest and were full of food and energy. They had decided to start early and see if they could make good time before the lawnmower-tank analog of Grabbit made its appearance.

The ramp road still led downward, and the going was easy and firm underfoot. Plenty of noises arose from the mist about them, and once in a clear patch Slater and Feng saw a large dark shape flutter out of the white fog with a great moth in its wide mouth. They both saw it clearly.

"That was one of those flying things from the cavern we passed through," the captain said as he made a few notes on his belt pad. "They don't seem to have eyes and they may not like the Martian days, so perhaps they use echo-radar squeaks on an ultrasonic level as bats do back on Earth."

"Don't need teeth either," Slater said, "if bugs such as that big moth are available. Wonder what they ate before the Central Country or someone or other dumped all those bugs here."

"Spare me the ancestral insults." Feng laughed. "If you are going to blame poor old China for misspent zeal, please remember you ate your fill of water-beetle steak last evening." Then he looked thoughtful. "There must have been small flying things in quantity here once, though there are not so many left now—of the locals, that is."

They had been tramping along, in and out of the opalescent clouds of mist and fog, for about three hours when a break came in their progress. Through the many calls and whistles, trills and clickings from the marsh on either side came a new one that froze them in their tracks. It was the long and echoing sound of something like a horn. It seemed to come from ahead. As soon as it began, the cries and sounds from the swamp ceased abruptly, at least those nearby.

A command whistle low and clear brought them all up and

back to where the colonel and the konsel stood listening with Danna and the two animals.

"That was certainly a horn or bugle or something of the sort, wasn't it, sir?"

"Certainly it was, Nakamura, unless it was something quite different. We are in the unknown here, Lieutenant, recall that. We could encounter a mushroom that sings operatic arias for all we know. That large replica of Slater's little guide made a sound like a steam whistle."

"The True People use small horns made from the horns of bulgotes," Thau Lang declared. "But the sound is far lower and not like that at all. That sound was deeper and far-carrying. Do you have any ideas, Louis?"

Muller's dark face was thoughtful and his brow wrinkled in a question. "I heard something vaguely similar long ago. But where and when I have no idea. But I do think that sound says 'Earth' to me, not 'Mars.'"

They listened in silence but the horn did not come again. Gradually the wildlife in the surrounding mists began to call as it had before the strange horn sounded.

The march continued for another few minutes, until another whistle brought them all up forward. The two warmen had found something.

Milla silently pointed and the others drew up and around. On the left side of the ramp stood a column, and atop the column was a head or face. The column, of some polished, dark-red stone, was about the height of two men. On the top a face looked back the way they had just come. Slater caught his breath as he looked up. He had seen that face before— short nose; ears like cones, blunt and short; great eyes, these carved of some yellow material tapering halfway round the skull. The head was the size of a human head, but it came to a dull peak at the back and there seemed nothing like hair.

And as they stared, the ambush hit them.

# CHAPTER 12

# The Dweller
# and the Lair

**F**ROM BEHIND THEM, THE HORN BELLOWED AGAIN. IT WAS close! Out of the foggy swirls on all sides came men, leaping and scrambling up the sides of the ramp. Big men they were. Their golden helmets came to a point and bore projections on the sides. Another line of them approached from up the causeway. From behind another raced out of the white mist, suddenly visible in the pearly light. They did not attack though all had long spears and some, swords. On their breasts gleamed metal too, for they wore breastplate armor. And they had beards and long, sweeping mustaches, which gleamed in the light over the kite-shaped shields each bore in the left hand. On four sides, they halted just beyond spear length, and then one of them advanced and held up his empty right hand. In the other he shook a curving horn, a half-circle of gleaming, coppery metal with a trumpet spout at one end and a mouthpiece at the other.

"Freeze and let me do the talking!" Colonel Muller rapped.

Then the light-brown mustache of big man in front lifted to expose gray teeth and from a deep bass voice came the words in accented but clear Unit. "Lower your weapons, all of you! Take off those that you wear on your persons. We are here to guard the Great Place. We can kill and we will!" The dark eyes shifted to fix on the straight shape of the oldest Rucker.

"You! You are a Wise One of the True People, those who war above on our enemies. Now you face the spears and points of the *real* True People! You may have heard of us. Maybe you have not. It makes no difference to us what you are up on the top. We will rule this whole world. You have a choice, one choice only. Be with us or against us! Come and learn how to fight the Terrans who befoul our planet. Or die here now!"

The deep voice went silent. With arms folded, the man stood waiting.

Colonel Muller hissed, "Do it!" and his party obeyed, discarding knives, bows, spears, rifles, and lasguns. Slater could see it was a terrible wrench for the Ruckers. As he stood with both hands in his hip pockets, he wondered if any of the others still had a weapon concealed. He thought of one item and smiled inwardly.

The colonel's hands flickered and Slater saw that the konsel also had noticed. Chevroned face impassive, the old war chief stood forward, arms folded across his chest like the leader of the foe, and an impressive figure too, though he had to look up to meet the eyes of the giant who confronted them.

"I have heard many strange rumors, I—a konsel—of a new clan of the True People. I have come and I bring five more of us also to find the truth, four men and a woman. Also, a strange, speechless one, who was found some time ago in Ruck by friends. We think, my friends and I, that he too might be a member of a new clan. Could it be yours?" The friendly interest in the konsel's voice was well done, Slater thought, as the older man pointed at the impassive face of Helge Nakamura.

The enemy leader seemed interested and stepped forward to look more closely at the big Norse-Japanese. Nakamura could and did look him in the eye. Slater noted a ripple of interest in the four lines that hemmed the colonel's party in.

The giants looked hard at Nakamura, and Slater could see that many were muttering to each other as they looked. Small wonder, the lieutenant thought, if he had a beard and was dressed right, Nak could disappear into the new clan's ranks.

"We will investigate this," the giants' leader said at length. Why don't they use the Rucker language? Slater wondered. "Much is strange these times and much to be revealed." Then his voice hardened. "So you are a konsel of the so-called True People. Well, let that be so. What then do you do with a group of the enemy in your following?" His hand swept over Muller and Feng and then passed to Slater. "Can these three be the allies and friends of the True People—especially one of their leaders?"

Thau Lang looked slightly puzzled, then his face cleared. "Oh, *them*?" His disinterest, bordering on contempt, was easy to read. "There have been many strange and new recruits to the True People, as you may know, you of this mysterious new clan. These three fled their base at one of the mines and seemed reliable. We had a new road and a strange one to travel and needed experienced men who could fight. They are not True People yet but if they do well, they might some day be voted as such—if they prove useful, trustworthy, and believers in nothing but 'Death to the Terrans and free Mars for those who love it and live there.' Were we not all Terrans, we or our forefathers, including your own, once upon a time? They are not important."

The tall leader looked unconvinced but thoughtful. Then his brow cleared and he smoothed his long mustache.

"It is not for us here to decide," he said. "We were warned that intruders were in our lands, which are sacred and not to be entered. We have many guards on our lands, some of which you might see and others not. Thus were you taken." He raised his voice again and gave commands. "You will come with us, you and your gotes. You will march in the middle, together, as you are now. We will see who and what you are and those who examine you will know the truth... all of it."

He rapped out a few orders to his troops in a tongue Slater could make nothing of. It had a lot of glottals and curious hisses that he had never heard before. The commands were terse and smooth and, in an odd way, repetitive, as if given by rote. It was as if the leader were somehow using a ritual language. Slater thought of the ancient Latin of the Christian Church of Rome and the even more obscure Geez of the Coptic Church of Ethiopia. Did the men speak this odd tongue or had they simply learned phrases of it?

Now they began to move, in the direction they were heading before the sudden attack. One rank of guards ahead, one rank behind, one on the left, one on the right, that was the order of march, with the party from the upper world and their two beasts in the center. Danna was on Slater's left, her pert face impassive in the best Wise Woman tradition. To his right towered Nakamura. One glance showed that the big man was excited. His face was flushed and his eyes glittered.

Slater was conscious of Danna's presence, but she walked in silence. Knowing women and something of Rucker customs, he knew she was very angry. Thau Lang had been addressed personally. But the leader of this band of the new clan had totally ignored a Wise Woman! This outfit was ignoring the protocol and the rules of a very tough people.

He smiled inwardly. His own Gilzai and Pathan ancestors had also made that mistake. It had done them no good either.

After they had been marching along for some time, Slater noted that the gentle downward slope of their mossy road was slowly leveling off. The calls from the mist on either side still kept up, but he had not heard a ferkat or a bulgote for a long time. Great reeds and lofty ferns thrust through the mist at intervals, and once he glimpsed a great cone thing like the one they had seen snap up a gote with such ease. The humming and buzzing of insect life was still thick, and several times he saw giant moths and once a flapping object with four wings and a body like that of a small egg, which he had never noted before.

As a matter of course, he counted the guards. Although the mist made it hard to tell, Slater thought there might be as many sixty.

A half hour more passed and then, in front of them, the note of that horn sounded twice. On all four sides the giants halted and so did the prisoners. Then, farther off, another, deeper, horn sounded three long calls.

As they resumed their progress, the mist before them seemed to grow thinner and lighter. Slater soon saw that the apparent change was quite real. A breeze had appeared also, coming from their left. From it he caught a whiff of new odors that were wild and strange. Then he noticed that the bulgotes were rearing and straining at their leads, trying to pull forward; yanking their guides off their feet. Several of the guards broke step and ran to hold the frantic animals, which slowly quieted. But their heads still pointed into the thinning mist, forward and to the left.

The tall, bearded leader bellowed something in the odd language and then walked to the little knot of prisoners. He eyed them coldly a second or two and then spoke.

"I must go back with my men to patrol. I send eight men forward with you, and they will be alert. Any trouble and they kill—quick they kill!"

"That is fine," Thau Lang said. "Where does our brother who leads this group of the True People lead us?"

"You go to be examined by the real masters of Mars. Be truthful and you may be permitted to live, even to join us." Then he turned and yelled another order. In a moment most of the guards were vanishing on the backtrail, the way they had all just come. The prisoners were alone save for eight of the new clansmen, four at the rear and four in front.

One of the four in the rear stepped out a little. "Go," he barked in Unit. "That way," and he pointed his spear in the same direction the gotes were straining. At a hand signal from Muller, the group resumed its march.

As they moved, once again the swirling opalescence of the mist thinned and grew lighter before them. Unexpectedly one of the gotes bleated as it strained forward. And suddenly, before them, lay the goal!

Danna gasped beside Slater. He could not help turning slightly to look at the younger folk of the Ruck. Danna and her two husbands were obviously stunned. For the first time in their lives, they were looking at a thing that they had seen only in pictures, and that rarely. They were gazing down a gentle slope and out over a great expanse of open water—blue-green water, extending far out until lost in the haze and fog.

The eight guards were calm. To Slater, they seemed amused. He moved closer to Danna and leaned over to whisper in her small ear. "It's only water, dear. You've seen water before, up on top, in your own kind of country."

"Oh, yes, Moe, yes, but not like this! You know what we have on the surface. Shallow ponds, sometimes marsh that comes and goes with the ice melt. None are large, ever. In a cave now and then we find ponds. But this, this is one of your *seas*! No one knew of this. If there were even any tales or rumors about such a thing, I, a Wise Woman, would have heard of them. This is unknown!"

Arta and Milla moved up while Danna and Slater were talking, and they had heard the last exchange. Milla broke in. "Warmth, plenty of water, and all together in one place. This is a country of the gods, this depth we are in. No such place is known; it should not exist!"

A deeper voice spoke from behind them, and they all whipped about like children caught doing something forbidden. To Slater's eye, even Thau Lang's iron countenance was visibly moved. The old Rucker chief kept his impassivity, but he too was shaken. His dark eyes were flashing. "I have seen wide waters in the bottom of a few of the big craters. Not like this, never like this. I have heard what you young ones said. This is indeed a land of the gods."

One of the guards reached down, picked up a long horn that lay by a rock spur, and raised the horn to his lips. Slater was conscious of two things. One was the bluish metal of the horn, which was like that of the strange weapon that Muller and Thau Lang had brought into Fort Agnew days before. The other was a memory; the whole scene was familiar to him. But before he could get the memory to surface, he felt Danna's hand on his arm.

"Moe," she whispered. "You Greenie dreamer—are you remembering? This was our dream when we took the Tea of Dreams together. It was like this, I think. Don't you remember?"

The sound of the horn broke in on her, long and echoing.

Three times it blew, then the man who used it put it down exactly where he had picked it up.

When he had done so, the guards fell back with leveled spears until they formed a line across the ramp with the prisoners between them and the short stretch of gravel that led to the water. The leader barked to them in Unit. "Wait now and stay in place. A thing comes to take you. Stay in place."

Slater sidled closer to the colonel. When near enough, he muttered to him. "Danna and I had a thing like this happen in a dream, under that Rucker tea back at the fort. I told you, sir."

"You told me. I wondered if you would recall it, boy. Now watch and stay alert. Let's see if the boat is the same, eh?"

And as he finished, the boat appeared. Slater shed the disbelieving expression on his face and tried to concentrate. He stared at the vessel that had emerged from the haze ahead of them and moved toward them across the calm water.

It was not the same as in the dream. For one thing, it was much larger and beamier. A quick look showed him that it could easily hold them all. Also, there was no steersman or pilot of any kind. The blunt-bowed vessel had only a boxy object amidships with a spike sticking up from it.

"Remote-control boat on a nonexistent lake of Mars. Not bad for this new clan of the True People, eh, Mr. Slater?" Muller's voice betrayed his great interest.

As the boat came closer, Slater saw it had four thwarts. From the box in the middle a metallic snake went over the floorboards aft until it disappeared in the stern. Slater figured that the boat had a rudder of some kind controlled from the box.

Soon the vessel was close upon them, heading toward the gravel of the little beach a few yards away. It went aground, bows on, and there is stayed. It was a muddy brown and gleamed as if it was made of plastic.

The voice of the senior guard broke the silence. "Step into the middle of that thing. When you get in, do not move until it comes to rest on land once more, or you will die when it turns over. There are other guards of the real True People . . . some of them live in the water. You would not like to meet them."

"Get in everyone," Muller said. "Thau Lang and I will be up front with Danna Strom between us. Gotes in the middle. Have them lie down. Stay still and don't rock the boat. We'll await events until the other shore or wherever this thing takes us."

They clambered in, quieting the animals and sorting themselves on the thwarts. Then they sat, waiting expectantly. Slater, in the stern with Nakamura, watched as the same man picked up the metal horn and blew a single note.

From what seemed far off in the hazy swirls from which the boat had first come, another note sounded. It did not sound like any horn they had ever heard before. It was more like a strange wail, mournful and yet resonant and echoing, higher in pitch than any of the horn noises. It made Slater's skin crawl. As he tried to focus on the sound, he saw Danna turn on her seat up front and stare back at him over Milla's shoulder. As she did, she raised a hand and made a drinking motion to her lips. He nodded. The sound was a reflection of their dream. Mournful and strident.

"Familiar, eh, from your teatime?" The colonel had been watching them. "A little precognition, I imagine. Have to get you to the telepathy group at I-Corps Center if we ever get back. They might have ideas."

With hardly a spasm of motion, the strange boat had smoothly backed off the beach and freed itself. Then it glided into a turn until the prow was facing into the mist, when it began to move and Slater sensed the faint hum of whatever was propelling them. As he felt it, he saw out of the corner of his eye that their guards were moving back the way they had come. "Now that we're alone for a bit," Colonel Muller said, "check your holdouts and then conceal them again."

They quickly inventoried what equipment they still had. Nakamura and the colonel had tiny boot knives; they and Slater, three or four miniature grenades of the kind Muller had used on the cave monster with the immense tentacles.

Thought of the cave monster made Slater stare at the smooth blue-green water over which the boat was calmly moving. It was not fast, not much faster than a man could run, but it was steady.

*What was in that water?* As he stared about, a motion to his left caught his eye. The bulgotes turned their heads also.

A tall, whitish spike, thicker at the base, stood out of the water and towered high over their upturned eyes. As Slater watched it, the end curled and a ripple ran down the thing's length. Slater's scalp crawled.

"Everyone stay still; do not move!" came the sharp tones of Thau Lang. "They said back on the land that we were safe if we stayed in the boat. We must believe that. We were not brought all this way to be killed before they can question us. Don't talk, don't move, stay still!"

As they watched, other spikes, all aripple with movement, appeared near the first, until eight or ten of the ghastly arms were waving and writhing above the water. The boat moved steadily on until the faint mist hid the writhing tower of palps. Only then did Slater notice the acrid reek hanging over the water.

Nakamura put the thought into words. "That stink and those arms! Why, it was the same thing—"

The colonel cut him off. "Probably not same one, lad. Interesting, eh, Feng? The Martian variant of an Earthly squid can live out of water for long periods and move about on land. Wonder if the damned things are that big on Earth, or if they still exist in the deeps of the sea."

"It was the same kind of thought-life," the Wise Woman beside them said. "That animal was like the one in the tunnels. But something held it off here. It fears something—maybe this." She slapped the gunwale of the strange craft that bore them.

Muller also stroked the boat's side. "What do you think, Thau? Feel anything odd about this boat?"

"Plastic only, but plastic with a strange feel to it. I don't see how it could bother a terrible beast like that one. But, Louis, what about sound? The hum of this box which sends power, that might be a warning to the animal, one that it fears like a bulgote fears the distant howl of a hunting pack."

They sat in silence as the boat prowled on, each lost in his or her own thoughts. Danna looked over her shoulder at Slater and silently pursed her lips in a kiss. He did the same, then looked over her head for he saw a shadow looming. Then the boat left the mist. Land lay ahead. The shadow Slater had seen was the rising ground covered with vegetation.

Before them lay a shore that only two of them had glimpsed. The view was as clear as it was eerie. None of the viewers was a child and four of them had known two planets. But the men of Terra were as new to this landscape as the three Rucker males and the young Wise Woman.

Before the prow of their moving vessel, and no more than a kilometer away, an alien view rose before them through thin steams and wisps of fog. Great reddish fronds hung low, nearly to the shore, from lofty, blackish trunks whose bark looked strangely scaled. Among the strange trees, Slater noted other growth. Great barrel cactuses appeared here and there, and some of the vines that hung down from the taller plants were vaguely familiar. But along the shore, save in one place, grew things like giant reeds that were new to any of them. From their lofty crowns, where an Earth plant might flower, burst a mass of whiplike purple tendrils, which, as the boat drew closer, could be seen to be in constant movement.

"Something like a Terran sea anemone," Feng ventured. "The tendrils sting its prey to death. Watch out when we get close."

As they drew closer to the shore, one of the reed whips snared a giant moth and enfolded its catch in a ball of shining purple.

"Damned if I think that's even Martian," Feng muttered.

"Perhaps Old Martian, eh, Captain?" Muller asked.

Just then the craft began to angle its approach to the shore, slanting a trifle to the left. There Slater saw an opening appear in the growth. The strange reeds did not block the opening, nor did the more ordinary and smaller ones he now saw among the others. As the boat entered the opening, they saw a small pebbly beach that sloped up to a gap in the strange verdure and a path, wide enough for three persons to walk abreast, which led up the gentle slope a ways before disappearing into the darkness.

The boat grounded itself with a *crunch* on the little strand of smooth pebbles. Muller's party sat quietly for a moment. Slater noted that the big gotes' eyes were wide open, their nostrils flared. He himself was conscious of strange perfumes, some wild and some sharp and bitter.

"Milla and Arta, get out and keep watch upslope," Muller rapped. "Slater, you and Feng next—take the bulgotes under one of the big trees. We three will make up a rear guard."

Slater realized that Nakamura had been given no assignment, so he was not surprised when he saw Muller whisper to the big man. Without a word, Nakamura faded off to one flank and vanished. Slater let his four-legged ally lick his ear and part his hair with a long wet tongue, and the remainder of the team stood and waited.

They did not have to wait very long. Out of the shadows near where the two young warmen crouched, there was a long hooting wail like the cry of a mourning Marswolf crossed with the rippling voice of some large and very strange bird. As a sound, it was as alien as any of the peculiar plant life about them. More so, for it had in it something clear and beckoning, which caught at one's nerves. It was a summons, and Slater looked at Danna, who nodded. She was on the same wavelength as himself, remembering the dream.

The colonel's voice came to life. "Let's move out. Burg and Breen first, then you three and the gotes, Thau and me last." His voice shifted and dropped. "What say, Slater? Is this the same as your pipe dream? What of yours, Danna? The same?"

"Not quite, sir," Slater said, as he led his beast forward. "But very close in lots of ways." He moved up the path under the trees, Feng and the other gote coming next. As he did so, he heard Danna's voice ripple out.

"In the dream, I had to go or come as the boatman wished and as the voice called. Here I feel the pull, yet I do not *have* to do anything. I am stronger here than I was then." Slater agreed. He felt an urge but no compulsion to do anything. Muller's next words were quite clear, and he knew were meant for him as well as the girl.

"The call may get stronger," Muller said. "You two may

be able to resist better than others because of the dream. But behave and act as if you were as strongly held as anyone else. Stay captive unless I say something or you can't help it for a stronger reason."

They moved up the clearly defined path, which wound among the trees. The long, reddish fronds, which sometimes trailed from lower branches to the ground, were like huge, coarse feathers, as wide as Slater's head but several meters long. The bark was odd also, like a mesh of oiled metal links as much as anything. The smells were odder still and they changed, so that one second, one's nose wrinkled at something acrid, the next, something sickly sweet and cloying. An adapted Martian starling, bigger than an Earth crow, peered at him from a branch once and seemed quite at home. At intervals he could hear things rustling in the darkness under the tree boles. Once he saw a pallid spider as large as his head run up a vine. Strombok was alert and nervous, and his big yellow eyes flickered first one way and then another while he sniffed and snuffed at the unfamiliar scents.

Insects were abundant, and the biting flies seemed far larger than any Slater had encountered before. They hummed and buzzed hungrily. Occasionally he saw the strange four-winged thing with a body like a fat brown pear flap by. After some time, the two gotes snorted and checked, and he heard Feng's voice.

"Did you spot that, Lieutenant? It had six legs at least, but I saw what looked like ears. Nothing in the books or files like that."

As they climbed upward, they kept a steady and easy pace. Half the time he could not even see the two warmen in advance. Slowly it grew lighter and he could see farther through the undergrowth.

Then he heard a quick whistle from ahead and checked the gote he was leading. Back came Arta Burg, one hand raised in warning.

"We are approaching a place where there are no plants, only grass. And there is a building of stone, a big one."

The colonel had moved up from behind, and the other two

as well. When he heard the news, he simply made a forward motion with one hand and faded back with the others.

It was quite a sight indeed, Slater found as he advanced. They had got to level ground and the big plants simply stopped. Before them in the misty, amber light reared an odd structure surrounded by twenty-foot walls of red stone, smooth yet weathered. Above and within loomed four domes, of the same material, set like a clump of mushrooms. Metal structures, like strange blue antennae, quickly appeared at the tops of two of the domes. At the same time, the section of the stone wall at the path's end began to roll up and back like a flexible metal sheet.

A gasp from Danna was silenced by Muller. "That's not stonework there. It has to be metal, camouflaged to look like the rest of the wall. Anyone get a feeling of time about this place?"

Age, incredible age! That was what radiated from the structure. Over the whole place, at every angle and curve, there lay like a blanket of impenetrability vast, stupefying age! Slater had seen many ancient relics like the pyramids of Egypt, but he had never felt the shadow of the aeons that this unknown place cast. Old, very old it was, so old, he felt, that its true age lay almost beyond human reckoning. And yet it was alive— the movement of the strange metal antennae and the rolling up of the gate proved that.

As they watched, spellbound by the mystery that lay before them, a sound broke the hushed silence. It was a voice and it came loud and clear, but with a strange crackle behind and under it. It spoke in Unit, and only one word. "Come!" it commanded. "Come!" it repeated and, after the fifth or sixth time, at the sides of the gate green, glowing flames burned like two great round green eyes.

"Hear that purring, crackling noise?" Muller asked. "I think we're hearing a recording. Let's go. Do what it says. Let's go through that gap." He motioned Slater and Feng first, and they went pulling their two gotes.

As they moved forward, side by side, Slater looked back quickly and saw the others following. He thought of Danna and choked off a curse in his throat. If only she could be saved from whatever peril lay before them! He caught himself and stifled his emotions. Muller knew what he was doing. Besides, he remembered Muller's words on the subject of Danna. He, Slater, was not to hurt the Rucker girl. Why? Because Muller was strangely fond of her. That gave him comfort.

Across the low green and yellow moss of the open sward they went. As they drew near the strange gate, Slater suddenly realized why the turf was so familiar. It was exactly like the covering of the ramp road over which they had come to find this place. It was *mowed* by a vast replica of his tiny pet, Grabbit.

They saw and heard nothing as they approached the open gate. Only the very faintest breeze moved the cloudy mists above their heads, causing the amber and pink light of the day to change slowly, now darkening, now growing brighter.

Then they were at the gate itself and Slater could not help but halt. Feng did the same, staring ahead. Before them lay more level ground with close-trimmed moss. Across a short bit of green and gold carpet lay another entrance, one with a real door, into a building. The building was topped by the largest of the four domes they had seen from the wood.

Slater noticed something else. Above the door of the building was yet another of the blue metal appendages. It was ridged and flexible, as if constructed of endless socketed joints, and it was moving, like the tentacle of some mechanical octopus.

Its movement ceased when it was angled in a lazy arc pointing in their direction. At its tip was a swollen knob of metal as large as a closed fist. As they watched, a sliding shutter flicked up over the end of the ball and a green lens fixed on them. They were under observation.

The voice still repeated its monotonous command, but the volume had lowered. The source seemed to be directly in front of them, just below the observation lens.

"Go ahead," the colonel said.

Slater and Feng moved out, the two bulgotes obediently behind them. They crossed the short space that lay ahead and entered the doorway side by side. Their feet began to ring on stone flags, and Slater soon heard the others in their wake.

Before them lay a short passage with an arched ceiling in

the reddish stone. Ahead was a bright light. They emerged together in a large and very high-ceilinged room, brightly lit from overhead by long blue-white bands of light that seemed to be immense tubes unlike any fluorescents Slater had ever seen.

But he and Feng were looking straight ahead now at a raised metal platform in the middle of the great chamber. On this platform sat a lone figure behind a broad panel of what looked like instruments. The figure was familiar to Slater at least, a thin, bony shape, which by its length, even when seated, must be very tall. The head was hidden by a round metal helmet with two peglike projections where a man's ears would be. A black band of glass or plastic ran across the helmet where human eyes might be. The body covering was a metallic robe that fell to the shod feet and the gloved hands, whose fingers were long and strangely twisted.

"The dream!" Danna exclaimed. "It is the one—the boatman of the dream sea!"

## CHAPTER 13

# The Last of
# the Attendants

*E*VERYONE WAS STARING BY THEN. AS SLATER WATCHED in fascination, the figure began to move. The hands lifted, one to each side of the ball helmet. The fingers were twice the length of a man's and there seemed to be too many of them. Even the creature's sleek gloves did not disguise their strangeness.

Both hands fixed on the underside of the helmet rim and lifted. The helmet rose higher and higher and, when totally free, was gently laid on a shelf near the owner's chair.

Two immense eyes, lambent jet in color, ran far around each side of the large, rounded head. The head itself came to a blunt point at the top rear. It had no hair and its skin was a very light blue. Two vertical nostrils pierced a nose that was more of a muzzle, short and blunt. Higher than human ears would be were the blunt cones, such as those they had seen on the column head and the helmets of the "new clan" that had captured them. The mouth was a long gash above the round and fluid-looking chin and now it opened.

The sound that came from the dark gap was no surprise. It was Unit, accented with a trilling—high and strange, but easy to understand. It was the same voice that they had been hearing, the voice that said "Come."

"I am Satreel," the being said. "I am the one you seek, whom *all* must seek, on this fourth world of the system, the world you call Mars." The voice was slow, and somehow Slater knew it was repeating things it had said many times before. He felt numb. He did not need to look at the others to know it was the same for them. From those black, glowing, impossibly large orbs, intelligence gleamed, and the intelligence was alien, utterly different, from outside human understanding. Allah aid us, said Slater's mind to his pounding heart, the Old Martians are real and we stand before one!

The voice went on, the strange purring, trilling voice, and while it did, the odd head swiveled slowly and the enormous eyes, those incredible eyes, took them all in.

"You see before you a judge. I, Satreel, am the judge of all this world. I come from beyond, and I serve those you will never see, the Masters of the Universe, the Le-ashimath. I have studied your race for long, as we of the Far Places have been here for long. You are young, you who were bred on the third planet, young and unguided. I shall show you how things must be done. All things, for everything must be done in the correct way. The only way—for this planet, this small Solar System, is but a step on the road, a mere stop on the way to the ultimate road, the road that was traced before your pitiful race existed . . . the path to the stars and beyond."

The humans and the gotes stood unmoving as if Satreel's words had placed them all a stasis field. But Slater heard a familiar penetrating voice from behind, and the voice awakened his nervous system. It was the colonel and he sounded reflective.

"So we're a way station, are we? And this is the secret of the Old Martians. No more Martian than Mercurian or Jovian. They come from Outside."

The voice of their strange interlocutor had fallen silent though he watched them still. Colonel Muller stepped forward. "Why do you not speak in the language of the True People? Why use the tongue of the Earth enemies? Are not the True People over all this planet your allies? . . . Or your servants?"

"I use what tongues I choose. From the third planet, I can listen to anything, and this installation has done so for so many *thousand* cycles of these planets that you could not understand. I use the tongue of the bipeds with some glimmering of science. I know them and I know their history. From when they first began to build things that could be seen from space, they have been watched and studied. Long ago, so long it would mean nothing to you here, we went down to that third planet and watched as you humans became what you think of as intelligent. It was from curiosity alone that we went. We needed nothing from you in this system." The voice gave a long keening note then, sounding like a strange and mournful bird, but with a grating, reptilian hiss at the end.

"I think I see," Muller said calmly. "You had a base here and it was forgotten or bypassed long ago. You and yours are only the last of a lost colony. You are the guardian of a long-defunct way station, forgotten by the ones who sent you here in the first place." He paused. "What makes you our judge? You are not of this Solar System but only a living remnant— like some of the strange life-forms of this world—which is no more Martian than you are. With your trees and your foreign animals about you, what gives you the right to judge us, who were born and bred under this Sun?"

Slater braced himself for movement. Satreel rose to its full height and a red flame seemed to glow in the heart of the strange, long eyes. Slater could see a ripple of tiny scalelike spots on the alien skull, as if the alien's skin were the hide of some delicate glassy-blue lizard. The wide mouth opened and then closed several times before an answer was given. The eyes stared fixedly at the colonel.

"What are *you*, then?" came the rippling, hissing voice. "Never has one of your kind ever addressed me so. You are no native of the Ruck, nor of this planet. You are of the third world." The great black eyes narrowed as if in thought. Then Satreel spoke again.

"I have had new things twice in this cycle. You interest me, for you have used your head in a way that few I have seen on this world could. So, you have concluded that some of the life here is not native to this world? Clever, that thought. I would question you at more length. But others have been brought to me, and they too are not of this world." He fell silent and then one of his long arms moved sideways, and Slater could see what looked like seven fingers. One of the long, slender digits touched something on the panel behind which Satreel stood. There was a buzzing noise and then a series of sounds that were a mixture of clicks and muted bell tolls. They died away and Satreel folded both arms across his front and looked down at the humans. Nothing happened for a half minute.

Then a panel slid aside to the right and behind where the tall figure stood on its dais, leaving a large round opening in the far wall of the great chamber. From this walked a group of figures, four in all.

Striding at the head of the new group was an unmistakable figure, white-haired, hawk-faced, and arrogant. No one who had ever seen Junius Brutus Pelham could ever mistake him. He was JayBee, and he paused to stare coldly at his enemies.

The tall figure in the center broke the unfriendly silence. "Here are more new humans from your Earth, who have come through the barriers around the Deeps. They must be taught as this place has taught many others. They must learn the truth of the Rulers from beyond the Rim, as you have done. Can they accept the laws of the Rulers? Can you work with them? Shall I, who speak for the Ancients, accept them? What are your thoughts, you who would rule Mars under my guidance?" The strange hissing tremolo died away. Slater got a good look at the three who had entered with JayBee. One of them he knew all too well, but he remained impassive as he took in her ample form now barely covered in wisps of some blue, silken material and her long, flowing hair.

Pelham broke the silence, his face set in a mocking smile as he spoke. "Lord Satreel, wisest of all who breathe, living spirit of this ancient planet, you have done wisely as only you can do. Behold, you have captured the chief enemy of Mars, of both your ancient rule of this world and my hope to revive it and increase its power." JayBee pointed at Muller, his face contorted with hatred. "There stands the secret leader of the Terrans, the one who hates the True People, who would do anything to block our reconquest of your domain and your emergence from the depths to the surface." He paused for effect.

Mohini Dutt-Medawar was looking at JayBee as if he were God incarnate. Her father, JayBee's chief acolyte, stood nearby. A vital and strong trio, and as Slater thought this, he looked at the fourth in their party, as JayBee spoke again, and his own jaw dropped, for there was a new surprise.

The fourth member of JayBee's group was short and very wide, but had no head, only a dome speckled with dots of light. More than anything else, the thing looked like an upright cannon shell or giant bullet gleaming with a metallic blue shimmer. Where the lights sparked was something more clear, like a smoky plastic. A metal spike rose from its blunt point and three pointed tentacles of coiling metal sprang from its midsection.

JayBee spoke again. "Lord Satreel, you have no reason to fear us three, who are your servants. Do not have your guardian robot waste its strength on us, but rather devote its energies to the disposing of this crew of enemies whom you have been clever enough to capture. They should live no longer, for they oppose the great plan. Destroy them all, unless you can convert the three younger ones of the True People of the planet's surface. Kill the rest." He stared hard at Louis Muller. "Kill them at once, those who are older."

Mohini Medawar chimed in. "Kill that female too! She is one of the so-called Wise Women. Kill her with the UN men! Kill *them* first though, especially that one!" Her outstretched arm was thrust at Captain Feng. Glancing at him, Slater saw the captain was impassive.

Slater could not help speaking to Mohini on the spur of the moment, though it took an effort. "What's the matter, hot stuff? Haven't found a good bedmate down here? Frustrated?" She spat in his direction but stayed silent.

After a momentary silence, the hissing purr of Satreel broke it. "So, they are enemies and not those who would join the

House of the Overlords. This one you call the greatest enemy of all is no fool, JayBee. He has glimpsed something of the past, I think, and of the ages of the dead stars that you have not. I will question them, for much might be learned that you do not know."

"Then, Lord Satreel, I beg of you, search them well and keep them in the most secure of your prisons! They are very dangerous, more so than you can imagine, you who have not fought, yourself for, for—" he hesitated—"well, for a long time."

"Satreel from Beyond, you may kill us and no doubt can do so with ease." As Slater listened to Colonel Muller, he saw that one of the alien's unbelievable hands was hidden by the metal of the instrument panel's back. He saw this and braced himself, then went back to listening.

"You have never tried to see whether our planet, of which I am but a trusted servant, is really your enemy at all. Why should it be? You are great and strange, but perhaps, with all of your vast knowledge, you lack something that we, not our criminals, can give you." He paused, then continued. "They could not find you a path to return. Our knowledge and yours together—such a combination—might find such a trail, to out and back, over the lost years."

There was a long silence now and it was JayBee who broke it. "He lies! Do not trust him, Lord Satreel. Kill him at once! Kill them all!"

"Silence!" The hissing rasp of the alien throat shut JayBee up instantly. The alien did not like being argued with, that was obvious.

The alien spoke again. "All of you new ones, you who have just come, stand still, well apart from one another. You will slowly take any weapon that you have upon you, anything at all, and any communication device of any sort, and lay them with care and slowness on the floor in front of your feet. When you have done so, move those two beasts over to the left side of this chamber. If any one of you attempts to disobey, you will all die, at once."

When the sibilant trill died away, Muller spoke clearly.

"Remember your training. I now give you an order. Do exactly what this lord has said to do."

The little group separated so that each was standing at least two arm lengths away from any other. Muller set the example by placing a little pile of things at his feet: tiny bombs, a boot knife, and a duplicate homer, such as the one in the butt of the knife the outer guards had taken from him. The others, without a word, began to do the same. Slater had managed to move closest to Danna. While divesting himself of anything that might be thought a weapon, he looked at the wild girl and she looked back. *Had he seen a wink?* He placed a boot knife on his own pile while he thought.

When everyone had divested himself of hidden weapons, in apparent good faith, Satreel spoke again. "You have done well to obey. Now lead those two lower things to the wall and secure them to the loops." The alien turned. "JayBee, you and your two servants go now. I will deal with this."

Without a word, the Master Mind of Mars walked to the back wall, followed by Mohini and her father. Only the squat robot stayed behind. The door opened and they passed through and vanished. Meanwhile, Feng had tied the bulgotes to large metal rings on the right wall. Slater saw splotches of a different color on the wall near those rings and also on the shining floor beside them. He had an idea of what was coming.

"Observe the doom of those who disobey," came the purring tremolo. One hand stroked the instrument board. There was a humming sound, and a broad beam of light struck the tensed bodies of Strombok and Breenbull, and before the horrified eyes of the humans, the two gotes began to dissolve. Ripples ran over them and their outlines blurred. Their legs vanished and became blunt mounds of ichor, their frantic heads melted back into the bodies and became more of the viscid mass. In seconds two masses of slobbering jelly lay on the floor where two large animals had stood. Slater felt a squeeze on his arm just as a vile stench struck his nostrils. He glanced down and saw Danna was clutching his arm, her face bleak with grief. "He turned Strombok into that! He could do it to you, Moe, to all of us!"

Her low, shocked murmur was cut off by the alien voice.

"Beware you who may think of disobedience. The Outer Lords left me, their good servant and guard, many powers and many weapons. You have seen what one, the Ray of Dissolution, can do. Stand now, and be searched."

There was the clicking hum again and from one side the strange robot approached. It rolled smoothly up to the colonel, who stood quite still, and its three metallic tentacles began to stroke his body from head to foot. When it was done, the thing moved on to the konsel.

The creature worked very quickly. In no time, it had done the males, all of them, and was making a start on Danna. After a second or two the robot stopped and stood facing its last target. From inside there came an angry buzz, the first sound the robot had made since its appearance.

"So, you have a weapon concealed upon or perhaps within you" came the singsong hiss of the robot's master from his mount. "I have told you what comes to those who defy me and you have seen your beasts, of whom I made an example."

"Wait!" Colonel Muller cried. "Wait, Satreel, you may be committing a grave error. Why does this machine say that the female of our company has a weapon?"

"I know not." Satreel seemed disinterested. "Perhaps it senses mood and can see treachery and rebellion. I can replace the power units in this mechanism and it will obey me. I can even repair it, in simple ways, should some external device be broken or fatigued." His strange voice paused and a faint sadness seemed to come into it. "But I did not build it. The Leashimath built it and others, long ago. I do not understand how it was constructed internally, nor all its purposes."

Muller's voice exuded confidence. "Has it ever examined a female of our species? This is a great woman, a leader of those who war on the enemies from the third planet, up on the surface. She has much mental power, much seeing-far-off, which we need to obey you properly and aid you in your quest."

For once the alien seemed hesitant. His purring trill seemed to check and catch as he spoke. "If you think her not an enemy, take her with you. I will have you all placed in secure quarters, whence you can leave only when I bid you to do so. Go then!" As Satreel said this, his hand pointed at Muller. "You, the leader, you stay! I would have speech with you, who seem to know much. none of the others do. I will return you to their midst after we have communicated alone."

He pointed one immense, lank arm at the group and indicated an opening in the left wall, opposite the horrible piles of reeking slime that had once been their two gotes. The konsel moved out at once and the rest fell in behind. Slater took Danna's hand and held it. In single file they went through the opened door and heard it slide shut behind them as the last passed through.

Looking about, Slater saw they were in a straight corridor. To right and left were doors, all of them shut. A fluorescent band in the center of the ceiling provided adequate light.

They had gone a little way when the konsel suddenly stopped. He held up his right arm, palm reversed, and they stopped at once.

Slater could see what had halted them. From a side passage a robot had emerged that looked identical, except for its color, to the one that had just searched them. This one was a baleful green-yellow.

With one of its sinuous arms, it was beckoning them forward, toward the opening from which it had just come.

"Follow where it says," the konsel ordered. He stepped forward and the others followed in silence.

The group turned to the right and entered a corridor that seemed identical to the one they had just left. They walked along it for ten minutes or so, and then the robot halted, blocking the passage and pointing past a hinged door that opened out into the corridor. Slater saw the metal locking bar that slid into it.

Led by the old warrior, the group came to where the robot waited. It pointed to Thau Lang, Milla Breen, and Arta Burg. When they had entered, it waved the others back and slid the metal bar in place, firmly sealing the door shut. Then it beckoned the others to the next door on the other side of the dimlit passage. Into this one it sent Feng, Danna, and Slater.

As the door shut behind them, Slater suddenly remembered that Nakamura was still on the loose. He could have kicked himself. Since Nakamura had been given his quiet instruction by the colonel and slipped away in the forest before they ever got near the place, he had vanished also from his friend's mind. He saw that Feng and Danna were looking at him strangely.

"It's all right. I was just thinking about Nak, out alone in that creepy wood. Hope to Allah he's not hurt. That lousy ray our friend Satreel used on the gotes . . ."

"The lieutenant is a trained officer, a bush fighter as good as any we ever produced—and we don't know what the colonel told him to do," Feng said. "Personally I'd like to see if we could find some egress from this hole we're in. While locked up here, we are easier targets for that repulsive beam than the lieutenant!"

"I might add," Feng continued, "that any talking we do ought to be as cryptic and unclear as possible. For all we know, listening devices have been planted in here."

Danna nodded and said, "This is a funny place, isn't it? I think we should look all over through our clothes, very carefully, in case the temperature is lowered. We might get very cold." The wink that she gave made her meaning quite plain to both of them.

Feng smiled frostily. "Good thinking, Wise Woman. I wonder what we have left on us that might keep us warm. Let's lay what we find on the floor, shall we?"

Out of his belt, Feng slid a polished stick of some very dense wood with a delicate curve, about two and a half feet long, with one end swollen into a slight knob. "Call it a knobkerry," he said. "I've carried it for years and the wood is African. Like the detects in banks and travel ports, our jailer's mechanical sleuth seems unable to find simple wood."

Flinching slightly as she extracted the thing, Slater watched Danna pull a flexible knife, in a flexible metal sheath, from under her curly hair. "I don't know," she said, "but maybe that's why that machine made noises at me." She smiled merrily. "What about you, Moe? Got any Greenie secrets hidden away?"

"Only one, I'm afraid." He took off his belt and placed it on the floor and then uncoupled the buckle. At one end, hidden in the belt, was a three-inch, double-edged dagger. "Rather old, this one," he said. "It was a present from my cousin."

"Let's look about and see what this prison has to offer," Feng suggested. It was not a large cell and seemed to be made of the same unyielding plasticene as the door. It was very dusty. There was no furniture at all save for a stool, also plastic, and a bucket of similar material. The temperature was constant and warm, and the air seemed to circulate through a row of small holes in the plastic ceiling.

Feng examined the door carefully. "Hah," he said. "There's a trap at the bottom of this thing. That's how food and drink must be put in."

Danna started to say something and got as far as "Moe, you've forgotten your other thing—" when they heard metallic sounds just beyond the door. They all sprang back, and Feng at the same time swept up the things on the floor and upended the bucket over them in a back corner.

As they watched, the door swung open. Colonel Muller stood in the doorway, a smile on his face, hands in his pockets, and seemingly at ease. Behind him there bulked the form of the mechanical turnkey that had shut them all in.

Muller walked in casually through the open door and did not even turn when it shut firmly behind him. They could all hear the *clunk* as the metal bar was slid into place and locked home. "You seem well, all of you." He smiled at them. "How are you feeling?"

"We're fine, sir," Feng said. "We wondered about you and our absent friend."

"We were thinking about what we had to keep us warm, if the heat went off," Slater said, grinning. He removed the overturned bucket so the colonel could see the extent of their resources.

"We've examined this whole place, Colonel," Feng said. "I doubt if we can get out with what we have here. Have something useful?"

"I fear not. So that's what we have, eh. Not much to play with."

The sound of a gurgling laugh, soft and deep, filled the little room. They looked at Danna in surprise but she was choking on her laughter. At length she pulled herself together and bent over the pile of weapons. Still choking, she held up

Slater's belt, ignoring the detached buckle knife. "I'm ashamed of you, you big Greenie warman." She was still giggling as she pointed to something and Slater felt indeed like an awful fool. How could he have forgot the tiny metal box on the belt and its small inhabitant?"

It was Feng who saved him. "Damn, I totally forgot your pet, the animal compass, the miniature of that monster that passed us back on the ramp road as we came here. I wonder if it can be used."

Muller had been looking about while they talked but he missed very little. "I think we must try the door. Nothing else seems to be of any use. The walls, ceiling, and floor are simply heavy sheeting of some synthetic, laid over stone."

Slater opened the box and Grabbit scuttled slowly out onto his palm. Danna cooed at the strange little creature and his single red eye blinked up at her. A tiny humming came from him, a note Slater had seldom heard the little creature make.

"He likes Danna," Captain Feng said.

"I think that's the equivalent of a cat's purr," Muller added. "Let's see what we can do with him. Can you get him to chew what I want, Lieutenant?"

Without hesitation, Slater passed the little thing from his open palm to his love's. "She can do anything better than I, sir. Remember that trick of making him a compass?"

"Right here," the colonel said, pointing with his forefinger. "We'll keep it simple. I want him to gnaw through the plastic or whatever it is and then go to work on the bar that locks this door—if he can. If he can't, we're going to have to think up another idea."

Without a word, Danna held the tiny animal up, then thought at it. Grabbit was happy to help, and his little claws came out and began to cut away at the place his new mistress had laid her finger. He went into the plastic on the door as if it were cheese.

While he was boring in, Slater turned to his commanding officer. "If you don't mind, sir, can you tell us what you and that . . . Satreel talked of, while you were alone?"

"Oh, yes," Muller said. "No problem about that. I wanted to learn whether he was alone here, or whether there are more of the aliens about the premises." He sighed. "Also, I must admit to being selfish. I simply had to talk with the first intelligent alien that man has ever encountered. And I wanted to clear up a final suspicion. I was afraid our dear friend, JayBee the clever, might have thought up a robot or dummy of some kind that could pass as an alien."

"I don't worry about that," Danna said flatly. "Whatever he, she, or it is, it is not from this world." Danna turned to Muller. "You are all Greenies, but the konsel and my two husbands would know. Colonel, though you are more at home here than these two, you do not know the feel of this planet as we who are born here. I should not laugh at you—but honest, couldn't you smell that strange smell?" She turned to Slater and smiled tenderly at him. "If I'm going to be in love with a Greenie, I guess I must learn he can't do what I do. The smells of this whole place are foreign and that of Satreel is the most strange of all."

Slater caught Muller looking at Danna and was intrigued to see both an air of affection and something else. Could it be pride? he wondered to himself?

"She's right, of course," said Muller. "I get occasional whiffs of a strange odor or so but, like you two, I was born in a city complex and raised surrounded by machine odors and chemicals. Danna wasn't and she has the keen nostrils of those born in the wild."

"I bow to you, sir." Feng smiled as he did so. "But what did you and the honorable alien have to say to one another?"

"I listened mostly," the colonel said. "I also asked what questions I thought possible. You all heard what I said in the big control room. This is indeed the last of a lost garrison. Where those masters of his came from, I can't guess. But they are from far, far away, that's for sure. Satreel is very, very old, impossibly so by our human rules.

"I also think he may not be alone. He made references to other guardians—attendants, he calls them. Damned if I know who or what they are. They could be like him, but cryogenic cases subject to recall from deep freeze or some kind of stasis that has a similar effect. We have to be careful."

"But, sir, why did he want you alone? He told JayBee and his two to get out. And how did they get here so fast?"

"The latter was simple. I fear we must bounce the I-Corps, Captain. The former Miss Dutt got a UN chopper out somehow. And through JayBee's contacts with Satreel's so-called new clan, JayBee made contact with this place and was vectored in past or through any screens or baffles."

As Muller talked, he leaned over to watch Danna's hand and what it held. There was now an oval hole in the oily brown plastic and Grabbit was in it. As they listened in silence, they could hear a tiny, whirring, crunching sound.

Muller patted Danna on the shoulder. "Good girl. He's through the plastic and into that bar already. Keep it up. Now, what *did* interest our friend from Out There about me? I tried to make myself interesting. I think he's desperate to get home. He is as loyal to his absentee masters—what does he call them? Oh, yes, the Le-ashimath. He is as locked to them as any good dog to a master. Plus I think he's homesick. Doesn't mean he ever saw what he calls home, you know. Maybe it's not our kind of 'homesick' either, but he misses something and it might be the whole culture complex that spawned him. Or a sun he never saw but his mother told him about. Call it pure loneliness and you do as well as I can."

"That's how I figured it," Slater said. "He wants to go back and he never met anyone before who could make him think he might get there."

"Precisely. For once, Mr. Pelham, the Master Mind, has missed a point. But this one he missed seems to be Comrade Satreel's weak point. I guess JayBee never felt that way about anything in his thorny life, so he couldn't recognize it in anyone, let alone an alien being."

Three of them stood in thoughtful silence, staring at the oily sheen of the brown floor. But the fourth broke in on their thoughts with a sudden squeal of joy. As she did, she held up her open palm on which a small shape was waving its pincer claws and humming quite loudly.

"He's through, Moe, he's through! I can get his think. He

cut the locking bar that holds us in and he came back to me and said so!"

Very gently, Muller exerted pressure on the door with his left hand. The others each picked up a weapon. Slight as the pressure was, their path, or its first step, was now open.

# CHAPTER 14

# *Conflict Throughout Nowhere*

IT WAS AN UNQUIET EVENING AT GRAND BASE, ORCUS Prime. As men and women of the UN Command moved through the long and echoing corridors, many were armed— and not just with sidearms.

In a small, well-guarded room just off the main Control Room of Base Central, the two top men of Mars Command sat staring at one another briefly. Marshal Mutesa looked hard at his second-in-command, General Scott, and Scott returned his gaze.

"Blast and curse everything and everybody!" the marshal said at length. His face was twisted with frustration. "We know too much and too little at the same time. Robert, where *has* that freelance Muller got to?"

His junior shuffled a small deck of recent reports, obviously searching for a sensible answer. "Look, Philip, I get everything as fast as it comes in, and *you* get it as soon as I can get it to you. Neither of us knows anything the other doesn't." He turned back to the reports and then continued. "I'll compress

176

what we know and if I miss anything, jump on me. The Ruckers are quiet—as quiet as they can be, that is. Space Force claims that it has caught all the arms-smuggling ships and blasted the asteroid base they were coming from or to. Okay? Next, Earth Central has raided five of the big corporate headquarters that were, they *think*, providing the arms and the same ships. 'Investigations continue' and all that police nonsense." He looked at another tab sheet and his ruddy face grew a little more strained.

"We cannot find any trace of JayBee. It took too long to trace the escape of that woman from Fort Agnew. She killed a man and took a jet-heli into the wilds. Because of her Indian background, it looks as if she is linked to Medawar, Pelham's chief of staff. Finally, we have lost Louis Muller. The spy-eyes, the hovering Air Scouts, the airwaves being monitored, have all come to nothing. The one link we had in the big Rucker meeting says JayBee was there, he thinks Medawar, some woman who might be our I-Corps traitor, Miss Dutt, and all the people sent from Agnew by us. All gone and probably in the Dead Zone around or in Cimmerium." He laughed bitterly. "We Greenies are stumped, baffled, and bewildered."

The marshal's powerful face grew impassive. "I have alerted the whole command, Robert. A strike force of five hundred of our best is on instant standby. You and I sometimes think alike. Let's hear what you'd do with them."

"Sir! Put 'em all on float-ships, ready for a snap putdown. Have the ships hang over the center of Cimmerium."

The last hereditary ruler of a long-vanished African kingdom also sat back, but on his face was a wistful smile. "You forgot something, I think. For two credits I'd forget my age and my job and go instead. Don't be proud. You don't have to beg, not with me. Robert, take command of the group and report to me when aloft."

The Duke of Buccleuch was out of his seat, out the door, and running while his superior officer leaned back and stared at a picture on the wall, a holograph of a particularly tangled piece of the Ruck. "Wish I could go," he murmured aloud to himself. "Wonder what's going on down there. Ah, hell, the Venus Transplant should be ready to go in a year. I'll go on that if things work out here." He turned his attention to another stack of reports.


Very slowly, Muller pushed open the door but he did not step out into the corridor. He listened and the other three waited in silence. At length he beckoned Feng forward to lead then the girl and Slater. The colonel brought up the rear. With two signals, he posted Feng facing to the right up one direction and Danna and Slater to the left on the other. With his guards out, for whatever it was worth, he crossed to the other cell and silently slid the locking bar back.

Before them lay a dimly lighted, boxlike cell. Thau Lang stood facing them, arms folded, and beside him, the two young warmen, Arta and Milla, one to a side. All looked ready for death. When they saw who had opened their prison, joy shone from their eyes.

"Quiet! Not a sound! Move by my signal until I speak," Muller said. He took a plaspad and scripter from his blouse, wrote for a minute or two, then showed the results to Thau Lang. The konsel read for a moment, then showed the message to Breen and Burg. Muller nodded to Danna and handed her the plaspad. She took it and stepped back between her two excellmates. Danna held up four pages of the small pad for Feng and Slater to read. It was quite clear, and in plain Unit script.

1. *We're going to snatch Satreel. Burg and Breen go first. They can smell better, hear better, and see better.*

2. *Thau Lang and I come next. Slater and Danna follow. Feng is rearguard.*

3. *Carry your weapons at the ready. If we see an enemy, use them fast. Very fast!*

4. *We'll retrace the way to the control room. There are sound detectors all over this place from what I heard Satreel say. Pattern and location are unknown.*

5. *There may be monitors or beam-trip devices. If you see anything like that, stop us all. Let's go—and win!*

Silently and stealthily down the ancient passage, illumined only by the dim glow of the ceiling strip, they went. Slater and Danna had just turned the corner to the first passage when they heard a mechanical murmur to one side. An oval door suddenly slid aside at the juncture of the two passages and out of it, metal tentacles whirling, came the bullet shape of the robot jailer. Its only sound was a humming buzz as it rolled after the group in the main passage, at about the speed of a running six-year-old but far more silent.

The machine could not count or it did not bother. Possibly its instruments and sensors were defective. Ahead of it fled six humans and it pursued, its rollers turning. Behind it sped the seventh, and that one was a *Kendo* man, though his stick was less than a yard long.

Slater turned at the savage hiss and saw what he had hoped would come end even better. Behind the opaque translucence of the robot's dome he saw Captain Feng run up and strike forward with his deadly stick, just below the forward curve of the plastic bullet cap. The knobkerry was as hard as Feng had said. With two lethal blows, the dome split, big shards falling off and flakes puffing away in a cloud. As the machine tried to deal with its new adversary, the third blow struck home in the maze of lights and circuitry that made up the robot's control center. In a matter of seconds, Feng's onslaught had reduced the dangerous mechanism to an immobile pile of scrap. Its lights were out, it sank to its round base, and the flexible arms sprawled like wet spaghetti on the floor of the passage.

Muller walked back quickly and took a careful look. Then, smiling, he punched Feng's nearest bicep and nodded. A rare broad smile split the usually impassive visage of the I-Corps captain, and with no more celebration they all went on, exactly as before.

Along the main corridor down which they had passed only hours before, they ran in utter silence and as wary as aroused ferkats. After what seemed like days, the upraised hands of Arta and Milla, who were well up front, brought them to a poised halt. The team moved up slowly at Muller's signal. Ahead was the panel of the door to the great chamber of Satreel.

Slater squeezed Danna's arm and looked carefully at the

door. It was as they had seen, a sliding panel, which, from inside, looked just like any other part of the control room wall. From the rear, though, it looked very different. Continuous bands of sturdy metal ran across the plasticene of the door and a pair of round, bright-blue knobs was set in recessed sockets to one side.

"Those must be manual controls," Muller whispered. "But for whom? Maybe only one of the robots can use them, and if we try we may set off an alarm. Everyone think for a second and see if we can stir up an idea."

Milla Breen said nothing, but he stepped smoothly through the other six and pointed. At the end of his forefinger was a well-concealed but perfectly visible outline in the right wall of the passage, perhaps two feet from the door they had been examining. Moreover, the camouflaged side door had what looked like a very simple recessed manual handle colored the same dull brown as the rest of the blank wall.

"Good man, Warman Breen!" It was the konsol who gave muttered approval, but Muller smiled and tapped Milla's arm. The young warrior drew himself up proudly, managing to give Arta Burg a derisive look as he did.

"Probably nothing more than an access corridor or just a closet for tools." The colonel stepped forward and carefully freed the almost invisible catch. He then slid the narrow door to one side. It moved without a sound. Muller stepped aside with a smile and they could all look.

It was not a closet. Inside was a very narrow passage with room only for one man at a time. It was far too narrow for the bulk of either of the two robots they had seen. It ended in a perfectly plain curve, which seemed to taper away to the left. They all looked to Muller.

"I want the UN people first this time. There will be machines, and we have more training in spotting or using such things. Slater at point, then me, then the four True People and Captain Feng's sharp vision as rear guard. Let's go."

A thrill went through the Anglo-Pathan as he took the lead. He touched Danna's arm as he passed her and entered the narrow tunnel. Satreel or one of his kind could use this, he thought. Or a robot of a kind we haven't seen yet. He paced on slowly and carefully, trying to miss nothing. He heard the scuff of movement at his back and finally the faint sound of the access door sliding shut.

The tight space seemed featureless, with the usual dull-brow plastic on the walls, ceiling, and underfoot. Suddenly Slater checked. He had been wondering if the narrow passage went round the whole control room of Satreel when he saw something in an alcove in the wall to his right front, no wider than his chest and at his shoulder level. It was dark but something was on the curved shelf that formed its floor. He waved the others back. Then he went forward and looked carefully, wishing he had a pocket beamlight. But those had gone to either Satreel or the "new clansmen" he used as guards.

On close inspection, he could see that it was a dust-covered tool of some kind. He examined the bottom of the shelf with great care, but he could see nothing that resembled an alarm.

He signaled behind his back and he knew Muller would come up. With great care, he picked the object up and held it out to his chief. They looked at it hard and Muller looked at him as well. They nodded and smiled. Both of them were veterans, and the younger was not stupid. It was a weapon.

The butt was huge, and when Muller took the thing in his hand, he could not reach the trigger—a button the front of the grip—with his index finger. Under the dust was the alien blue metal of e barrel, which was short inproportion to the grip and came to a blunt point. At the tip of the point was a small hole, and the edge was worn on this opening, worn and fused looking. Finally, on the plastic of the side of the device a strange stamp was embossed. It looked like a circled bullet with arms, made of some different metal.

"Could be used for welding or maybe it's an odd cooking utensil," the colonel said gently. He winked at Slater and then turned and murmured, "Found a gun of sorts" to Thau Lang, who was next to him. The konsel passed the word back. Meanwhile Muller had tapped Slater's shoulder and urged him to move on.

As Slater went on, he began to notice that he could actually "feel" the left curve of the strange passage. That they were indeed going around the control room of their captor finally came home to him. On and on went the slow curve, but no more niches appeared in the walls and the strip of light in the narrow roof caught nothing but greasy dust as it rose in sluggish swirls under his careful feet. He was suddenly conscious of a very dry throat and he knew it was not fear but thirst. They had not had any water for a long time, he realized. *How long had it been and how was Danna holding out?* His thoughts did not slow his steady progress, and he checked instantly when he saw two things that drove all other thoughts from his head.

First, he saw that the passage ahead lay straight. And not only was it straight but at the end of visibility it was crossed at right angles by a barrier. In an instant he knew what he was seeing—it had to be the passage into the dome of the alien control room, the one down which they had all come when Satreel called to them. He *knew* there had to be another door there.

From three openings on the left side of the passage, and not so far from his position, there came a glow of intensified light. He was not conscious of signaling to Muller but the colonel was immediately beside him, looking past him intently.

"They must be sealed. I hear nothing. Never noticed them when we were inside there. Might be one-way glass, or could be views of another room just outside the big chamber." He paused. "No point in brooding. Go on, boy. Be careful."

As Slater moved on, he thought of the strange find that the senior officer now carried. Probably empty and tossed away a hundred and fifty years ago by Satreel's mother, said his mind, and then he forgot all about the thing for he had reached the first of the light sources. He peered around the near corner with one eye and blinked as he did. The dim light he had grown used to in the corridor was a different strength from what he was now getting. There could be no mistake about that light, if it had been seen even once. It was the eerie buish-white glow that lit the great domed control room in which they had seen their helpless animals turned into slime.

Slater instantly ducked down until he was below the port. He hurried on until he was at the third and last of the openings, then carefully rose to one side. Looking around, he saw the colonel at the second opening and Thau Lang at the first. Muller smiled and clicked his fingers once. Then they all three bent to look carefully at the corners of the view.

Slater saw at once that no one had used the port for a long time. The fine dust lay heavy over its surface. He gently began to stroke it away with one finger so that he could see. A side glance showed Muller and the konsel were doing the same at their's.

As he smoothed away the dust, he saw something else. The instant he did, he spun and clicked to Muller. When Slater had his attention, he pointed to what he had seen. Muller looked down at his own port's edge and then looked up and nodded. He then turned and signaled to the konsel.

Slater had found a small, corroded lever on the bottom of the port, a simple manual catch, inset but easy to grasp. Obviously it was a way to open the thing. Slater looked at it again and then made a mental estimate of the opening's size and shape. A horizontal oval, it was quite large enough for a man to get through, and he could see the floor on the other side was no farther down than on his. He bent again and peered through the now-clean corner.

He had a plain view of the control room's central dais and its instrument board. There sat the tall alien in his metallic robe and he was speaking, for Slater could see the mouth purse open and shut. But as if that were not enough, there stood JayBee Pelham, Mohini Dutt-Medawar, and her father.

Not only could they be seen, but they could be heard. The ancient view port allowed sound to come through plainly, if there was no other noise to interfere. During pauses in the conversation, Slater could even hear their footsteps. But now Satreel was speaking, the strange hissing tremolo coming over plainly.

"You know nothing yet, JayBee! Nothing of me and mine or what I have in the way of power. This is not the only center on this forgotten world. I am under orders given by those neither you nor any of your new little world ever knew or guessed at. There are allies to be brought from ancient sleep, in ways and methods you know nothing of. And this is not the only world with installations left by the Le-ashimath. You who come from the third planet know little. The second planet has things you never knew and cannot know. Its heat and clouds cover much."

"Lord Satreel, all is as you say. We are your ignorant servants. We only wish to help destroy all or any who threaten you. I urge you again to kill those who came last, especially their leader, the most dangerous Earth agent on Mars. Only thus can we be sure of complete safety while we plan to take over the planet and restore your rule." JayBee sounded sincere, but Slater wondered whether Satreel truly understood human treachery. His handling of the colonel's party certainly left a lot to be desired. Pelham wanted to rule Mars himself, not as anyone's deputy or servant.

"I will destroy any who do not do as I wish. Make no mistake about it, JayBee. Anyone!" Pelham fell silent. The strange high, purring voice continued. "That man you fear is guarded and secure, as are the others with him. He is the one I must talk further with, for he alone has guessed what I really am and what I want. He may be able to help and I want his knowledge—all of it—so that I can plan to go to the ancient stars."

Pelham made a short motion behind his back with one hand and his two allies went into action. Mohini drew a small lasgun and fired instantly. Her father whipped a small knife from a sheath at the back of his neck and threw it straight at the pale blue of Satreel's head. The thin beam of the pocket laser missed Satreel and hit the edge of his control board, but the knife buried itself to the hilt just below the alien neck, at the collar of the shimmering robe.

Instantly Colonel Muller threw the catch on his port and slammed it open. He aimed the peculiar old thing they had found on the corridor shelf, and with both hands managed to grip and fire the piece.

Warned by the noise of the port's being slammed aside, JayBee fell to the floor. A brilliant streak of violet light passed over him and struck Medawar in the side as he leaned forward and blasted a hole in him the size of a man's hand. Medawar fell as if hit by a steel fist, his mouth open and silent, a black hole burned in his side. From the distance, a faint roar, like that of a lion, came to their ears.

Slater wrenched his port open. Ahead, JayBee had gotten to his feet and was moving away while Mohini was turning her lasgun in their direction.

"Mohini! Look left, you fool," Slater yelled as he fell to the floor of the giant chamber. His diversion worked and her laser beam swung toward him, but well wide. Now she too moved and he saw her race after JayBee, who was almost at the far back wall where a door gaped open.

As Slater rose and began to run, Arta Burg flashed past him. Burg hurled something bright and metallic, but he was too late. The opening slid shut, and his projectile merely bounced from it.

"Stand fast, everyone!" The colonel called. "We can't follow them now. Let's get weapons and stay ready for whatever is tried next."

In the few seconds all the action had taken, they had all got through the three portholes in the wall. Danna ran over to Slater, squeezed his arm, gave him a grin, and turned with the rest of them to gather round the central platform.

Colonel Muller and Thau Lang were kneeling by a long shape.

"How in God's name does one give first aid to someone bred on a planet we couldn't see with a telescope?" Muller sounded as unsure of himself as anyone had ever heard him be. He was supporting Satreel's thin, wide shoulders in his arms and Thau Lang was examining the place where the knife hilt jutted from the pale-blue skin. The great eyes were open and flicked from one to the other, but the first member of an alien race any human had ever seen did not appear able to move.

But the alien was not dead, and it seemed his brain or whatever he had to think with was still functioning. The great dark eyes turned up to Muller and the toothless mouth opened. "Use the board. Press the lever marked with"—he paused, trying to put it in human terms—"marked with three crooked marks, marks which point down." Something like a sigh came from the strange mouth. "They are marked with colors but your color sense is not mine." He rallied and kept speaking but his vocal apparatus was losing power. "Listen, they will go around and out through the corridors. They know them not and they must search. Press that lever. I have strange pets here, such as none of you ever saw, and yet some came from your own world long, long ago." The eyes like black opals sought the ceiling. "To be killed thus, by primitives with missile weapons! I have much to do and this is not the only base that the absent masters left on this world. There are others and things sleep in them, sleep until this whole world dies." Another pause. "Or unless they are awakened. I myself cannot read all of the codes left me but I think the masters may have left—some of themselves! I had hoped if that were so to awaken them some day. They understood these things, the mighty Le-ashimath. They could stay anywhere, sleep in vaults in any place, on almost any world. In my searching I have found hints of yet another hidden, well-protected place, on the second planet from your sun, where you have never been, you humans."

Another brief silence followed. Then the strange mouth opened again. "Beware! When you press that lever, beware of leaving. It will release life-forms you must be wary of, release them into the outer and the under corridors. They are things bred from seeds preserved many cycles ago, both from your own world and from this one. Look for weapons such as you used on that dead human. They are hidden but they are about. You will need them, for JayBee may find them too. And those things of the ancient past which I bred back and you can release. For them, too."

The voice from beyond rose in a last dying tremolo. "I go, who am alone, and so young too. Only a thousand cycles of your sun have I lived since wakened from the storage cells. I go, my work unfinished, I go to my ancestors beyond time, I, Satreel, the last of the Attendants."

There was silence in the great, high-ceilinged chamber and Muller looked at his friends. "I guess he's gone. The movement of his thorax has stopped." He rose to his feet and looked down sadly. "Poor devil. All alone and trying to do a job he thought sacred, with no help and incomplete knowledge. For all his power, he must have been the loneliest thing in all of space."

Slater thought it a very decent epitaph for the first and the last of the entities from beyond the stars.

# CHAPTER 15

# *Animals, Aliens, and Close Combat*

T HEY LOOKED ABOUT THEM WITH INTEREST AND TREPI-
dation. The great domed room was empty save for themselves and the two dead. One had been an outright and familiar
enemy, and he was human. The other, who lay at their feet,
his great, gaunt arms spread out, the seven-fingered hands half
curled, was more of a mystery dead than alive. It was the girl
who first put it into words.

"He is dead, poor thing. So strange, so alone. I saw him
in a dream at first, and now it all seems like a dream, a terrible
nightmare we are having, and it can't stop or end." Danna
moved next to Slater and took his hand, looking forlornly down
at the strange face of their former captor.

"Yes, my dear, it may still be a bad dream—that is, if we
don't do a thing or two and wake up!" The vibrant tones of
the colonel broke into the strange hush like a bugle call in a
sleeping barracks. They all stared at him, even the impassive
Feng, as if they had just come on an alert.

"Slater," Muller went on, "I think you heard what he said last. Let's find that control with the three marks. We're sealed in here and we must use any weapons we can find, and fast." He turned to Feng. "Captain, you look for a weapons store." He faced Thau Lang next. "Old friend, get everyone to looking at anything that might be a com set. We have to break the shroud of silence that hangs over this whole area, so we can get in touch with the outside world. No one touch anything, just look. We could probably explode this entire point or island or whatever it is simply by pushing the wrong button. Call me at once if you see anything promising, and, meanwhile, I'll prowl about. All clear? Then let's move!"

And move they did, everyone fanning out but Slater, who went to the vast half-moon of the control board. The words of the dead creature raced through his mind. *Three crooked or bent marks, which faced down . . . Pull the lever!* The search was not easy for many controls were marked with bright symbols, in red, blue, orange, green, and purple. He closed his mind to the colorful distractions and began to count marks and slashes. It seemed as if an hour passed before he made his choice. "Colonel!" he shouted. "Come quick, sir. I think I have it!"

Muller was there instantly. "Are there any others that look like that?"

"No," Slater said as they stood looking at the tiny coppery lever. Next to it, colored mauve, were three raised vertical symbols like lightning flashes.

"I'll do it." Muller snapped the lever over as far as it would go. "Let's hope we understood Satreel." He smiled as he spoke.

At first they heard nothing and when they did, it meant nothing. It was simply a humming sound that came from the panel in irregular beats. After a few minutes, the sound stopped. Once more the board was silent and might have been inert, save that here and there a few lights glowed.

A shout came from far over on the right of the vast room. It was Feng. "Found a cabinet with three of those projectors like yours, Colonel!" The three short, bulky things he held out appeared identical to the one Muller had used on Medawar, but far cleaner and newer looking. Slater pointed at one of them.

"This one has different colors on the butt, and the trademark or whatever is red instead of blue. Notice?"

"Yes, I did," said Muller. "I'll give you mine, boy. We know what it does, at least so far. I'll take the odd one. Feng, the other dupe is yours. Give the last to, lessee—well, give it to Thau Lang. He saw what it could do. Now, let's—"

His words were interrupted by another yell, this one from Milla Breen. It was a wild whooping yell, in which the only word clear was "door." As the three on the dais looked left, to where the young warman had been, nothing more was needed.

A concealed door had slid silently open. It was a large door, big enough for three abreast and what was emerging from it was also large. Out of the dark opening had come an enormous head, coarsely furred in gray and brown and with pointed ears. The snout was massive and yellow tusks glinted in the light. Red eyes glared about in baffled anger and the great shoulders of the animal moved out into the open. They were as high as those on a horse, but this was no horse. It looked to Slater like a horrid cross between a large pig and an enormous wolf. Slowly it lurched on into the room and large hooves went *clack-clack* on the floor as it did. Its vast mouth opened and let out a raging grunt, deep and rasping at the same time. It had many great teeth as well as enormous tusks. The hooves were like those of some distorted deer. When the thing first appeared, Danna had raced toward Slater. She was peering around his left arm as he tried to sight the peculiar weapon, when Muller called, "No one else shoot while I try this thing of mine out!"

The monster had made up its own mind by this time and gathered on its haunches. At the colonel's voice, it began a charge. Muller crouched, used one arm as a rest, and pulled the firing button. This time no violent heat ray shot out. Instead, a stream of silver needles flew from the muzzle. When they struck the foaming jaws of the great brute, they exploded.

The great body collapsed on the spot where it had been hit, the head and much of its chest simply dripping shreds of meat. One instant it was alive and charging, the next its body had crashed to the floor, streaming blood in every direction. Everyone stood agape at both the creature itself and the amazing way it had been killed.

"What do you think, Feng?"

"Well, Colonel, hard to find a nicer device for an anti-personnel weapon." While he spoke, Feng had walked forward. He was kneeling by the dead hulk of the monster, his eyes gleaming. "Fantastic! Who would have thought Mars concealed such a thing as this?"

Muller and the others had moved up to join him, and all were staring at the huge body in fascination. It was the size of a horse, though shorter in the legs. They had trouble avoiding the pools of blood and the animal's own stench was rank and sharp, as coarse to the nose as the thing itself was to the eye.

Muller looked thoughtful as he studied the body. Then he turned to Slater. "I think we two have the only clue, young man. This thing could be from anywhere, but I think it's a neighbor of ours, from Earth. Look at the split hoof, like a cow's but narrower... This is probably one of the creatures Satreel warned us about when he mentioned things from seeds, preserved in time, both from this planet and Earth. If I'm correct, this beastie is an extinct mammal from Earth."

"No wonder that this new clan thought they were in the hands of a god," Thau Lang said. "If I understand you, Louis, these animals and many more have been preserved alive for many centuries, kept as even we, who are no scientists, keep food in the cold and see some of the fishes that Earth sent here stay alive frozen in ice, ready to go away when it melts or someone melts it."

Muller broke the hush that had fallen after Thau Lang spoke. "Remember two things, both important. We want JayBee and we want out. Find the switch that frees this area from the communications blackout."

He turned to Slater. "Have you considered what Prime Base must be at right now? *JayBee* gone, *us* gone, that *traitor* gone, and no word, no report, no *nothing*!" He wheeled on the others again. "Thau Lang and I will provide a roving guard. The rest of you study any controls you can find. Keep looking for more weapons, too."

Slater spoke to the colonel as the others moved out again.

"Sir, I do think Captain Feng ought to stay right here. He is I-Corps and they know lots we don't. Wouldn't that master control be likely to be on the control board?" He felt abashed for even vaguely correcting Muller but he had a strong feeling.

Muller eyed Slater appraisingly. "Feng, check out the big board here. I think that the Wise Woman might need a special sort of guard, don't you?"

Slater grinned. Then he and Danna joined the prowl, looking for anything that might be useful. But the next surprise found them. Danna was a few yards to one side of him and had begun to walk around a mass of metal higher than her head when she halted, stared for a second, then stepped back. As she did, she yelled, "Quick, Moe!"

He spun and moved to her, beamer up and cradled. Around the corner of the machine she had been passing, well above their heads, a great limb reached down—an olive-green limb ending in a hooked claw. Along one side of the limb were huge spikes like the teeth of a tremendous saw, but thinner and longer.

"Get behind me, Danna!" Slater shouted. "Look out, every-one! There's a great beast coming out over here!" Then he jumped back for the head of the beast was emerging from behind the unknown machine and was looking down at them from a height three times their own. It was roughly triangular, that head, mostly taken up by two great balls of shining almond eyes. Under the eyes, pointed mouthparts moved delicately. As it came slowly into the strong light, the great goggle eyes seemed to look everywhere and another giant arm also came into view. The towering almost neckless body, which sup-ported the yard-wide head, was emerging steadily and a few of the tremendous, sticklike legs, set far back on the torso were also becoming visible. Utterly silent save for the faint scrape of its claws on the floor, the towering horror seemed, in some ghastly way, familiar. Puzzled, Slater backed slowly away, shielding Danna as he did.

Then it swept forward with its great bony arms, and he pulled the firing button.

The intense beam of violet heat lashed out of the beamer once again, striking the body just below the head. Whatever the composition of the creature's skin, it was not so strong as human epidermis, or as Muller pointed out later, a human survival suit. Almost decapitated, the great tall shape simply fell forward, with a series of feathery clicks and thuds, landing just in front of Danna. The two bulging eyes, pupilless and shining, looked exactly the same as before. No life seemed to have left them, but the whole long shape, which now was seen to have many legs, lay limp and unmoving in seconds. A thick green slime flowed sluggishly from the wound.

The others had all come up by now and were staring, but it was Captain Feng, his face alive with interest, who spoke first. "Incredible what those star rovers had in the way of science!" He turned to Muller. "This is impossible, Colonel, even with the lighter gravity of Mars. No insect should be able to even move at that size, nor should its circulatory system work. Quite apart from whatever growth it was bred to, how under Heaven did they do it?"

Muller looked at Slater and smiled. "I had a few tribal ancestors, long ago in the extreme southern part of Africa. They thought the praying mantis was a god. Here's one they never met but which might qualify, eh?"

Slater turned to Danna and put one arm about her shoulders. "Look, Wise Martian Woman. Here's something from the home of your ancestors, a thing I used to catch and squash when I was young. I squashed this one for you, so it wouldn't pick you up in those claw arms and eat you. Now who's a stupid Greenie?"

"Ugh, horrible!" She smiled up at him and returned the one-armed hug. "Please stay and protect me, Moe. And keep any of those pets back on Earth."

Thau Lang moved around the immense insect's corpse, then called out. "Here is another open door. How many of these doors can there be, Louis? And why are they now open?"

"Because, my dear fellow, Slater and I opened them. It was the last thing Satreel did for us, telling us how to do it. Before you ask why it would be 'for us,' think a second. JayBee and that very nasty girl are also in this building. With this crew of killer beasts loose, we have two chances—one of having them killed by the animals, the other of killing them ourselves before they kill us." He turned to Slater who was nearby. "Recall that interrupted humming noise when we pulled the lever? It must have been opening and shutting cage doors. So, my friends, let's get back to work and find whatever else is around. We found good weapons twice. Back to work and find more."

They spread out and began to examine everything they came across. A few strange-looking cabinets were sealed shut, and no one dared try force on them. All appeared to be metal, though coated with some plasticene covering. Some were blue, some yellow, and a few even purple.

Suddenly Arta Burg's choked cry made the others stop their roving and turn. Three tall shapes had unexpectedly appeared, their bearded faces furious. In seconds Arta fell, transfixed by a spear he could not dodge.

Danna screamed as the new clansmen, in full battle array, shouted as one man, "Kill the Earthlings, kill them all!" Spears, swords, and shields ready, they rushed to the attack. And behind them more burst from the wall in a milling, tangled crowd, all yelling and waving weapons.

"Shoot to kill!" Muller roared. Even as he said it, he was crouched, firing the alien pistol that shot exposive bullets. He sprayed the new clansmen with silver death. As Feng had guessed, it was a superb anti-personnel weapon. A whole section of the advancing horde's front rank went down, shredded dead on the spot.

Meanwhile, Thau Lang and Slater had begun to fire their beamers. The three-part barrage of explosives and superlaser fire stopped the wild rush in its tracks. Those new clansmen not hit fled back to the wide doorway from which they had just burst, leaving their wounded and at least twenty dead behind. Blood, charred meat, and fragmented flesh and bone were spattered all over. The battle was over in seconds.

"It seems that JayBee has found allies or servants," Muller said. "These poor devils didn't come here on their own, they were sent. He is somewhere around, taking care not to get hit himself—and I want him! If he gets any real weapons, anything like our stuff, we're dead! I want *him* dead, not us, and I don't want to give him a chance to escape—which he'll do if he can't get us first." Muller paused while he looked about with cold rage. He tried to not listen to the moans of the wounded giants who lay among the dead and pieces of the dead.

"Listen up, you guys. One thing I want you all to know about," Muller went on. "Outside, before we ever came in this alien hellhole, I gave Nakamura some instructions. Our mission is to finish this place. I hoped that if they got us, he, with his size and his knowledge, might get away somehow as a member of this so-called new clan. I had to take as few chances as possible, and Lieutenant Nakamura was my last hope of getting the word out if we ended up dead. So, look out when you shoot or hit anyone, just because he's big. Nakamura might be in with them."

Slater was wondering if Nakamura was still alive when he noticed Danna and Milla Breen kneeling by a limp form that lay in the middle of the fragmented dead. Realizing who it must be, he ran over to them, trying not to slip in the gore.

Danna looked up, her eyes full of unshed tears. "He never had a chance. Poor Arta. He had just become a warman and he guarded me all his life." She buried her face in both hands. As he looked down, Slater realized that young Burg could not have felt much. The point of the heavy spear was deep in his upper chest. He sensed movement at his side and saw Thau Lang had joined them.

"Come, up, both of you. Milla, you are the last husband now and have more to do. No time for mourning here. We must avenge him. Later we will sing his praises."

The young Ruckers got up, and Slater put his arm over Danna's shoulder. *Allah! To think I was once jealous of that poor dead kid* went through his mind as he hugged the shaken girl. But before he could get maudlin, Muller interrupted.

"Over here, all of you. We may have found something we can use." Muller was pointing to a lever in a hollow on the floor under the central panel.

Slater crouched and studied the heavy, dull-blue lever that thrust up at a slight angle from a depression on the floor. Next to it, a raised, square-ended projection protruded from the underside of the panel. On the face of that a strange mark was deeply incised in the metal, a hemisphere with lines from the pole to the diameter line. Across the whole thing was something that looked as if it might be a word in a strange script.

Slater looked up at Feng and saw the I-Corps captain was excited from the expression on his face. He looked down again and an idea came to him suddenly. "Might be a picture of a shelter of some kind, like a domed tent. But maybe it stands for a grid, a dome over something. I don't know—"

"Why not a power grid? Over all this area?" Feng asked.

"We know there is one," the colonel said. "This whole area of the rift is one of the Dead Zones; has been since we first came to Mars. There are others. There's one about or near about the mountain. But this is the one we've known about the longest."

They stared at the enigmatic lever until Muller broke the silence. "Let's go. We'll have to take a chance and hope we won't blow ourselves and the whole place sky high. We can't read their script and we have no time to go to school. Pull it over—all the way, Lieutenant."

Slater grinned at Danna and yanked the lever. A long moment went by, in complete silence.

"All right, Feng. Try the thing you think is a radio or whatever." He smiled at Slater who still crouched by the lever. "The captain is reasonably sure he has located a comm of some sort on the top left over there. Let's see if *that* blows us up."

Feng turned a knob and spoke loudly into an oily cable that ended in yet another knob. "To any UN force within sound of my voice, come in please! This is an I-Corps FLASH. I repeat, this is an I-Corps FLASH."

Nothing happened, so after a brief pause, he rotated the knob and repeated the call.

The response was immediate but not too loud. Even Muller jumped a little when they heard it. "General Scott here, Captain. I read you five by. I have a fix on you. What's your status? Over." The new voice was projected from under the panel in front of Feng, but Slater could not see from what.

"We need help, sir—" was all Feng got out before Muller leaned over and took the mike from him.

"Colonel Muller here, General. Are you nearby? What's your strength?"

"Almost directly over you," came the answer. "Six floaters and five hundred troops. A crash force I put together. What's the situation?"

"Come straight down, sir. JayBee's here but I think he has little in the way of weapons beyond knives and spears. We killed the communications blackout. He seems to be in control of the new clan. I don't know how many there are, but they are armed with only crude hand weapons. We are holding an al . . . we are holding the archaic control room of this fort. Tell your men to touch no controls or odd-looking devices at all. Might blow us up and them too."

"We're descending now, Colonel. Anything else?"

Slater was gesturing wildly and pointing to the body of the hairy monster that had appeared first. Muller nodded. "Strange life-forms wandering about here. Many of them, and they can be very bad news. Instruct the men to kill on sight."

"Very good. Keep this channel open."

Muller leaned back against the control panel and let out a sigh of relief. "I know Scott, a good man. Tough and quick when he needs to be." He looked around with a fresh light gleaming in his eyes. Slater could see a new plan forming even before he spoke.

"We have to get JayBee and this new clan he's inherited. We don't know where they are, or even if they believe enough in JayBee to follow him." He looked searchingly about the vast room. "Captain Feng, you stay here with the com and keep watch. Danna Strom, you stay too. Lieutenant Slater and I will form one team, Thau Lang and Milla Breen the other. We'll fan out through the side corridors and keep looking for JayBee. Feng, you tell General Scott what we're doing."

But Danna would not stay if Mohammed Slater went. And she carried the point with ridiculous ease, Slater thought, considering that she was opposing Colonel Muller. All he did was listen quietly, smile, and nod. Feng shrugged and settled at the panels of the control board.

And so they set off, the two Ruckers down the tunnel from which the giant mammal had come, the other three down the larger one from which the praying mantis had emerged. Even as they passed through strange doors, they could hear the roar and whistles of noncoms as the UN strike force formed up.

Muller went first, Danna next, and Slater brought up the rear. For a long time the corridor ran gently down on a curving slant. Eventually Muller held up his hand; they halted and drew together, weapons at the ready.

"Listen," he murmured. "I heard something move." As Slater peered ahead, he could see that the dimly lit, featureless passage curved yet again, this time to the left. Further, when he had stared for a few seconds, he had the impression that a larger space lay beyond, from which came a very faint light. He muttered this to Muller who bobbed his head. Then, as they listened, sounds about which there could be no argument burst upon them. One was a high, piercing scream that rose until it hurt the eardrums. The other, which underlay the scream, was something else. Part shrieking roar, part grating hiss, it was a horrid sound and its volume alone gave an impression of great size as well as appalling savagery.

"Let's go!" Muller snapped. They raced for the curve that lay ahead, the two men in front with weapons poised and the girl just behind, her spear ready. They whipped around the shallow curve and burst into a great underground room, a sunken cavern of a place with rough walls arching overhead and a floor of earth and rock littered with small chunks of rubble.

Yet the place was not entirely natural, and it had at least once been used. Overhead a few large fluor lamps glared and here and there were strewn bits of furniture and utensils of some sort. But it was the scene before them that gripped them.

Three persons were backed up on to a low mound of debris, some distance away to their left. They could be seen clearly in the lights. One, taller than the other two, was their greatest enemy. Alongside JayBee, her face twisted in fear, stood Mohini Dutt-Medawar, all beauty gone in her stark terror. And in front of them, her arms held behind her back by JayBee, stood an unknown quantity!

She was young and seemed, in that flashing instant, to be lovely in a strange and unearthly way. She was straining against Pelham's grip. A lovely young woman with orange hair! It did not seem to be dyed hair either, though one could not have said just why, but a flame color that verged on a fire yellow. Her mouth was open and she screamed again, high and piercing. Her teeth were clearly visible and to Slater they looked somehow wrong, though white. But his gaze and that of the others was really fixed elsewhere. The flame-haired woman in her swirls of blue robe was incidental.

Crouched a little lower than the three on the mound was the creature that had made the ghastly roar. As they came in the tunnel entrance, it turned to look at them and it bore the head of a nightmare!

The creature was the size of an ox or one of the extinct giant bears of Earth. Its huge head had small ears, vast jaws full of great teeth and a pair of upper canines that looked like huge tusks. From its lower jaw stuck bone flanges into which the great upper teeth obviously fit when the mouth was closed. The massive body was powerful and bearlike but with a long tail such as no bear ever has or had. The mighty legs had vast paws with longs claws, and the whole close-furred body was striped along its length, white stripes on a reddish background. They could smell its reeking odor, pungent and rank.

Alien fauna, Slater thought. Something they brought from the stars and it got loose when we pushed Satreel's button? But there was no time for much thought. The thing had finally focused on the new prey. That hissing bellow erupted again from the gaping jaws, and it hurled itself at them.

"Fan out!" Muller screamed as he fired. Slater tried to step in front of Danna, but, to his surprise, the colonel beat him to it, so the lieutenant ducked the other way and crouched to get a better aim.

The two weapons did the trick, but not by much. The explosive needles from Muller's gun tore into the giant chest of the oncoming behemoth, while Slater's ray burned through the great right shoulder, which was nearest to him, and he fanned the weapon a little to spread its effect.

With a last coughing, choking ripsaw of sound, deafening even as it gave way to gasps of pain, the creature fell so close to the colonel that a spray of saliva from the dying jaws fell across Muller's feet. The two men ceased their fire but stayed in a crouch, weapons ready in case the monster had some last strength in reserve. Suddenly Danna noticed movement ahead. "Moe! JayBee's getting away over there!"

Behind the mound of earth and rubble JayBee and Mohini had been standing on, was an opening in the rough wall of rock. Mohini had already entered it and JayBee was right behind, dragging the strange girl by one arm.

Slater leaped forward, his pistol raised. Behind him, Muller yelled something, in which the only word he caught was "*alien!*"

Pelham was out of sight and Slater could see only a rough crevice in the wall. As he rushed forward, the stare of the strange girl, who was pulling in his direction without effect, met his eyes head on. The eyes filled his vision and sent a chill down his spine. Large eyes they were, and reddish. The pupils were narrow, jet black, and vertical. No human eye ever had such a pupil!

The girl disappeared in the crevice before he could reach her. Without a pause Slater ran into the opening but found it was dark and lightless. He rushed on as fast as he could and he heard a grinding noise in the blackness ahead, a noise that ended with a heavy thud. Seconds later he ran smack into a hard barrier and bruised his outflung left arm badly. He tripped on a piece of loose rock and fell to the floor, annoyed and blind.

Then, suddenly, a light went on behind him and he whirled, heat beam ready, just as Danna and Muller rushed up. Danna was holding a small pocket beamlight.

"Found it on the mound," Muller said. "JayBee must have dropped it while struggling with the girl."

They carefully checked the great door that had blocked the passage. It was made of some dense, dull metal. There was no control or latch, nothing but blank, immobile metal in one huge slab, which closed the rocky tunnel from floor to roof.

"Shouldn't we go back to the big room, sir? We might find another of these openings there." Danna's hand slipped into Slater's own behind his back.

"We may have to." The colonel was using the small beam to examine the vast block in the passage very carefully. "May still have to," he went on, "but let's try something first. We'll all get our hands flat on the surface and push. First, this way, to the right."

Under their pressure, the great slab was quite motionless and inert. "Now the left," Muller prompted, and to Slater's amazement, the huge thing began to slide.

When a narrow opening had appeared on the right, the colonel made them stop, while he reconnoitered, peering around the corner very carefully. "Nothing," he said at length, standing back. "Just an empty passage, dimly lit, but a smooth one, not like this at all. Plastic coating all over, I think, under the dust. The footprints went straight on and there were broad smudges. JayBee must have been dragging that very odd captive of his. Anything about her strike you as peculiar, lieutenant, aside from the startling hair?"

Slater gulped, his mind racing. "Well, sir, her eyes. They had vertical and very long pupils. Like a ferkat's, only bigger. Maybe something strange about her teeth too, although I can't think what it was."

Muller laughed softly and the laugh wrinkles about his eyes crinkled in the reflected torchlight. "They were fangs, young man—pointed, very sharp fangs. I missed the eyes myself but you got closer. Good observation." The laughter died from his face and it grew solemn for a moment. "Glad to see Danna's man has good vision. Makes an old fellow feel better."

At their look of joint incomprehension, he smiled again. "I have a responsibility to Danna, lieutenant, quite apart from my job and rank and this search of ours." He paused and then reached out his free hand and patted the girl's shoulder. "We won't go into the details right now. I had never seen her until she came to Fort Agnew. But I knew about her long before." His powerful arm left the girl's shoulder and slipped around her slender waist as he pulled her in close to his body.

Grinning over her shoulder, his clear gaze met that of the startled younger man. "Not to worry, boy. She happens to be my daughter. I think I ought to begin worrying about her choice of a man, don't you?"

Danna pulled loose from Muller and stared at him. "But, but—what do you say? My father was a great warrior of the True People. He was from a foreign clan from far away in the

North. When my mother bore me she died, but all have told me this and Thau Lang, he . . ."

Muller smiled but a sadness was mixed with the smile. "I posed as a faraway clansman, my dear. I loved your mother and Thau Lang knew who and what I was. He was her father, after all."

Danna looked at the colonel and her mouth was soft and her lips just parted. "You speak the truth, I think." She turned to Mohammed Slater and he saw a hint of the tears in the amber eyes as she came to his arms. He stroked the short ruffled mass of her hair and she said into his shoulder, "I am half a Greenie myself and so it is all right." He murmured as he would to a child and held her tighter.

It was Muller who brought them back to reality. He had been watching the narrow gap of the great metal door and now he spoke. "We will have a long time together to discuss family matters. But first and now—JayBee!"

The man and the woman drew apart and, at his orders, fell on the door again and pushed it open wider. The dusty corridor led down.

They watched the walls closely as they went and kept their weapons poised. The very weak line of fluors in the ceiling on that side of the sliding door was enough to follow the trace they sought. It was all gray and extremely gloomy, that untenanted road to nowhere, yet they felt stronger just because they were together.

Slater's wristchron said they had been on the sepulchral route for about fifteen minutes when Muller, who was leading, held up one hand and pointed—the sloping passage leveled off ahead and another barrier seemed to seal it.

"This may be it," Muller said quietly. "We'll go down with care and look that door over. I want JayBee and I want that *other* even more." Slater had no doubt that the "other" his superior meant was not Mohini.

## CHAPTER 16

# *The Last of
the Best*

$T$HE NEW BARRIER WAS QUITE DIFFERENT FROM THE ONE
they had encountered higher up, just a dull plastic finish
with transverse bars of metal cutting across. But Danna pointed
to the wall on the left side of the passageway.

Sure enough, under the dust, there was another small door,
just as there had been by the Control Center. And it too had
a recessed manual catch.

Muller released the handle, opened the narrow portal slowly,
and beamed his torch into the dark interior. After he had checked
the darkness that lay beyond as well as he could, he said, "I'll
lead, Slater will bring up the rear. You, daughter, will stay in
the center. Watch my light and anything else you can see. I
think we're getting close to our quarry and I want to avoid
accidents."

Silently and slowly, they filed into the dark, the colonel's
beam providing the only light. The walls and floor were the
same dull plasticene as those above, but dustier. They walked

202

for a considerable distance, and all that kept Slater hopeful was the gentle righthand curve of the walls. It seemed the corridor circled a much larger space, just as had the one above. But no shelves, openings, ports, or lights were apparent on this one. They went for minute after minute until Muller suddenly stopped.

Ahead of them, the surface of the floor had changed. For a stretch of about thirty feet, it had become a bluish metallic surface, which looked as if it had been oiled. Beyond that as far as the light could show, the old floor wound away into the darkness.

"What do you think?" Muller asked.

"I don't know, sir," Slater said. "It looks as if it had just been cleaned."

"I don't like it," Danna said.

"I don't like that smooth bit at all."

The colonel looked reflective as he mulled over the situation. Finally he spoke. "I think we have to try it. Going back gets us nowhere, and we are sure JayBee came this way. He must have guessed we'd follow even if he hasn't yet been alerted about the troops Scott is landing up above. If we try to force the big door back there and he is inside it, he'll be waiting for us. I'm afraid we'll have to look for another entry—hell, there has to be a reason for this thing we're in to keep going on."

Muller walked carefully out on the metal surface and the others kept him covered from behind. Nothing at all happened. The floor was quite solid. He turned and waved the other two on after him, and soon all three were standing on the dust-free surface. Muller was only a yard or so from the other side when the floor tilted sideways.

Danna screamed once. The two officers remained mute, but in that blinding moment when the footing suddenly vanished, Slater just braced himself for sudden death. The result of the fall was certainly sudden but it was not death.

Almost as quickly as the foothold had vanished, another hard surface took its place beneath them. Without any real impact, the three bodies jumbled together and all three continued downward together, but this time on a sharp slant. They slid, with increasing rapidity, down a long and very slick tube.

Even as he twisted and writhed, trying to find a foothold or a hand grip somewhere, Slater was, in another part of his mind, reasoning. Was it for *them*, this collapsing floor trap, or for others? When had it been set first, and by *whom*? And as his mind raced, he managed to get Danna's arm out of one eye and Muller's heel out of his left armpit. But that was all, and still the fall went on, on and down.

Unexpectedly they fell to a stop, all three in one tangled mass, but quite unhurt and on some soft surface that had cushioned their arrival. The long slide down that corkscrew chute and its sudden end had done them no harm at all.

As they freed themselves from the tangle of their own bodies, Slater felt heavy plastic under his groping hands. A large mat lay beneath them, and he could stand on it even though his knees shook. But no sooner was he erect than he was half blinded.

Trying to focus through aching eyes, he watched as one wall of the pit began to move upward. And strong light flooded under it. The illumination grew stronger as the curved surface rose above their heads, and to add to the confusion, there were shouts, raucous laughter, and catcalls.

"Look at the Greenies! All in a cage! Burn 'em down, JayBee—fry 'em to a crisp like they did us." Finally Slater's eyes were beginning to adjust to the intense light.

He, Danna, and Muller were in a nearly circular space with a padded floor. A row of massive bars rose higher than his head from floor to the roof of the aperture. Outside the bars, which he immediately realized were not close enough to stop his passage, was the enemy.

None was close but all were within easy distance. A mob of the new clan giants in the usual uniform danced and waved along one side of a huge subterranean chamber. Vivid blue fluor tubes blazed on the arched ceiling above the giants. On a platform at the far end of the domed cellar, JayBee Pelham crouched over a UN-issue heavy lasgun. Over the heads of his impassioned followers, his black eyes were gleaming in malignant triumph. His waving white hair was disarrayed and he looked as if he had run hard and fast. He had won and they had lost, and he revelled in his moment of victory.

"Silence, all of you! JayBee commands here!" His voice had not lost its power or charm, even in curt commands. The thirty or so new clan warriors fell silent at their leader's order.

In the quiet that followed, Slater could hear the breath of the two behind him. He moved very slightly, shuffling his feet on the pad, and managed to move in front of Danna.

"I do believe it is my dear friend Colonel Muller. You took me once, I recall, and put me behind bars. Now you are the one behind bars, and I shall not make the mistake you did. The Master Hunter of Mars himself, and two flunkies! What a downfall, eh, Muller? Strange how life always favors the better man, right?"

Louis Muller's voice was calm. "I told them to execute you, Pelham. I said you were as dangerous as plague spore and ought to be expunged. But you know how politics is—perhaps better than any. Your judgment and sentencing had to be done by the letter of the law. I live under rules and the law. You live under nothing but your own desire to be omnipotent. And you are not stupid. So the plague bacillus escaped and like any kind of disease germ, found itself a wound to fester in. And, of course, you found allies as well, like these poor men who don't know you or even what they really want or what's good for the planet. I'd call it a bad turn of the dice, Pelham, that's all. And don't try to lie to me and tell me you had us trapped!"

There was a surge of the muttering now. The savages who glared at them picked up the contempt in Muller's voice. They understood little Unit, but keen ears could easily detect the lack of respect and the cold dislike in their imprisoned enemy. So could Pelham, and he lost his temper.

"You fool! You are in *my* grip and you have the gall to say *I* didn't trap you!" His voice rose in anger and Slater could see that Muller was provoking him. The longer he could keep the Master Mind busy and arguing, the longer it gave Scott and the strike force to penetrate down to their underground prism.

The colonel's level voice, unexcited yet very audible, was quick to reply. "This slide is too big for just a few people and you know it. Satreel's race and what came before them must have built it for something else. Probably a trap for any of the big animals that got loose which could be herded into that passage or lured in with food."

He laughed, a sneer evident in the sound, and then waved at the men assembled across the room from JayBee.

"I could see that they all were *surprised* as well as impressed by your great cleverness, Pelham. I'd be willing to bet you had no idea where we were at all until this tube spilled us down here. Sheer dumb luck—so of course you're claiming credit for it. Bah! Spare me your boasts. Impress these peasants as you did the more stupid colonists up top when you were still a respectable petty crook on the make."

Slater watched the play of emotion on JayBee's furious face, then scanned the other members of the audience. Something registered on his brain. One of the tall, scowling figures—a very tall one, dirty and unshaven—was known to him! Their eyes met for an instant and he had it. It was Nak!

Slater turned back to warn the colonel but he was distracted as Pelham, his face livid with rage, was preparing to fire. He was obviously aiming at Muller who stood to Slater's left. But Pelham had forgotten something. Suddenly a small door behind his platform whipped open and first one and then another figure darted out.

The flame hair of the first was evidence that the strange captive was loose. Behind her ran Mohini Dutt-Medawar as she tried to catch the fugitive. "Stop her, JayBee, stop her before she does something!"

The big clansmen merely gaped and even Pelham seemed momentarily paralyzed. But one brain did not freeze. "Run, now, through the bars," Muller hissed.

The incredible orange-fire hair had come to a sudden halt, at an angle of the wall between JayBee and his followers. She leaped up and to the side and seized a thin lever that jutted inconspicuously from a boxlike bulge in the wall. The rod was a strange mixture of flaming pink and subtle blue. With both hands, the fugitive wrenched at the thing and it descended with a loud, grinding sound. A strange low hum became audible.

At this point, Pelham seemed to come awake. He wheeled the big lasgun and took aim, but he was too late and too fast on the trigger. Mohini had just grasped one arm of the captive when a line of white light and inconceivable heat struck both bodies. In a second they were ash, the wall behind them molten plastic and stone.

Slater had lost his alien gun in the fall down the shaft and had not had a chance to find it. But Muller, with the instinct of the born old fighting man he was, had not lost his. He took aim now and yelled as he did so, for he was out past the wide-spaced bars and in the room.

"Try this for size, Pelham, you butchering bastard!" Then he pressed the button to release the explosive bullets. Alas for the colonel. Nothing happened at all. The fight with the last monster had exhausted the load.

Pelham whirled to fight, but another was quicker still. One of the new clansmen had drawn back his arm at the colonel's shout and hurled a light spear like a striking snake.

Slater had turned and grabbed Danna's sword then leaped forward, but he was not fast enough. The spear drove deep into Muller's body, and he staggered and fell at the impact. The crowd yelled and JayBee's voice was higher and louder than any.

"Good shot! Now let me get the other Greenies and that's it, True People!" He turned and leveled the lasgun. Slater braced himself for a hot and instant death, but he had forgotten something and JayBee, sure of triumph, had never known it at all. A bull's bellow shook the whole room and a giant figure leaped high, in a way no one born under Martian gravity could have done. "Try this one, Pelham," Helge Nakamura roared. And as he reached the summit of his upward leap, well over the heads of the crowd around him, he hurled a spear with all the power of his great arm. As a balancing act, despite the lesser gravity, it was superb. It was also accurate! The spear flew like an arrow, and it took JayBee Pelham to death, hitting him at the base of his corded throat with such an impact that he was hurled off his platform and hit the floor with an audible thud.

The mob of Rift-dwelling clansmen froze in horror. That one of their own should slay their new leader held them numb and shaken with combined amazement and horror.

Slater was already on the move. He had a clear path in front of the stupefied warriors and he took it straight to JayBee's platform, now empty of its occupant. In ten or so strides he was there and had vaulted up. Spinning and stooping, he levered the fallen lasgun onto its tripod and leveled it at the new clansmen, his finger in place on the trigger.

"Freeze or I kill!" he yelled. "Any of you move and you all die!" He kept the barrel swiveling back and forth. They flinched as he did. "Get up here, Nak, while I have them covered!" His second yell was unnecessary for Nakamura was already moving to him, keeping to the side so as not to interfere with Slater's field of fire. In an instant he was beside Slater with a great sword in his fist.

"Drop weapons! Drop all weapons! Do not move or I kill all of you!"

The new clansmen obeyed.

"Take over this thing, Nak, and keep them quiet. I have to see to the colonel."

Slater ran to one side and raced to where Danna keeled beside Muller's prostrate body. As he ran up, he could see the spear was still protruding from the colonel's chest and wondered why she had left it.

Muller's calm voice answered the unspoken thought. "Hurry up, my boy. That spear caught me cold. If she pulled it out, I'd be gone in a second. I have a little time and I want to use it well.

"Be good to each other. I loved Danna's mother and I would have left the service for her. She died when I was far away. Get Thau Lang to tell you about her, dear. He knows it all. You two can bring a new message to the planet to the True People can live in peace without losing their independence. Look up the history of the treatment of Amerindians of that area today called the United States of North and Central America. Learn what the rulers did wrong and the few things they did right." He smiled wearily, but his strength was fading. "I wish that damned maniac had not killed the redheaded female. She wasn't one of us or Satreel's people. I think you'll have to find who and what she was, Slater. Perhaps one of the ancient rulers of Satreel's race, frozen or something. . . . Wish I knew."

His voice was growing fainter and they bent over his head, straining to catch every word.

"Now, listen hard and move fast— That lever that she pulled. I think it means death, death and destruction. It's what *I* would do in that place she was in. Hear that droning hum? I think something's running down or winding up. The three of you, leave me and go. Go now, That's an *order!*"

Slater took Danna's arm and she gave no trouble, just bent and kissed Muller on the mouth once. Then she was up and following her man.

"Nak, we're getting out and fast. Give me that weapon. You lead. The colonel thinks the whole place is gonna blow."

Nakamura handed over the lasgun and bellowed once at the silent and disarmed men. "We are leaving. All should follow. This place becomes a place of death. Those who stay will die, die in agony. Follow us!"

With that, he led off at a fast trot and the other two followed. Slater cradled the lasgun, which was heavy but not impossible, once he had freed it from the tripod. As he followed Nakamura into the large tunnel upward, the group of new clansmen began to follow. And he saw the prone figure wave one arm and then let it drop. Moisture burned his eyes and he blinked rapidly to clear them. Then he and Danna rounded a corner and the scene was lost.

They ran upward at a steady jog, and he could see over his shoulder that the men of the Rift were following. They were not too close however. They knew what he carried in his arms and they thus kept back a little.

As they ran, Nakamura shouted over his shoulder about how he had managed to mingle with the giants. "Colonel Muller told me to wait outside until I decided you weren't coming at all—then I was to try to get out and get the word to base. I stood it until I saw this bunch coming through the woods. They weren't any we'd seen before, so, when they left a guard at the tunnel entrance I waited, until the sentinel was alone, killed him, and ran down. They were so hyped up no one even noticed me. It was simple, really." He led on, panting only a trifle.

When they had made several broad but easy loops up the tunnel, they emerged into an open space like a high-ceilinged warehouse or a great barn. They had run steadily upward all the time and Slater was sure they were close to the surface if not on it already. Any doubts they might have had were soon brought to an abrupt halt.

"Freeze, Ruckers! Drop that piece, you in front. Anyone moves and they're dead!"

"We're officers from Fort Agnew in disguise," Nakamura shouted, dropping his sword. Slater had let go of the lasgun with relief. "Take us to your chief and get moving, you guys, get moving fast! This whole place may blow in a few minutes!" Nakamura's voice was a help. In seconds they had been checked out and were explaining to a grizzled sergeant and his squad of Space Marines. They warned him of the disarmed men following and to lead them out in a hurry.

They were led to Scott. Captain Feng was with him, as were Thau Lang and Milla.

"We've got to get out of here, sir, and get out damned fast," Slater explained to the general.

"Give me details on the way out," he snapped and issued instant orders. "We'll get everyone in those ships, crowded or not. I'll take as many of those disarmed locals as we can. If Muller thinks this place is mined somehow, then, by God, I listen."

"A steady drone from the control board started about twenty-five minutes ago," Feng said. The general nodded and kept up his crisp volley of orders. Out of the various tunnel openings, men began to pour, mostly Marines but some of them pulling members of the new clan and even a few women and children.

Noting the bafflement on Slater's face, the general explained. "We found a village back in the woods behind this place. Took as many as we could alive. Some wouldn't surrender at all. Regrettable."

In less than a quarter hour, they were all in one or another of the big floaters that were grounded outside.

As they lifted off in the command ship, Slater suddenly felt the exhaustion of the last few days wash over him. He slumped by a port, staring out foggily while Danna hummed to herself and stroked his weary head.

"We're well away and getting farther," Nakamura yelled.

"If the colonel was right, we may have done it. Place looks peaceful, though, and I—God almighty! Get down and hang on, everyone!"

The whole point of wooded land on which the alien base lay was sinking into a smoking crater that had come into existence in a second. Steam rose about the edges of the vast and horrid subsidence, but the waters of the strange lake, whose shape they could at last see, rushed into quench any flames. They could make out the ground and the trees rippling at the land's edge where the point had once thrust out. And that was all, really. In only a few minutes, the swirling and discolored water, its murky rim growing wider as they watched, was the only trace of the lost colony from the stars.

"A good tomb for the colonel and a peaceful memorial," he heard a strange voice say. As he fell into total exhaustion, he knew it for his own voice.

The conference held several days later was tightly restricted. Aside from Marshal Mutesa and General Scott, only Captain Feng of I-Corps and Senior Lieutenants Nakamura and Slater were present of the UN forces. By invitation there were some odd guests, however. An elderly war chief of the Rucker clans was one. Another was a young native woman, the recent wife of Lieutenant Slater. And the third was a young Rucker warman, who, apparently mixed up, introduced himself as Mrs. Slater's husband.

"I'll start off," Scott said, "since I was there, at least for the last round. The marshal says we'll be informal. Just raise your hand if you want to ask anything or comment. Clear enough?" He was smiling and the others were also.

"What about that last bomb, the one that wrecked the alien's whole base and sank it, sir?"

Nakamura's answer came from the marshal. "Your unknown female seems to have done that, son. If the colonel was right and she was actually a revived alien, she knew her tricks. As well as my experts can figure it, there was a big fissure or cavern way beneath the base, and it may not have been natural. Whatever she blew off simply knocked the floor out from under everything. So the whole place just sank. There was no trace of atomic power in use. What they had there, we simply don't know."

"What about the animals, sir? Were any identified? Were any of them left, either dead or alive?" Feng was a zoology nut and his interest was intense.

"Nothing alive, but quite a few floating bodies that rose to the surface," Scott said. "We have all your reports on tape as well, while my boys took a few pictures." General Scott smiled and looked at the marshal. "Sorry you couldn't have been there, sir." He turned back to business. "As you all know, we were mainly out to prevent a planet-wide rebellion of the True People clans.

"Well, some of the pictures have been transmitted to Earth and the science boys were called in. From the pics alone . . . the giant mantis, a miracle of breeding. That first big animal you killed in the control room: It sounds very much like a long extinct creature called *Dinohyus*, a vague ancestor of the pig, only much bigger and far meaner." He checked another page. "That one Slater and Muller got when you found JayBee pinned down by it sounds to them like one of the great carnivorous marsupials that lived in South America a million years or so ago, I think." He stopped reading and looked up. "Any questions? Those notes are on just the three animals you encountered before I got down with my men, and they're only guesses. There were a number of weird things no one can identify or will even try. The scientists don't think they were from Earth or even Mars. Well, let's have it."

Slater had his hand up, barely beating Feng, and got the general's nod. "Sir, what are the conclusions? That Satreel's people or their rulers came to Earth on collecting trips a million years ago? Then managed to save the embryos or adults as well and keep 'em alive somehow until now?" They sat in silence as the idea was voiced aloud. They had talked of it among themselves but were understandibly wary of others.

"It may be fantastic," the general said calmly, "but that's what the feeling is." He nodded to Feng.

"Sir, what have we concluded about the, ah, Le-ashimath, those rulers that Satreel referred to? *His* kind seemed little more than their servants, if we heard right."

Scott looked at the marshal, and he did not speak until he got a nod from Mutesa. "Frankly, we think you saw one of these entities yourselves."

"The red-haired creature who JayBee blasted sounds as if she may have been one, kept in stasis for God knows how long. We don't really *know*. But she pulled the destruct switch. If the ancient rulers did leave some of their own in some kind of hibernation or stasis, we won't find it in the ruins of the base. Still, some might be elsewhere. On this point, I am turning you over to the marshal."

Mutesa leaned back in his chair and he smiled at the group. His ebon face shone with bland authority. "I will tell you a number of things, my friends. I think they'll please you. I wish I were more junior in rank and younger as well. Anyhow, here it is. A top-secret team is being formed to investigate other Dead Zones. One, for instance, is to explore Mount Victory." There was silence at this. The lofty volcano of Mars was a grim mystery, and no one who had ever gotten there and stayed for long had ever come back. The marshal went on. "We have selected a major and two captains to head up this team. They will select the remainder from the UN service or out of it, whoever they think they need." He paused and surveyed the crestfallen faces of Feng, Nakamura, and Slater before continuing. "I think Major Feng, Captain Nakarmura, and Captain Slater might do, don't you? All three have exemplary records." He fell silent.

Slater knew they had all done well but the spot promotions were a bit stunning. He felt numb. He finally managed to mumble, "Thank you, sir."

The marshal continued as smoothly as ever. "There is evidence also that something lies buried on Venus. When you people finish on Mars, we will perhaps take a look there." He stopped and stared out the window. The room stayed quiet. Then he went on. "Wish I could go. Maybe you'd let me volunteer, perhaps without rank, eh?"

The room exploded in yells of triumph and excitement and all of them joined in except for Thau Lang. When his silence was noted, the others fell silent also. He smiled quietly.

"I know why you yell and you do well, for this is wonderful.

But I am old and I think only of this planet. I think also of a man not here, my friend. It may not be an Earth custom but I ask a minute's quiet for a prayer of thanks. To my friend Louis Muller, for due to him alone, we are all alive."

Every head bowed, then the officers rose and stood at salute.

## About the Author

STERLING LANIER, BORN IN 1927, GRADUATED FROM Harvard in 1951. When he was an editor at Chilton in the sixties, he published Frank Herbert's *Dune*, which went on to become one of the great sf bestsellers of all time. Lanier was trained as an anthropologist-archaeologist. He is also a well-known sculptor whose work is on exhibit in several museums, including the Smithsonian. He lives in Maryland.